Edmund Po
South Kilker
He works as a teac

THE LAST CHAPTER

Edmund Power

POCKET BOOKS

TownHouse

First published in Great Britain and Ireland by Pocket Books/TownHouse,
2003
An imprint of Simon & Schuster UK Ltd and TownHouse Ltd, Dublin

Simon & Schuster UK is a Viacom company

1 3 5 7 9 10 8 6 4 2

Simon & Schuster UK Ltd
Africa House
64–78 Kingsway
London WC2B 6AH

Simon & Schuster Australia
Sydney

Townhouse Ltd
Trinity House
Charleston Road
Ranelagh
Dublin 6
Ireland

A CIP catalogue record for this book is available from the British Library

ISBN 1-903650-47-X

Typeset by SX Composing DTP, Rayleigh, Essex
Printed and bound in Great Britain by
Cox & Wyman Ltd, Reading, Berkshire

THE LAST CHAPTER

CHAPTER ONE

'Two-five-six Easton Terrace, hello?'

'Brendan? Is that you?'

'Yeah . . . Dad?'

'That's right. Well, any news?'

'N . . . no. Not yet.'

'Not yet. Aha. I suppose that's a good sign, though, isn't it?'

'It's . . . Probably, yeah.'

'I mean, when they wouldn't take th'other ones, they weren't long about letting you know, were they? Not this long, anyway.'

'That's true.'

'Jay, it sounds to me like they're interested. Sure, otherwise, they'd never stay looking at it this length.'

'Please God you're right.'

'You'll see I am. So don't be worrying just 'cos you're not after hearing from them. That's surely no bad thing.'

'Well, here's hoping. Anyway, how's life?'

'Yerragh, struggling by like always.'

'What about the knees?'

'Sore enough, to tell the truth. Not as bad as they were but . . . still not great.'

'Sorry to hear that. Mammy's keeping okay, I suppose?'

'Oh, now, you know yourself – hang on a minute till I tell her.' He made no attempt to cover the mouthpiece, so I clearly heard, 'Moll – they never sent him back the book. They kept it.'

Nothing. Not a breath from the far end. Then, 'Brendan, still there? She says, "Congratulations and well deserved." '

'Tell her, thanks.'

'God, ye won't know yerselves when you start earning money again and there's two wage packets coming in. What'll ye do with the extra few bob at all?'

'Haven't thought about it really. I don't want to start counting chickens just yet. But I suppose a house would be nice.'

'Oh Lord, boy, the very minute you can afford one! Now, I know the price of property around Dublin, but you've got the little lad to think about as well. You can't expect to rear him there, without a green field to run in or a child his age for company. D'you remember that day we were up with ye?'

'That's a while ago now, Dad.'

'Whatever about that – what I'm trying to say is, I didn't see a single person in them flats who looked a day younger than myself!'

'Granted, it's not ideal. But the market at the moment, especially for a first-time buyer—'

'Oh indeed now, you may give up that poor-mouthing! Any day at all, this book of yours'll be out – and with your missus hauling in good money too! Listen, will you just promise me one thing?'

'What?'

'When you make your first million, you won't forget your poor oul' fella, will you?'

'One step at a time, Dad, eh? First it's got to be published. Then it's got to sell—'

'And why wouldn't it sell? God, boy, I've said it to more people around here that you were writing a book about the carry-on up in Barron's. And everyone I mentioned it to is mad anxious to read it. Honest, they can't wait. And country people everywhere'll be the same, you mark my words. 'Cos country people know the value of land. And they know there's no dispute as bitter as a disputed farm. Anyway, sure, I'll let you go. You will keep us posted?'

'I will. You might even call up some time.'

'Yerragh, you know now we don't care much for th'oul' bus.'

'Well, take the train then, you've got the free travel.'

'That's not right convenient either. The train doesn't stop here in Earlsgrove.'

'Fair enough, Dad, have it your way. We'll maintain phone contact.'

'Aye. And next time, for God's sake, you might ring us? It must be damn near your turn by now!'

'No problem.'

'Okay, good luck – oh, Christ, wait a minute, she's coming.'

A rumble as the phone was handed over.

'So you're buying a house, are you?'

'Hopefully at some stage we'll be—'

'What about buying one down here?'

'Where? In Earlsgrove?'

'In Earlsgrove, why wouldn't you?'

''Cos it's a hundred miles from Dublin, for one thing. It'd be difficult getting to work every day for my wife.'

'Ah, let her go be damned. And, anyway, sure you wouldn't have to live here. You could have it as a holiday home.'

'A holiday home? Mammy, it's customary in these cases to get the main residence bought first.'

'There's a few sites coming for sale near the railway gates. I'll say it to Paulie Flynn that you're interested.'

'Mammy, no!'

'He won't mind saving you one, being a neighbour. And sure if he says anything, we'll give him a few pounds of a deposit. You can fix us up as soon—'

'Mam, stop it! You've got to listen now. I will *not* be buying a site near the railway gates. I have no intention. More to the point, I have no money right now.'

'You're a foolish man. Property is not going to get any cheaper, mind.'

'That's neither here nor there. I just can't afford it.'

'Please yourself. I'd better go, or 'twill be God help us all when the phone bill arrives. How's my grandson?'

'Oh, getting big and brazen.'

'Good, good. I'll go. And we won't call again – not till you call first. We're pensioners now, y'know. You're the one who'll be raking it in.'

Click.

Our communal telephone was an A/B model, a throwback. Rickety and ancient – possibly pre-dating even the carpet that sat like scum on the stairs and hallway. With a heavy hand, I put the receiver down.

From above there came a noise, a soft shuffle of feet. Then, around the bend in the landing, one of my neighbours emerged. Like any, like all of the others: elderly, frail, open cardigan over check cheesecloth shirt, trousers belted just below the nipples. With his right hand on the banister, his other on the wall opposite, it would've been difficult for me to squeeze by him. So I leant back into the phone nook and waited. I smiled and nodded as he inched past and towards the front door. He smelt, I thought. Acrid, like urine. Like old age. Like any, like all the others. Or maybe it wasn't him – maybe it was the building itself.

Back in the flat, Robert sat in his playpen. He'd discarded the soother and was chewing the corners of an oversized plastic block. Contentedly. At least that was something.

By the boarded-up fireplace, I slumped in an armchair that much – far too much – sitting had moulded to my shape. What now, eh? What now? I reached to the mantelpiece, to the clutter of bills, of reminders, of miscellaneous, and drew it out. It wasn't likely to fill me with any great rejoicing, but such sarcasm, such perfect condescension surely deserved a second outing.

Monitor Press, Publishers
1008 Rathmines Road
Dublin 6
7th May 1996

Dear Mr Stokes
Please find enclosed your manuscript, *Fields of Fury*, which I hereby return to you.

This, I understand, is the fourth – or is it the fifth? – such endeavour you've sent for our consideration. I marvel at your persistence: evidently, you just don't know when to quit.

However, Mr Stokes, there appears to be so very much more besides that you don't know. Like how to write in clear, concise and coherent English. Like what constitutes a good yarn, a tale worth telling. Each of your books to date has been more turgid, more boring and more utterly pointless than the previous.

Take this latest. The plot, and I flatter you hugely by use of the very term, goes as follows: to retrieve monies owed, a national bank puts a South Kilkenny farm to auction. It's bought by an Englishman. The locals aren't happy. So the Brit returns whence he came, tail between his legs. And the land is restored to its original owner.

Not exactly high-concept, Mr Stokes. It could scarcely be called low-concept. More *no-concept.* You say it's a true story. You say you're a native of the area, and so have the idioms and nuances to pat. But this does not make it good. Even a competent author would struggle to turn this to vintage. In your hands, it's absolute ditchwater. Commercially speaking, it would be of interest to nobody, save those one or two misfortunates on whom this drivel is based. And even then there'd be no guarantee of book sales as I would have grave doubts as to whether any of those people can actually read. Indeed, Mr Stokes, illiteracy, at its varying levels, may well be endemic down your neck of the woods.

To conclude, let me give you some friendly advice. Let me put it in a way that's straightforward, unambiguous and not at all overwritten: the kind of language to which you have so obvious an aversion. Mr Stokes – forget it. You are not a writer, and you never will be. There are a thousand jobs out there, each of which would greatly value your tenacity, your industry, and your courage in the face of insurmountable shortcomings. For God's sake, choose one. Choose one today. If another manuscipt bearing your name should arrive on my desk, I will not read it. Insofar as possible, I will not even handle the thing. It will be dispatched at once, not to my out-tray but to my shredder.

Yours finally and forever

Kate Rooney

Chief Commissioning Editor

On hearing the key in the lock, I hastily folded the letter and stuffed it into a back pocket. Better not to let her see me reread it. Not that she'd have noticed: she'd been drinking – I could tell by the insolent swagger.

'Hiya,' she said airily.

'Fine.'

A little unsteadily, she lowered herself to her haunches, poked her head between the playpen rails and cooed, 'How's my best little man?'

'You weren't home last night.'

'Ah, no, I wasn't. Hey, d'you get that smell on the landing?'

'Any harm in asking where you were?'

'I was . . . am . . . at my Mum's. Seriously, d'you not get that whiff? Sorta . . . I dunno . . .'

'You were like Hell at your mother's.'

'Sure I was. Ring her up and check if you don't believe me.' With great ostentation, she went to her handbag. 'G'on – I insist,' she mocked, removing her mobile phone and handing it across. 'Give the woman a call. You know how she loves to hear from you.' I said nothing, bit my lip, conceded. 'No? Please yourself. Don't say I didn't offer,' and with a smirk she returned the mobile to her bag. Victories like these were too easy. Again, she began to look about discontentedly, 'Christ, how can you not get that bloody stink?'

'Well, I don't.'

'It's probably developed gradually. And you haven't noticed, being sat here all the time.'

'Well, that's something you need never worry about.'

'True. I'm usually out earning us a living.' She got to her feet and went to the armchair adjacent, inviting me to try another tack if I dared.

'You should've rung. I was worried.'

'When?'

'When you didn't come home last night.'

'Aw, change the goddamn record, will you? I didn't ring. I never do. You ought to know that by now. So spare me the I-was-worried crap.'

Another lengthy, uneasy peace.

'Where were you drinking earlier?'

'The Black Lion. The others are still there. I'm just going to stand under the shower a minute, then I'm heading back to join them.' Again she squatted by the playpen and twittered, 'Mammy is going to the shower, and then she's off for the night!'

'What others?'

'Eh?'

'What others? Who're you meeting down in the Lion?'

She stood. She shrugged. 'The usual gang. Finola. Brid. Sinead. Alan and Ger.' From a cupboard by the fireplace, she took a towel. 'The usual,' she repeated matter-of-factly, and left the room.

The skirt was too short and far too tight, the heels too high. Much, in fact, as they'd been when first we'd met. When she'd arrived at the mill all those years before, straight out of school, fresh-faced and flighty. And immediately taken up residence as the belle of the ball, the one to be seen with, the pearl before a factoryful of exuberant swine. What lengths I'd gone to, what charm and smarm expended, what competition I'd put to flight. And what a pyrrhic victory it since had proven. But we were younger then. It was difficult letting go of something so hard-fought and won. Easier far to hear her tell me how she loved me, and kid myself that I felt the same. A different time and place, a previous existence; tonight, she looked like nothing so much as a painted scrubber whose skirt was too short and far too tight, whose heels too high. Once or twice she came maddeningly, infuriatingly, close to going over on an ankle as she flurried about the room, fastening an earring, applying lipstick, locating her jacket, her purse.

All attempted at the same time, such was her haste to get away.

'This mother you spent last night with, will *he* be down the Lion too?'

'Look, Brendan, if it's a fight you're after . . .' she pressed a tissue between her lips, '. . . it'll have to be another time. Right now, I'm already late.'

'I don't want to fight. I do want to know why you're in such a rush out of here. And so anxious not to have me tag along.'

'What? Good God, I don't care whether you come or not. It's a public house, the more the merrier. You just arrange for someone to look after the child—'

'That's always left down to me, isn't it?'

'Well, yeah. 'Cos you're the homemaker, remember? I'm the breadwinner. I don't mean to threaten your masculinity, God between us and all harm, but that's just how things are.' With one final clip of her handbag, she went striding to the door. There, she about-turned and, 'So, if you can unearth a babysitter – oh, and a few quid to buy your round when the time comes – I may well be seeing you. If not, don't wait up, eh?'

It had gone one when the commotion started in the hallway two floors down. She'd deigned to come home. And she'd brought guests. Drunk or sober, she never forgot the right buttons to press. Because nothing caused my blood to boil like the thought of strangers invited back purely to gawp, to shake their heads and pity us at first hand. Our living conditions shamed me, *mortified* me, and ought to have mortified her as well. Yet, every so often, she pulled a stunt like this, knowing it embarrassed me more. Her latest tour party – I could make out two male voices – had now reached the flat door. I stood, fixing my sunniest, brightest, brassiest face. Important not to let it show how this fall had hurt the mighty. From outside there came the jangle of keys, some rustling, some small hubbub. I beat them to it and began opening the catch.

'Oh shit!' I heard her hiss. 'Now what the fuck's he doing up?'

Sunny, bright and brassy.

'Lads! Great to see yeh! Come on in, you're welcome. Keep it down a little bit, that's all. I've just got Robert off to sleep.'

She scowled, said nothing, went bustling sulkily by. With a nod and a salute, the other two went bustling after. There followed the wonted rigmarole as two kitchen stools were pulled alongside the armchairs to form a half-circle round the hearth. And we all sat. The three revellers had with them some carry-outs. Ger McEvoy tentatively, fearfully, offered me one of his large ales. For spite, I almost accepted. But before I could, Alan Bradshaw had cracked open a Heineken, placed it in my hand and said, 'Cheers, Coops.'

Alan was an old friend and neighbour. We'd been together through eight years of primary schooling, then moved on for another five to the famed De Le Salle College in Waterford. There we were to find ourselves both condemned to the pass class, to the also-rans: he for his lack of any great intellect, I for my total and ill-concealed lack of interest, along with a penchant for independent thinking that seemed to unnerve certain among the teaching staff. Following such dismal academic careers, the future was decidedly blue-collar, and we were somewhat fortunate to secure a pair of apprenticeships as fitters in a Waterford city iron foundry. Our time served, eighteen months on the dole persuaded us that there wasn't very much doing in or around the south-east. It was then we'd headed for Dublin, for full-time employment in Kilmainham.

Textiles. In recent times I'd married, had a child and quit the mill, so it was understandable that we'd grown apart somewhat. But Alan remained a kindred spirit. McEvoy, on the other hand, remained the same beer-swollen, obnoxious asshole he always had been.

'Pity you didn't make it down, Coops,' Alan opened. 'There was a right oul' crowd in the Lion tonight.'

'I wouldn't have said no to a pint,' I told him. 'But, y'know, trying to find a babysitter . . .'

'Aye, I suppose it can't be easy getting someone at such notice. Anyway, you probably had work to do, yeah?'

My wife jerked her head up. 'Pah!' she snorted, 'Work?' then rolled her eyes skywards, came unsteadily to her feet and stepped to the mantelpiece. Here she took a match from the outsize box and lit up. She'd just begun teetering back to her stool when McEvoy, all full of his fun, caught her by the waistband and pulled her on to him in the armchair where he sat.

'Let go!' she half protested, half laughed.

'Falling for me in a big way,' McEvoy cackled, as she attempted, without much conviction, to disentangle herself. At last she did wiggle free, straightened herself, straightened her clothing, and said, 'Ancient history, sunshine. You had your chance and you fluffed it.'

'Well, honey, I'm a great believer in second chances. And next time round, I'll make no mist—'

Then, and only then, did he seem to remember that her husband was present. And fully conscious. Mouth still open, but now sagging in a witless smile, he began scrabbling for something to say. Something diverting. Something light. *Something*. Eventually, after twice clearing his throat, 'Jayzus, *Coops*! Haven't heard that for a while now. Remind me, what's the story there?'

Bradshaw looked to me for a signal of approval. Angie sighed loudly, preparing to endure the tale one more time, preparing also her stock retort.

'Back when we were doing our Leaving,' Alan began, 'we got this new art teacher, a young bird fresh out of the uni. And she took a bit of a shine to the man here. Told him he looked like a young Gary Cooper.'

'With a nose like that?' My wife came in, bang on cue. 'Are you sure she didn't say "Tommy Cooper"?' She grinned directly at McEvoy, who was more than happy to cackle his own tuppenceworth in support.

'Gary Cooper my brown bollox! Some bleedin' heart-throb you are, right enough!'

'I've had my moments,' I said drily. 'Wiped a few eyes along the way. As you, my oul' flower, know better than most.'

That fairly knocked the smile to the other side of his face. Now again he sat scrabbling, this time for something altogether different. At last he spat, 'So how's this famous book of yours coming along?'

'Very grateful for your interest, Ger. I've finished it, as you ask.'

'And?'

'And it's with the publishers.'

'Is it now?'

'Tell the truth – it's been rejected,' my wife drawled. 'Actually, the letter he got back was very funny. Hey, read it out for the boys!'

At that moment I would willingly, *cheerfully*, have cut the woman's throat. She knew it too as she gloated on, 'Ah, do. Give us all a laugh.'

'I haven't got it,' I seethed.

'You haven't? Well, what was it it said again? Let's see. Boring, pointless, foolish . . . and turgid. *Turgid*? I don't know what turgid means, but it doesn't sound great. And then it ended with, "You're not a writer and you never will be. So do us all a favour, for fuck's sake, and get a job." Mind you, I could've told him that, and I'm only a machinist in a textile mill.'

The other two instantly sobered up somewhat, realizing that this was no joke, sensing a razor edge to the exchange. She merely sat back, her face contorted in as put-on a grin as I'd seen from her. Through clenched teeth I quivered, 'I-sent-out-four-copies. I've-had-just-one-back. *That*-is-the-truth.'

'There you go!' Bradshaw said. 'And sure, once down is no battle.'

But even as he spoke, Angie was shaking her head, slowly, emphatically. 'Oh, for the love of Christ!' she groaned. 'How long more must we keep this up? Lads, he's been turned down – turned down *flat* – by a crowd called Monitor Press. Monitor are this small firm, mostly for first-time authors, the only place in all of Ireland that'd ever be likely to have any dealings with a booby like him!'

Alan looked around awkwardly. 'Ah, now, Angie, you don't know that for sure.'

'Oh yes I do! He's said it himself – if Monitor give you the elbow, then the big boys won't even take the string off the manuscript. Tell 'em, Brendan. Tell 'em, and have done with it.'

'Ah, anyone for more?' Alan again intervened. 'Coops?' And he chucked me a second beer, even though I'd barely touched the first. The other two each took something from their own stash and, for a while, all four of us supped in silence.

I wasn't meant to see, but the drink made her careless so I couldn't fail to. First it was a wink, then a nod, obviously something prearranged. But not to McEvoy, to Alan Bradshaw. To my friend. He acknowledged in kind, then waited a second, coughed and began warily, 'Y'know, Brendan, I'm not saying your book won't be published or anything. In fact, knowing you, I'm sure it will. But if for some reason it wasn't, you might consider asking for your old job back. Yer man, Keogh, the old supervisor, he's gone.'

'Gone where?'

'Gone, *gone*. Left the mill.'

'Retired, y'mean?'

'Sorta. More pensioned off. Been diagnosed with cancer. And it's inoperable – apparently he's had it for years.'

I laughed. 'For years? Aw, shucks! And I thought it was just a great punch I caught him with!'

None of the others so much as smirked. Obviously not getting the reference. I went on, 'Ironic, isn't it? That day I decked him, everyone was saying how he should go to hospital to have himself seen to. And if he'd gone, y'know, they'd probably have checked him over, found the cancer, maybe even saved his life. Christ, what a twist in the plot that would've been!'

Still nobody was seeing the funny side. And when Alan next spoke, his tone was all self-righteous opprobrium.

'Yeah . . . an unfortunate business all round.'

'Unfortunate *how*, Alan?'

'It's just . . . ah, you don't like to be roughing up an old man like that.'

'Really? And what would you have done if he'd accused *you* of stealing?'

'Well, Coops, let's face it, he caught you. You were—'

'Was I fuck! Those remnants were being thrown out in any case. They were no good to anyone. So how, in God's name, can you call that stealing?' I wondered just how much porter Alan must've skulled to have him dare speak to me this way. And it seemed he wasn't yet finished.

'We were told from the first day we went in there that it was forbidden to take them or sell them on.'

'Alan, you can quote your precious rulebook at me till you're blue in the face. But the reality is, the money in that sweatshop was so absolutely piss-poor, they must've expected us to supplement it when the chance arose. And that's a different thing altogether from stealing. It's called using your fucking loaf.'

16

'May God give you sense, Alan,' Angie shot in. "Cos y'see the wall of the jail across the road? It's about a yard and a half thick. And you might as well be talking to *it* as to this arrogant prick.'

'Why don't you shut that tinker's mouth of yours until you know what you're talking about, you dirt—'

'Anyway,' Alan dived between us, 'all I'm saying is that we, the fitters, we're run off our feet in there. And the bossman claims he's all the time looking around but he can't get the right staff. A tradesman as handy as you? You'd walk back in the morning. All you'd have to do is apologize—'

'What? *Apologize? Over Keogh?*'

'C'mon, Coops, what's it matter? The bloke's on his last legs anyway.'

'And that somehow changes things, does it? The big, bad bug's got him, so suddenly he's one of the nice guys? Not in my book, Alan. I never liked that wanker, and dying's not going to make him any more appealing.'

'You wouldn't have to even mean it.'

'Alan, I won't apologize now, just like I didn't apologize then. And I didn't apologize then because I had nothing to be sorry for. Anyway, it all happened for the best — I wanted out of that dead-end kip, I did not care how. No offence, guys, I know it's your bread and butter but it's not for me, I'm afraid.'

'Oh, no!' my wife almost shrieked. 'Not for you. Nothing so common for our Brendan. He won't dirty his hands 'cos he's a writer, don't you see? He *is* a writer. Now, he gets publishers' letters here every other day telling him in no uncertain terms that he is *not*. Telling him that, even with two gallons of beer on board, he couldn't write his name in the snow. But they're all mistaken, aren't they? He knows he's something special. Something remarkable . . . You're not special, sunshine, you're fucking soft in the head. And the only remarkable thing about you is not that you're useless, it's that there doesn't seem to be anything anyone can do to make you appreciate just how useless you are!'

The others shuffled in seats, ran fingers through hair, examined footwear. If it had been my first time hearing this foolishness, I'd most likely have done the same.

Alan, good old Alan, at last broke the silence, changed the subject. 'Er, lads, like, I don't mean to be rude or anything, but are yeh sure your front door is closed? 'Cos I'm still getting a tiny bit of that smell.'

My wife craned her neck and replied, 'It's closed, yeah. But . . . rotten, isn't it? It's coming from the flat beside the phone. The one where the tramp lives.'

'Wha'?' McEvoy crowed. 'A tramp? Lives *here*?'

'Oh, yeah,' she told him, eyes to me, glinting with malice.

'Get the fuck, Ange! What kinda tramp?'

'The real deal, Ger, honest. Trousers and coat tied up with clothes line, toes out of the shoes, twigs in the beard – the works!'

'No way! Brendan – tell me that's not true?'

'Of course it's not.'

'Bloody right it is!' she hooted. 'And you know it.'

I ignored her, looked to the other two and spoke reasonably. 'There is a homeless man, who comes once in a while to visit the bloke living in Five-A.'

'Liar! That *is* the bloke from Five-A.'

'Jay-zus, Alan,' McEvoy said, with a toss of the head, thoroughly enjoying himself. 'I think we're after wandering into the bleedin' Simon Community!' I was on the point of telling that overweight boor he was free to wander out again at any time when he continued, 'That fucking whiff hit me before I was through the front door, but the lord of the manor doesn't seem to notice a thing. Bleedin' unreal!'

With considerable effort, I smiled. 'Actually, I do a little.'

I did. I had earlier, as I'd come off the phone. Only earlier I'd mistakenly put it down to the old man I'd passed in the corridor. Alan coughed, then sniffed, then asked tentatively, 'So what d'you reckon it might be?'

'Oh, that's no great mystery,' Angie sniped. 'It's that filthy, stinking hobo in the flat beside the phone.'

I exhaled long and weary. 'That guy calls once in a while. He does *not* live there.'

'All right then, smartarse, since you're such an authority. Who does? Live there, I mean.'

'You know damn well, you've seen him.'

'No, never.'

'Yes, you have. Early seventies, maybe older, bald . . .'
She shook her head vehemently.

'He's the man with, y'know . . .' I hesitated, fearing the worst if I finished. 'You know him. The man with . . . with the cat.'

She blanked a second then wrinked her nose, slitted her eyes and erupted. I made a despairing attempt to shush her, pleading that the baby was sleeping in the next room. But by now the other bastard had caught it and was guffawing just as rowdily. Even Alan could scarcely keep a straight face.

'He's right, he's right!' she gasped eventually. 'I've seen him. I *have* seen him. It was ages ago now – we weren't long moved in. This bloke in Five-A – bald, early seventies Brendan; I do stand corrected – brought home a cat that he found one day. Now, this was totally against house rules, so he let no one see, and thought to keep it on the quiet.' She sniggered to herself. 'Wasn't what you'd call the ideal man for the job, though. 'Cos not only is he a bit of a simpleton, he's an outrageous alcoholic with it. So he'd stock up on the cider and be out of his tree for whole days at a time. Leaving the poor moggie without food or water, going berserk around the flat. As well as that, he used to put down newspapers to catch the shit. But he wouldn't pick them up again, he'd just put down more on top.'

'God Almighty!' McEvoy gurned.

'Anyway, in no time at all the place was reeking. My husband, good citizen that he is, decided to go have a word. Of course, he got no answer, 'cos yer fella had been on the jungle juice, he was poleaxed drunk on the bed inside and he heard nothing. So our hero took aim and kicked the door in. But as he did, his foot went through one of the panels . . .' here she stopped to laugh, then to catch her breath '. . . through one of the panels and he wound up needing seven stitches to his shin. Then, while he was lying there screaming—'

'I was not screaming.'

'Lying there roaring his head off, the cat attacked him.'

20

'Huh? Attacked him how?'

'Scratched him on the face and the arms. But – this is the best bit – with all the hullabaloo didn't the oul' lad wake up, think he was being burgled, and begin beating him with a frying pan? Jesus, it was priceless!'

And the two pealed off to even greater hysterics.

'Oh!' McEvoy slapped a thigh as he sobbed. 'Oh, Christ! And what happened?'

'Well, along with the stitches he had to get a tetanus jab 'cos—'

'No, I mean to the oul' lad. And to this ferocious man-eating cat.'

'The cat, I believe, was taken to the pound. The oul' guy wasn't evicted – obviously not, if he's still here. But the flat had to be cleaned and fumigated. And he was warned never to bring strays home again. Mind you, he hasn't, to give him his due. Instead, nowadays, he brings home this down-and-out that he found wandering somewhere. Honest to God, you wouldn't see it on *The* bloody *Simpsons!*'

And away they went again. Eventually, after they'd dried eyes and coughed it all up, Alan, whose gaze had never left the floor, spoke soberly, 'On the level now, it does seem as if somebody's not keeping your no-pets rule.'

'What d'you reckon, Brendan?' Angie mocked. 'Smells like your old foe might be back in town.'

'For Christ's sake,' McEvoy chimed in, 'stay well away this time. Or if you are going to risk it, be sure you've got your safari suit and your big-game rifle. I mean, beating up a sick old supervisor is one thing, but this is a wild animal we're talking about. A case of kill or be killed!'

My wife, now firmly in her element, sneered, 'You should forget altogether about going back to that mill. I'm sure there's a job for you on TV. On *Pet Rescue.*'

'Or join the SAS,' was McEvoy's suggestion. 'You'd be a natural at storming embassies and—'

The end of his punchline was lost in another riot of hooting and braying. When at last it subsided, it was to allow me to hear my baby son cry behind the bedroom door. I stood.

'Right, lads, show's over. It's time you were going.'

'Yeah, yeah, sure. Fair is fair,' Alan said, as they both swigged off what remained in their drinks and set about gathering up those not yet opened.

'Hang on, hang on, sit down!' my wife demanded. 'Where're ye going?'

'Ah, the man is right, Ange.'

'The man's got no fucking right! I'm the one who pays the rent on this place. And you need only look around to realize we don't get visitors that often. So don't mind him, sit down!'

The pair hauled themselves to their feet. As they did, she grabbed fiercely at McEvoy's arm, attempting to wrestle him back on to his chair. I brushed past them and put a hand on the door latch. 'Alan, Ger, if ye wouldn't mind. We can do this again some other night.'

Slumped now on the far-off stool, my wife began to curse, at me, at them, in general. But even her vehemence was drowned by the furore from the bedroom. Leaving our guests to extricate themselves, I ran.

Robert, as ever, was easy. Even when startled this way, even at his most distressed, he was never too far from sweetness and light. In a minute or two, I'd cajoled him back to sleep. As he fell silent, so too did the flat. The men had made good their escape. Easing the door closed behind me, I tiptoed back to the living room. There she sat, with an especially bad look in her eye. 'That was mighty hospitable of you, I must say.'

I'd never in my life raised a hand to the woman. But, just then, I didn't trust myself to come within an arm's length of her. So I went to the front door where I applied the various bolts and deadlocks. I returned to find her mellowed not a whit.

'Did you hear me, you ignorant bogman? I invite friends back here only once in a blue moon. And when I do, you chase them off – good-for-nothing fucking waster!'

I took a deep breath. I took several. Then, quietly, 'This has to stop.'

'What has?'

'This. You going out every bloody night, blowing money that we can't afford—'

'Woah, woah! Have I got this right? Are you trying to tell me what I can and can't do with *my* wages?'

'I'm telling you this. There's a small child in the next room who's going to grow up barely recognizing his mother. It's bad enough that you're never here for him, but bringing those other drunks back at this hour of the night, terrifying the poor little bastard—'

She smiled a great lazy smile, caught the sides of the chair and hoisted herself to her feet. 'Don't call him that, it's not nice.' When she reached the bedroom she turned, the smile broader. 'May be true, but it's still not nice.' With that, she ducked inside and, at once, I heard the key turn in the lock. It took an instant for it to register – what she'd done, what she'd said, what she'd implied. When it did, I went charging for the door and wrenched at the knob till it rattled loose in my hands. 'Open up, I want a word with you!'

'Go to Hell! You're not coming in here tonight.'

'What the fuck was that supposed to mean just now?'

'There's blankets in the cupboard, you can take the cushions off the chairs. Or else find yourself a soft part of the floor.'

'Open up when you're told!'

'When I'm told? Who d'you think you are, ordering me abo—'

'Open the fucking thing or I'm coming through it!'

'You just try and I'll scream this house down.'

I stepped back a pace or two and charged, striking with my shoulder just above the handle. Blinded, numbed by rage, I felt scarcely a twinge. The door shuddered and shook; behind it my wife shrieked loud enough to be heard, not just in the next flat but in the next postal district. And when she'd done, the baby was off again, roaring like he was being disembowelled.

'It's okay, sweetheart . . . it's okay,' I heard her whisper. Then, 'He's awake now for the night – you ought to be bloody proud of yourself. I suppose this is your idea of good parenting? Jesus Christ, can you do nothing right?'

'Open this door, you cunt!'

'Don't be upset, honey,' she cooed, for both our ears. 'He can't help it. It's the way he was brought up. Like father, like son, they say. Which is good news, really. Means there's some chance for you.'

That tore it. Like it was a paperweight, I picked up the old armchair, raised it above my head and made again for the door. I was about to send it splintering through when, on the other side, the baby stopped crying. He chirped once, then he began to jabber, then to chortle. Slowly, slowly, I lowered my battering ram. Calmer, but still far, far from calm.

'I've not done with you!' I snorted. 'First thing in the morning—'

'Oh, fuck off,' she said, her words dripping with disdain. 'Fuck off, why don't you, and leave us alone?'

I spent the night under an old topcoat, curled up on the front mat. There was little prospect of any sleep, but I positioned myself to bar her exit just in case I did drift off. Some time before eight, she emerged.

When she failed to see me right away, she gave a small squeak of surprise, nothing more and then carried on preparing to leave for work exactly as always. Even when I stepped into the room, it barely cost her a beat.

'Okay,' I said quietly. 'I want the truth.'

Without looking, without pausing, she groaned, 'Brendan, I don't have the time, I'm late—'

'And you'll be later, honey. 'Cos you're not getting out of this flat until I know.'

She stopped, sighed loudly, dropped her arms to her sides, 'Know what?'

'Is that child mine?'

25

'Yes,' and she went to the wall mirror where she set about fixing her hair. When she'd done, she turned and pronounced, 'Yes.' More random fidgeting, more shuttling hither and thither. Then, seeing I'd still not spoken, she stopped and shrugged, 'Jesus Christ, *yes*.'

'So why did you say what you did?'

'Why?' She sneered, her patience evaporating. 'Well, because I'd had a drink or two, I guess. Because you'd been rude to my friends. Because, once again, you were shown up for the dull, tiresome old know-it-all you are. Because on nights like last night, I can't help thinking how much better off I'd be without you. But mostly bec—'

As if freeze-framed she stalled, then looked away and muttered, 'I've got to go. The boss'll be—'

I lunged forward and grabbed her forearm, 'But mostly what?'

'N . . . nothing.'

'Bollox! I know there's something more.'

She wriggled, she grunted, she strained, but she didn't answer.

I held on. 'I'm going to get the truth here, Ange. Or maybe I got it last night, did I? Is that goddamn child mine?'

'Yeah, he's yours.' Still she struggled, but not so much now.

'Is there some chance he might not be?'

'He's yours, for Christ's sake. How many more times d'you have to hear that?'

'But is there a *chance*?'

She opened her mouth, shaped to speak, then thought

better of it and suddenly began threshing and grinding mad as a collared alley-cat. Now I did let go. And, like I'd inhaled chloroform, went reeling till my back was against the near wall. For a long while, the world wobbled in and out of focus. I steadied myself with a hand on the table and faltered, 'G . . . Good Christ!'

She eyed me defiantly, still saying nothing.

'I . . . I know about now. And to be honest, Ange, I couldn't fucking care less about now. But back then? We'd only just got married?'

If there was any remorse showing, I was too shell-shocked to see.

'So, what're the odds?'

'Huh?'

'What're the odds that I'm not Robert's dad?'

'I don't bloody know,' she spat. 'One in a hundred – a thousand. I dunno, but just the one. Aw, for God's sake, why'm I bothering—'

'Just the one,' I mumbled, more to myself than her.

'Yes, just the one,' and at that, the old sneer returned with a vengeance. It didn't often happen but, for now, she'd got me on the ropes. 'Brendan, poor man, the child is yours. I *know* this, you'll just have to trust me on it, won't you? Now, you can keep me here all day, all week, for the rest of your pathetic little life if you feel like it. I've told you he's yours – beyond that, I don't see there's very much more I can do for you.'

'And . . . ah . . . who?'

'Sorry?'

'Who's this other bloke?'

'Oh.' She furrowed, looked to the ceiling a while and

then, 'You got me there. I don't know. He didn't stick it for too long – working in the mill one day, gone without a trace the next. I can't remember his name.'

'You what?'

'You want the truth, this is the truth. It was one time, a long time ago. I-can't-remember!'

'This man – he might be the father of your child – and you've *forgotten* him?'

'I have, Brendan. 'Cos whoever he was, he was only in competition with a screw-up like you. So he didn't need to be all that memorable now, did he?'

'You bitch! You cheap, dirty slag. You weren't even married six months. And already you were – what? – ducking into the broom closet with some stranger for a quick knee-trembler as soon as the boss's back was turned?'

She smirked. 'What a pity you can't write like you speak sometimes.' Then, snatching up her bag and coat, she swept past me and was gone.

CHAPTER TWO

There had to be some sense to this, some meaning – it was real life, after all. But those past forty-eight hours took a bit of believing. I'd had that damning rejection, signalling the end of the line with a publishing house where I'd been fancying my chances in a big way. I'd listened to – I'd even encouraged – the hopes of my parents, high as fireworks, false as fool's gold. I'd been held up as a laughing stock before an old friend whose respect and admiration I'd always enjoyed; and before a sworn enemy whose envy and resentment I'd positively gloried in. I'd had a confession of infidelity from my wife, although that wasn't headline news: the kick in the teeth came only in the timing, the starting date. Halfway through our first year of marriage. Or, put another way, even before – *long* before – I'd tired of her, she, it seemed, had tired of me. She, *she*, had tired of me *first*? There had to be some sense to this, but where? In God's name, where?

Oh, and, yes, there'd been one other thing. It had come to light that I might just be bringing up, be doting on, be mollycoddling, the child of another man. I was never overfond of children – indeed, it'd not be far wide of the mark to say I greatly disliked children – but Robert

29

was no ordinary child. Robert was different. Robert was my son, my heir, created in my own image and likeness. Inheritor of the name, the pedigree and the blood, he it was who would carry my genes and at least some small part of my genius to the next generation and beyond. Guaranteeing, in his way, a kind of immortality: if through some sinister miracle my writing failed to get me there, then an offspring surely was the next best thing. If all else failed, I'd at least have him to show. Except suddenly there arose the possibility that I didn't *even* have him to show. Still, one chance in a thousand, his mother had said; ninety-nine-point-nine per cent in my favour. Closer to a certainty than this world is generally inclined to offer. Maybe in time I'd have things confirmed beyond the last shred of doubt, but for now I'd take those odds. After the forty-eight hours I'd just endured, I had to take those odds, had to take solace from somewhere.

This close to rock bottom with so little to lose, decisions come easy, even the unpalatable ones. I was leaving her. And taking the child with me. It'd be no great problem, relatively straightforward. Step one would involve getting a job. As Alan Bradshaw had quite correctly pointed out, I was still a bloody handy fitter. My likes were hard to come by, a valued commodity any time, anywhere. I'd stroll back into regular, well-paid employment. From there, it'd be the simple matter of moving out, establishing an alternative base, and applying for custody. No judge in the land would rule against me. Especially if, in the meantime, I could find myself a new woman, someone decent, someone respectable, someone nothing like the trollop I'd been fool enough to marry. That didn't seem too high a hurdle either. In minutes I was decided, my plan formulated in broad outline. Now to get those wheels moving. And no time like the present.

A job, then. A return to the ranks of the wood-hewers and the water-drawers. No more the full-time, desk-bound author. I'd miss that. Even if the establishment had seen fit to grant me neither publication nor due recognition, even if so blatant and shameful a raw deal stuck in the craw betimes, I'd still miss it. For despite everything, it had always given me a glow, a sense of fulfilment I'd never known as a nine-to-fiver. But a nine-to-fiver I soon again would be. It'd make things difficult, but not impossible. And it'd certainly not defeat me, nor force any towels in from my corner. My writing time would be curtailed, but what of it? I knew I could accomplish more, and better, in my few spare hours than any of the current literati working flat out over five mediocre lifetimes. Could, and in due course would: a change of scene, a brief revisit to the jobs market, a general recharging of the batteries, and I'd come blazing back to claim my rightful place and station. The next move was strategic. It proved nothing, it settled nothing. Except, perhaps, that my dalliance with Monitor Press was best discontinued forthwith.

But even with them, I wasn't signing off just like that. No, sir, it was not in my nature to go quietly. There was still time for one last letter, a richly deserved and long overdue broadside at that sow of a commissioning editor. Over the years, she'd had her fun with me, I'd had to take my lumps and laugh. But not any more. I went to my desk, engaged the PC and got cracking.

Flat 8
256 Easton Terrace
Kilmainham
12th May 1996

Dear Ms Rooney
Just a brief note to wish you nothing less than viral meningitis, you dried-up, frustrated, menopausal, old cunt (hope that's clear and concise enough for you).

Good God, that smell again! I recalled the force with which my good lady wife had banged the door behind her as she left: it must have rebounded and come open again, allowing the reek from below into our dwelling. I went to investigate but found everything closed tight – whatever was coming in was coming underneath. So I took the mat, rolled it lengthways and bunged it into the gap at the bottom of the door.

Returned to my desk and reviewed what I'd written. *Dear Ms Rooney, Just a brief note to wish you nothing less than viral meningitis* . . . Nah, this was pointless. She'd immediately skip ahead to the end, see my name there and shred the thing as she'd promised. Unless . . . unless, of course, I didn't sign it. Which, when I thought about it, was, if anything, more pointless yet. An even greater waste of a stamp.

But how, then? From what angle might this parting shot be best delivered? I wanted it to find its mark – and

I dearly wanted it to wound. After much pacing the floor I retook my seat, deleted what I'd done and began again.

Flat 8
256 Easton Terrace
Kilmainham
12th May 1996

Dear Ms Rooney

I trust you've recently received my manuscript entitled *Fields of Fury*. It is with great regret, and no little embarrassment, that I must ask if you'd be good enough to return it to me at the above address. I've never sought to hide the esteem in which I hold both you and your remarkable publishing house, nor can anyone deny the help and support you've given to countless fledgling authors down the years. Indeed, it had long been a dream of mine that when, eventually, I made it to print it would be with none but Monitor Press.

However, I am in my mid-thirties, unemployed, married with a family and, Ms Rooney, sentiment is a commodity I can ill-afford. So when, just yesterday, I was offered a four-book deal and a sizeable advance by another publisher, I felt I owed it to myself and my dependants to take up that offer. I do hope you understand. I'm not at liberty to disclose the name of my new employer, but I should keep an eye on the daily papers in the coming week if I were you; deals like the one I've struck tend not to stay secret for very long . . .

There! That was more like it. Pretend I'd not yet had back the latest from her poisoned pen. And let her think she'd just passed up pure gold! Let her believe she'd made the kind of decision that would not just return to haunt her, but would go on haunting, and taunting, her for the rest of her natural life. Let her contemplate the ridicule she'd flung in my direction; let her brace herself for more of the same, rammed back her own smart mouth. If only for a short while, let the bitch sweat.

Now for a suitable ending, trowelling on a few more compliments and heartfelt best wishes. Something along the lines of . . . Christ, there it was again! It was now leaving traces of a taste at the back of my throat, while my eyes were watering just slightly. With a thumb and forefinger, I wiped them clear and refocused.

> For this, I know, I have you to thank in huge part. So, even though we will not now be working together – I suppose we are, in a manner of speaking, competitors – I would like you to know how grateful I am for your encouragement and your unshakeable belief in me down the years . . .

Before me, the screen blurred. On the floor, my child began to hack, then to gag, then to cry. With a slap of open palms on the table, I sprang to my feet. Enough was enough. I considered myself as reasonable as the next. But if any tenant was fouling up the building with an illicitly kept pet, I'd see both him and it evicted. It was tough enough living here, even when everyone stayed on the right side of the rules.

My toolbox lay at the bottom of the hot press where I'd discarded it some years earlier. From it, I armed myself with a two-foot-long jemmy bar and made my way downstairs.

The source, once again, was 5A. No functioning set of nostrils could've mistaken that. With a jumper sleeve clasped across my lower face, I came near and knocked.

I knocked again, louder.

And again, loud as my knuckles could stand. Nothing.

Nothing else for it, then. Grasping the bar with both hands, I plunged it between bolt and jamb. Ancient design and built to last, it was as stubborn as I'd expected it to be. But on the fourth heave the wood relented, the fittings gave way and the door splintered open.

The stench, I'm certain, was absolutely overpowering, but I didn't notice it – when a bloke sees his first dead body, other things tend to slip the register. I was no expert, of course, but I guessed he'd been there a while. He was on his back, arms and legs at peculiar angles like he'd been struck down breakdancing. His skin was green here, purple there and black almost everywhere else. His mouth and eyes were open and garish, the skin about shrunken tight. There seemed to be swelling in the region of the abdomen, and some dampness around the crotch and seat of the trousers. He was dead all right.

My stomach never was my strongest feature and, to this day, I don't know what kept me from turning and running. But something did make me linger. Perhaps the knowledge that this chance would not come again: once I'd raised the alarm the place would be swarming. But now, and at my leisure, I could enjoy a thorough rummage, and maybe get an insight into the world of a man who, it seemed, had virtually retreated from our world a good many years before. I closed the door behind me, secured it with a chair under the knob and began.

Flat 5A was a single room. A damn sight cleaner than when last I'd been in it, though that wasn't saying much. The floor was covered with worn, patchy lino, while a single-bar electric fire sat by a hearth boarded up exactly like my own. A grime-caked Baby Belling cooker stood by the sink in one corner, a narrow bed in the corner adjacent. There was a window, painted shut, with a diagonal crack wide enough to push a penny piece through. The walls were a sickly, candyfloss pink, without any adornment save for a rectangular mirror that hung over the mantel. And it was there I saw the first indication that a life had been lived here, that the resident had some connection to the greater human race: stuck in the mirror frame was a Polaroid, small and old. It depicted a teenage girl, sandy-haired, smiling cheekily, mischievously. Maybe a relative? Without looking round, I considered the pitiful husk on the ground behind. Certainly a relative, I decided. What else could she be?

Thinking no more of it, I went ahead with my once-over. On the mantelpiece itself, there wasn't very much. A Chef sauce bottle had been washed out for use as a moneybox. I could see it held a note and some change; when counted, it amounted to £18.04. His need for this had well passed; my need, however, was present and pressing. Anyway, no right-minded person could expect me to do what I'd done for nothing. I pocketed the money as my due. Alongside there was a table lighter, medium-sized, made from cut crystal. As I stashed it, too, I saw it had been obscuring a Claddagh ring. I couldn't say for certain, but it did appear to be genuine gold. It also appeared to be made for a finger far smaller than mine or, indeed, his. Now who would've expected to find such a thing among the possessions of this old recluse, this near destitute? Exactly, I thought, as I dispatched it the way of the lighter and the cash.

I was still short of being compensated for my troubles, for what inconvenience the old man had put me through in death and in life. I was surely owed more. But there didn't seem to be much left worth having. A radio, held together with green insulating tape, sat on the dining table. The sink overflowed with dishes almost as mouldy as the corpse on the floor. At the foot of the bed was a large black refuse sack; it contained empties of various ciders and spirits, all of them cheap and rough. But now, about the bed, one other thing caught my eye. There, by the headboard, a grey milk crate was turned tallways, facing out, to serve as a bedside locker. And what should there be, perched atop this crate, but an electric typewriter. A Sharp Q-110, no less. Quite the thing in its day, even the secretary at the mill had had one when first I worked there. But she'd ditched hers, not long after, in favour of a PC and wordprocessor – as for that matter had the rest of the planet at large.

So I never seriously thought of stealing it too; but what I couldn't help thinking was why on earth the John Doe should've felt the need to own such an thing.

Then, half-hidden on the floor beneath the bed, my

answer was revealed. A sizeable sheaf of A4 paper; I did have some knowledge in these matters and, from where I stood, it looked awfully like a manuscript.

I got to my knees and hauled it onto open ground for a better look: '*Remember Me, Fair Eleanore*. A novel. By Andrew Whitty, 256 Easton Terrace, Kilmainham.'

Fair Eleanore. A reference, no doubt, to that dirge of a showtime from . . . from which musical I couldn't offhand say. Or, indeed, care less just then. A second look. Oh, good Lord Jesus, I sniggered; what a title. What originality of thought. And laid low in his prime this way; what a black day for the world of contemporary fiction. With a wince, and a morbid curiosity, I gave a flick through the pages. There seemed to be more than 250, comprising some fourteen chapters and, towards the end, an epilogue. An *epilogue,* indeed! He had scarcely a friend in the world, a decent stitch of clothes or a pot to piss in. But he had an epilogue. And why not, when all was said and done? Delusions of grandeur cost nothing. Idly, I turned the title page: 'Shafty McDermott had the kind of face women dream about. Directly before screaming themselves awake, laddered in sweat and fumbling for a bedside light . . .' *Laddered*. The less common past tense of the verb 'to lather', I assumed. And if he was making howlers like this in the very first paragraph then, Heavens above, what must the rest of the piece be like? But yet . . . that character's name wasn't half bad. Shafty McDermott! Now, that had a ring to it. And the gag itself – well, as openings went, I'd read worse. A bit on the pedestrian side by my own standards, but I *had* read worse.

At my back, there came a rap on the door.

'Mr Whitty? Mr Whitty, are you there?' croaked a voice from the hallway. At once, I restored the loose leaves to the tidy bundle, which I pushed up my jumper and down the front of my trousers. Then I went to answer the knock. Outside was the old man I'd seen by the phone the evening before. 'Oh, God, 'tis yourself! I thought it might be that quare fella that comes calling on him now and again.'

'You mean,' I smiled, 'the homeless guy? The tramp?'

'Aye, the very man. I didn't see him in a while, so he must be due a visit. Anyway, is Mr Whitty in there? 'Cos, y'see, I'm getting this oul' smell, and I'm thinking 'tis from—'

'You're quite right, it is from Mr Whitty's. In fact, it's from Mr Whitty. He's dead.'

'D . . . dead?'

'I smelt it too, so I broke in just now. You can have a look, by all means, but I think it'd be better if we let the cops handle it from here. I was just about to give them a call.'

He blessed himself, muttered something, then shuffled away. I went to the phone and, using the man's own money, summoned for him the emergency services.

Back in my own flat, after I'd hidden my booty in a drawer of the TV unit and given the baby a feed, I reopened the manuscript on my work desk and read on.

Shafty McDermott, it quickly transpired, was not himself the hero. Rather, he was the sidekick of one Edward J. Lynagh. Ned and Shafty leave their native Mayo in the mid-seventies, both intent on seeking their fortune, neither possessed of anything more than a tolerance for hard work and hard living. They make for Luton, a medium-sized town not far from London, where they soon find employment on the buildings, surrounded on all sides by drunkards, degenerates and weirdos. Indeed, the entire first chapter was anecdote after anecdote, some of them funny, a surprising amount involving food. A mouse, killed in the storage cabin, winds up in the sandwich of the canteen glutton. On another occasion, a pig's eye somehow finds its way into his teacup. And, in what seemed to be some kind of initiation rite, Lynagh himself, mortally hungover this particular lunchtime, is approached by one Comer Joe, a blackguard of high renown. Joe seems to want nothing more than a chat and is the very soul of civility till, mid-conversation, he removes the cooked ham from his roll, vigorously blows his nose in it, returns it to the bread and proceeds to scoff the lot. Reading, I was unsure whether to laugh or puke. Lynagh, in the telling, had no difficulty deciding.

*

The police arrived. It was I who admitted them. I briefly explained myself, why I'd done what I'd done and what I'd uncovered. They thanked me and assumed responsibility.

*

Before long, the friends find their feet. But while remaining close on a personal level, their paths diverge on every other. All around it's strictly subsistence, work to pub to bed to work again. Shafty thinks he's died and gone to Heaven. Lynagh, on the other hand, aspires to something better. He's punctual, conscientious, and stands out a mile from the herd. So while Shafty and his fellows have nothing to show but bloodshot eyes and beer bellies, Lynagh is promoted to foreman.

*

'Hello – anyone home?' came the tentative voice.

I turned to see a youngish policeman, with prominent buck teeth and a hatted head craned round my door. 'Come in,' I said. 'Are ye done downstairs?'

He stepped into the room. 'Yeah. Bad business, y'know. Can't be much fun having your number come up all alone like that. I'm Denis Cambridge, by the way.'

'Brendan Stokes,' I told him in reply. 'D'you want a cup of tea or anything?'

'Please, if it's not too much trouble.'

'None at all. I was about to brew up anyway.'

'There's a great boy!' he called cheerily, as I filled the kettle next door. 'It is a boy, yeah?'

'That's right,' I called back. 'Robert.'

'A topping great chap!' he boomed. 'What's the story? Is his mam not around?'

'No, she's working. I suppose one of us has to.'

'Okay. And you're a writer?'

This fairly knocked the wind from my sails: if it was a guess, it was nothing short of miraculous.

'You're a writer?' he repeated, louder. 'A novelist?'

'Well, yeah.' I came through, carrying the tea tray. 'Sort of.'

'Oh, now, you're being modest, I feel. A four-book deal, by God! *And* a sizeable advance. Congratulations, and fair fucks to you!'

'Eh?'

41

He nodded. 'I've just been reading the letter on your PC.'

I swallowed, feeling extraordinarily foolish. 'I really do wish that was the case, Garda. But, unfortunately, I've not been published. That's just me having fun. Daydreaming.' He stood, frowning slightly, saying nothing, inviting me to please elaborate. 'Ah, y'know, some guys stick "Sultans of Swing" on the stereo, pick up a tennis racket and pretend to be Mark Knopfler. This is how I . . .' now it sounded daft, even to me '. . . this is just what I do.'

But he was smiling toothily, nodding his total under-standing. 'You're not alone in that, believe me. There's this big old skillet in the house I share. And the other day, when he thought no one was looking, one of the lads was shaking hands with some imaginary bigwig, raising th'oul' pot over his head and saying how proud he was to accept the European Cup on behalf of the victorious Sligo Rovers side.'

He did seem to be speaking English: beyond that, he'd lost me.

'Not a football fan, I take it,' he said, blushing puce.

'No . . . not really.'

'That isn't a sports book, then?' and he indicated to the manuscript on the table.

'Th . . . that?' I flustered. 'That's . . . No, it's not.'

'But it's your latest, right?'

'Kinda . . . yeah, it is.'

'Finished?'

'Just yesterday . . . This morning, actually. I'm proof-reading it now, y'know, looking for mistakes.'

Cuppa in hand, he stood, walked back to the desk and

said, 'D'you mind?' Before I could bar his way, he'd begun aloud.

' "What?" Lynagh laughed. "You've been sacked again?"

' "Not at all," said Shafty. "Not sacked. Resigned. A simple difference of opinion with the ganger."

' "Oh yeah?"

' "Yeah. He seems to think he's not the biggest wanker in Europe." '

He turned, giggling. 'Brilliant! Very, very good. Great name, Shafty,' and he faced away again, intending to read more.

Hastily, but careful not to appear too hasty, I rose and came to his side. 'Please, it's not quite . . .' and I went about closing the manuscript. Just in time, I remembered. To do so would be to reveal the title page, the name of the author. Instead, I pressed a palm firmly down on each of the two leaves facing. 'It's not quite done yet . . . and I don't want to, y'know, jinx it.'

'Sure, sure, can't say I blame you. But, Christ, if it's all as good as that, I do look forward to reading it some day.'

'Was there . . . anything else, Garda?'

'Oh, sorry, Mr Stokes,' he said. 'You're mad keen to get back to work, and here's me wasting your time. I just called to thank you for what you did. It was a decent and neighbourly thing. Now, can you help us out at all with next-of-kin?'

'Fraid not, Garda. I didn't actually know . . . What was his name?'

'Whitty. Andy Whitty.'

'Mr Whitty. Didn't know him at all, didn't know

anything about him. There was this man who used to call on him every once in a while . . . I don't want to sound uncharitable, but he was, well, he was a bum.'

'Yes, I've heard that from some of the other tenants. But it seems this geezer hasn't been around for a spell – it's all possible he may be dead too. They tend to go pretty suddenly, his kind.'

'So there's . . . am . . . nobody, then?' I asked, fingers crossing.

'Well, we've had a quick sift through the assorted garbage round the flat, and it does look like he had someone. A niece, maybe. There were birthday cards—'

'Oh, that's right,' I said brightly, determined not to show any deflation. 'I remember seeing a small photograph stuck in the corner of the mirror frame.'

'That was well spotted.' In his tone, I sensed just the slightest accusation. 'You must've had a good look around the place before we arrived.'

'Not at all. But when there's only one picture of a human face over the entire four walls then, yeah, I'm going to notice it.'

He thought, then he nodded slowly. 'Aye . . . Mr Stokes, thanks again. We may be contacting you for a formal statement but it's fairly cut and dried. Foul play is *not* suspected.' We shook hands. 'If you need anything from us, you can contact the Kilmainham station.'

'Very well. Bye then, Garda . . . ?'

'Cambridge. Denis Cambridge.'

I listened to him along the hallway and down the stairs, still not at my ease. Out of nothing, that had ended up a pretty close call. Once I'd heard the front door slam, my first act was to destroy that goddamn title page. Not having an open fire, I burned it in the sink. As the flame danced, Robert whooped, rattled the bars of his cage, and then remembered how hungry he was. I fed him on my knee, all the while reading ahead.

The two continue further down their chosen roads. Shafty goes from bad to worse, and is soon mixing it with some of the greatest rakes and reprobates in town. Lynagh shacks up with a girl from Donegal, one Cathy Rowland. It's a very prosperous union. She earns steady money as a shiftworker in the nearby Vauxhall car plant. He's a tremendous success as a foreman; the men like him, the bosses love him. He's affable, he's approachable but, bottom line, he gets things done.

His folks back home in Mayo are kept abreast of his career, but not his domestic arrangements. This is rural Ireland of the 1970s: living over the brush is severely frowned upon. His girlfriend's people are similarly kept in the dark. So there's trouble on the horizon when, in the summer of '77, Cathy's younger sister announces she's coming for a visit. A holiday. She's fifteen, still at school, stunningly good-looking, and has no idea that her sister's bloke is a live-in.

But any and all fears prove groundless. Young Ellie takes the entire situation in her stride, and has the time of her life. She and Lynagh hit it off like a dream; a little too well, in fact. He may be a full twelve years her senior, but on those long nights with Cathy shiftworking at the car plant, the two begin a clandestine affair. And fall helplessly in love.

I hadn't heard my wife come in. She breezed past me,

through to the bedroom. 'All right, Ange?' I said distractedly.

She poked her head out of the doorway, seeming surprised, confused, even, to find me so agreeable, so disinclined to start aggro.

'Hiya,' she ventured. 'Anything strange?'

'Am . . . no. Divil a thing.'

'Apart, of course, from you finding a dead body *and* having the police in the flat.'

'Oh, that? Yeah, there was that.'

And, again, I buried my face in the text. From the corner of my eye, I saw her head go to one side, her hands to her hips. 'What're you reading?'

I looked up a long moment, then casually closed the pages over and said, 'Nothing much.'

'Nothing much?' she repeated, as she sauntered to the desk.

'Just some old thing I wrote a long time ago.'

'Oh, well, in that case you certainly aren't lying.' She stopped and she squinted. 'The writing, it's strange. Very . . . I dunno . . . kinda hard to make out.'

'I suppose it is.'

'How come it looks so different from all the other stuff you've written?'

For a time I could only get my mouth to make shapes. Eventually, 'It was when I got the PC first. I didn't really have the hang of it. So the typeface isn't the best.'

'Hmm,' she said. Then, with a shrug, she began to walk away. 'I'm going out tonight.'

'Fine.'

'In fact, I'm heading off this minute.'

'Have a great time.'

'I may be quite late.'

'Don't worry about it.'

'You'll . . . you'll be okay with Robert?'

''Course – amn't I always? Don't give it a second thought, you go and enjoy yourself.'

Again from the corner of my eye I watched her frown, scratch her chin, then shrug again and go.

The affair remains undetected as Ellie heads back to Donegal for the start of the new school term. Without her, the transformation in Lynagh isn't pretty. Gone is the personable, popular old Ned; in his place is an ogre, who treats his superiors with insolence, his underlings with contempt and his common-law wife with relentless antagonism. The pair split up, he moves into Shafty's house, the consequences are entirely predictable. Before long, he's carousing with the best of them. Before very much longer, he's lost his job, his drinking is out of control, his life is in total tailspin. Tuesday afternoon in The Painter's Arms, his fall from grace is complete – broke, drunk, and has just cadged a pint from a disabled ex-serviceman – when he gets a tap on the shoulder.

It's young Ellie. She's run away from home.

From outside I smelt the fish and chips, then my wife came swaying in and collapsed on to the armchair behind me. 'Still reading that thing?'

'Am . . . yeah.'

'D'you want the rest of these, or will I throw 'em out?'

Only then did it occur to me that, since I'd come into possession of the manuscript, I'd not eaten a crumb. I devoured the remnants of her takeaway; as I did, I took a time-out. I couldn't concentrate properly with her around. 'Good night, yeah?'

'Not bad.'

'Alan and Ger there?'

'Nah. Ger was for a short while, but he left early. A hot date, I'm sure.'

'Well, why not? There seems to be a lot of hot dating going on from that mill. A regular ballroom of romance.'

'Stop it, will you?' she groaned, then closed her eyes wearily and sat back in the chair. I remembered how I wanted her: not energized by the prospect of a good row, but in bed and out of my way. So I said, 'Sorry, Ange. I didn't mean—'

'That's okay.' She opened one eye a sliver. 'Any trouble with Robert?'

'Oh, Christ, Robert!' I jumped from the desk and rushed to the playpen. There he was, panned out on the rug, absolutely conked.

'You forgot the child!' she crowed.

'I'm afraid so. I was kinda . . . engrossed.'

'In that book? But how come? You wrote the thing, didn't you, you must know who dunnit?'

Choosing to disregard this, I gently took the baby in my arms. He woke, looking groggy and disorientated.

'Here, gimme the little man. Bedtime, fella!' Then to me, 'You ought to come too.'

'I'll be along shortly.'

'Ah, come on now.' She twinkled through the beer glaze. 'C'mon, Shakespeare, whaddya say?'

'Five minutes,' I told her. 'Gimme five minutes and I'll be done here.'

'Don't leave it any longer – this may not keep!'

He quits Shafty's and the couple, Ellie and he, set up home together. At once, the reverse transformation is total: he cleans up his act, returns to work, is reinstated in his old position by delighted employers and, for a short time, everything is beautiful. Then, one afternoon, there appears a delegation from Donegal. Ellie's father, along with a selection of her brothers, each a greater redneck than the last, come to take the young girl home. The locals don't know the whys or the wherefores, but don't care a whole pile. They see a friend in need and outnumbered, they immediately wade in behind him. On the road beside The Painter's Arms, a mighty pitched battle ensues, which ends with the raiding party being put to flight. Indeed, when the cops call next evening, Ned assumes they're investigating the brawl. They're not; they've come to arrest him for carnal knowledge of a minor. Statutory rape.

He vows to fight the charge, to surrender his love for nothing or nobody. But that stance proves unwise. As word goes around that he's facing prison, people become wary. As word goes around as to the *reason* he's facing prison, those same people become hostile. Men refuse to work for him or with him. In the canteen, as in the pub, he's ostracized. There's talk, and not all of it behind his back. Still he battles on till, one day, Shafty comes to him with an offer. He's been in contact with Clan Rowland. They've intimated that, if their daughter is returned home to Donegal, they won't proceed with the criminal charges. Ned is enraged that Shafty would dare insult him with such a proposal. But his old mucker talks him round. Pointing out how Ned's life has fallen to pieces since meeting Ellie. Pointing out the considerable difference in years. Reminding him that a teenage girl will change heart as often as she changes hairdo; what odds Ellie sticking around for the long haul if her boyfriend is sent to jail and she's left high and dry in a town where she knows scarcely a sinner? Clinching it with the sworn guarantee that, if he is sent to jail convicted of sexual deviancy, then he's ruined for good and all.

Reluctantly, Lynagh folds. He must end things. However, he can't bring himself to tell the girl face to face. So he waits till she steps out of the flat next day, writes her a letter saying he's been called away on business, and that he'd better not find her there when he returns. He then hastily packs a bag and heads to the station, intending to leave for London and lose himself in the city till she's gone.

But as he sits waiting for the train he gets to thinking. To considering what it is he's walking away from. For the first time in his twenty-seven years he loves, and is loved. He's found the one he wants to grow old with. He knows with absolute certainty that there is only one: nobody could ever replace what he had with this girl; anything from now on would at best be a pale and sorry sham. Yet here he was, casting her adrift. And why? To get his life back in order? But what was life, how could it be endured if she wasn't part of it? What was a spell in prison when compared to a future without Ellie Rowland? He leaves the station and races back home to destroy the letter, to undo the damage. But he's too late. She's already seen it, read what it had to say, taken a knife and slashed both her wrists. She's dead.

Shafty, gazing idly out the pub window, notices his friend go charging up Hightown Road at a time when he should be on his way to London city. After finishing his drink, he decides to pay Lynagh a call, for fear something's up. When he gets there, he finds that Ned has joined his young lover. The pair are huddled on a bloodsoaked hearth, together in death. Together for ever.

Taking us to that epilogue, which didn't now seem so great a conceit. Shafty McDermott sits by a gravestone in a bleak and blustery Mayo churchyard. It's Ned's final resting place – Ellie's too, we learn. Shafty relays to him all the *craic*, the gossip and the scandal from his old pals in Luton. He berates the pair for having so little consideration as to check out in the very dead of winter: if only they could've seen their way to wait till the weather picked up a bit, these anniversary visits home would be that much more agreeable. Then, bidding them farewell, he turns up his collar to the wind and away he goes. His first steps on the journey back to Luton town.

'Back to the land of the living. Back to the grind.'

As I rose to walk the floor, my legs all but buckled. I'd practically lost their use, so long had I been sat in that same position.

'Back to the land of the living. Back to the grind.'

In the distance, the Oblates' clock chimed four. A couple of minor interruptions aside, I'd been at the desk sixteen hours straight. The going hadn't been easy. The spelling was less than perfect. The writing was ordinary at best, woeful in places, with no real flair or turn of phrase in evidence. It further suffered from being told in the third person; a first person account seen, say, through the eyes of Shafty McDermott, would've been far more effective, more punchy. And, worst of all, it was set in the late seventies. The seventies, I ask you! The decade that style forgot even then, and that the world has been trying its damnedest to forget ever since. What a field day my old nemesis, Kate Rooney of Monitor Press, would've had if she were to lay hands on the likes of this.

But for all its faults, one fact spoke volumes: I'd completed the entire tome at a single sitting. And why? It was no mystery. An untidy mess it might have been, but it was backboned by *some* storyline, a cracking old yarn. Despite itself and its many, many imperfections, it was a real page-turner; the plot made it so. The plot, that was the thing. Even now, rough-edged and raw, it was engaging. But, God, if a real writer were to cut loose with such material, the possibilities were mouth-watering.

As it stood, I knew it was not publishable. However, I also knew an uncut diamond when it sat open on my desk with a blank screen facing. Here was a story in need of an author. This day, it had fallen into the lap of an author crying out for a story. It was destiny, plain and undeniable. It was history minding her children.

By now I'd been awake for nearly a full twenty-four hours. But the thought of sleep had never once entered my head, so fired was I with adrenaline, with purpose. Opportunities like this didn't knock every day. When they did come calling, it was best to let them in on the first rap.

However, I was not so blinded, so caught up in the rush, that I didn't foresee pitfalls. Or one pretty deep pitfall in particular: namely, that another person, or persons, knew of this manuscript. Knew of its existence, knew of its content. Old Whitty might have been a shut-in, but that didn't preclude the possibility that he had at least an acquaintance somewhere, a confidant even. If this were the case, and I tried one day to pass off this book as all my own work, then somebody somewhere would be sure to cry foul. After all, I intended changing the story plenty, but not quite beyond recognition. It wouldn't take much to deduce that I must've stolen the old man's work; I had the opportunity and, Christ knows, I had the motive. It was like starving to death while sitting on an oil well.

CHAPTER THREE

Over Dublin to the east the the sky began to pale, the sun
about to rise on a life-defining dawn, on one of those
proverbial forks in the road. I could grab a few hours'
sleep, then go about setting my affairs in order, go looking
for decent, regular, honest-to-goodness employment as
I'd pledged. On the other hand, I could say to hell with
that plan. And I could say much the same for that pledge:
an undertaking made in haste, in anger and, doubtless, in
error. For here, in the clear-headed quiet before
daybreak, the way forward was pikestaff-plain. If I was to
crack it at this writing lark, now was not the moment to
turn part-time, to show anything less than full and fierce
commitment. The iron, I knew, might never be this hot
again. I could give it my all for one last mighty heave. I
could, couldn't I? There had to be a way.

And so I began my calculations. It was I who picked
up the mail each morning after it had fallen through the
letter box. I would *surely* have recognized correspondence from a publishing house, had there been any. But
no, the old man had never submitted his work, I was
pretty certain of this. Or if he had, he'd not received a
reply. Perhaps one would arrive, posthumously; if one
did, it'd not be a problem intercepting the letter. And I'd

soon know whether best to proceed, or to abandon the whole idea, with no harm done.

Next there was that bum to consider, the guy who made occasional housecalls on the late Mr Whitty. Maybe he, too, was dead. Even if he wasn't, he didn't worry me unduly. I felt that book could've been published under my name, then gone on to outsell the Bible and still not registered with an old derelict like that. Which left only the niece, the next of kin, the single fly in the ointment. If her picture was anything to go by – I was assuming that was her in the mirror frame – then she was a good deal more savvy than that uncle of hers. This was no mental defective, rather a feisty young thing with all the appearance of being best not trifled with. Nor, for that matter, swindled out of what was rightfully hers. But did she know what was rightfully hers? And if she did, then what did she know? How much, exactly? I decided there was only one way to find out.

Five in the morning and Inchicore Road was deserted, all the way past the Royal Hospital and on to the Kilmainham cop shop. When I rang at the front desk, I was attended to by that same young Garda I'd spoken to only the day before. 'Mr Stokes,' he greeted me. 'Nice to see you again.'

'And you, Garda . . .' I'd forgotten his name.

'Cambridge,' he reminded me. 'Denis Cambridge. And, may I say, 'tis you're up fine and early.'

'I'm afraid I've not been to bed yet.'

'No? Oh, pardon me. A writer, yeah? I guess you're allowed to be eccentric. Anyway, what can I do for you?'

'It was only after you left yesterday I remembered that

I had some stuff belonging to the old man. To Mr Whitty.'

'Stuff?'

'Yeah. Nothing of any value. Just some odds and ends.'

He rested an elbow on the desk counter, his chin on his open palm and said, 'How did you come by them? You told me yesterday that you didn't know the old man at all.'

'Well . . . I didn't. But you don't necessarily need to have bonded with a bloke to borrow a can opener or a cup of sugar, do you?'

His expression didn't change. I went on, 'You said you thought he had family. If you manage to track any down, could you have them call on me? I'm sure they'd want what I've got, for sentimental reasons. I mean, he didn't leave a whole lot to remember him by in that flat.'

'I noticed that too,' Cambridge said, again in a tone I didn't much care for. 'There was very, very little left lying around by the time we got there.'

I didn't respond, he didn't follow through. After a few uncomfortable seconds, I said stonily, 'You think you can do that, then?'

'Sure, his niece is going round there today. I'll have her drop in on you. Any particular time?'

'Doesn't matter. I'm there all day.'

'Oh, of course,' he said, his good grace returned. 'A writer, where else would you be? Certainly, Mr Stokes. I'll pass on your message. And best of luck with Shafty and the boys.'

It must've been the lack of sleep at last taking its toll

because, for one awful instant, I could only stand and gape.

'Y'know, Shafty. The character from your book?'

'Y . . . yeah, of course,' I stammered. 'I just didn't think you'd remember, that's all.'

'Oh, I remember, don't you worry. I just hope you remember a signed copy for a poor hard-working rozzer when you're top of the bestseller list.'

With a grin, and a massive inward sigh, I left the station and set sail for home.

I'd just come in the door, barely taken my coat off when she appeared. 'Okay, what is it this time?'

'What's what?'

'What's the bone you have to pick with me now?'

'Sorry?'

'Look, let's not mess about, eh? You've waited up all night *again* to ambush me. So what's this latest beef of yours?'

'Nothing. Nothing at all.'

'Well, why did you not come to bed, then? You couldn't tear yourself away from the book, is that it?'

'Yes, actually.'

'Ah, pull the other one, will ya?'

'Seriously. I wrote it that long ago, it was like seeing it for the first time. And it was impossible to put down.'

'Something written by *you* was *unputdownable*? Well, that'd be a first,' she said snottily, as out the door she swept.

I needed sleep. But I dared not go under too deeply, for fear I'd miss my visitor if and when she called. Which set me thinking, if she did call, it'd be no harm she find me with my sunny side out. In the first flush of youth no longer, maybe, but I still scrubbed up a damn sight better than most. And a good first impression is never a bad idea. So I shaved, changed the shirt, then liberally applied the cologne all over. After that, I snuggled up in the armchair and drifted away. How long I was out, I don't know. But the room was full of sunlight when I was roused by the rapping on the door.

Outside there stood a woman, low-sized and slightly overweight, her dark brown hair cut in a bob. Late twenties, I guessed; at least ten years older than the face in the picture. However, there was no way that the passage of even ten years could've equated the two. Quite simply, this wasn't the girl in old Whitty's photograph. I'd concluded as much beyond doubt in the moment it took me to ask, 'Yes?'

She smiled and said, 'Hiya. I'm expected, I think. Carla Whitty. Niece of . . .'

I looked again, more closely this time. In a different light, perhaps? With streaks in the hair, and maybe less make-up? No, I decided. These were two different people.

'You are Mr Stokes?' she enquired, that smile wilting just a little.

'Yeah . . . sure. It's just, you're nothing like . . .'

'Sorry?'

'I mean to say, you're nothing like . . . as old as I was expecting. Come on in.'

As I closed the door behind her, she laughed, 'And why would you be expecting someone older?'

'I . . . ah . . . well, Mr Whitty was quite elderly, so I

didn't imagine him having a niece as young as you.'

'I'm flattered. But I'm not that young. And he wasn't that old. Fifty-two, as it happened.'

'Is that all? I would've said—'

'That he looked seventy-five? Well, that's the drink for you.'

'I suppose. Whatever the case, may the Lord have mercy on his soul. He never did me any harm.'

'I'm glad to hear it.'

'To be honest, I didn't know him at all. He tended to keep to himself.'

'That's kinda what I figured.'

'Good God, where are my manners?' I said, realizing. 'Have a seat, please, Ms Whit—'

'It's Carla.'

'And I'm Brendan. Sit yourself down there. Can I get you tea? Or coffee? Or are you in a rush back to work somewhere?'

'Not at all. I'm a nurse in James's Hospital, and this week it's the nightshift. So I've got hours to kill, and a cup of tea would be lovely, if you're offering.'

She may have been a tad on the roly-poly side, but she had very attractive features, remarkable blue eyes, and a most disarming manner. All in all, I was quite taken. But it still wasn't her in the picture.

If not her, then who? I was trying to compose a subtle phrasing of the question when she called, 'The cops reckon you've got some of my uncle's gear?'

'That's right,' I said, as I came from the kitchen and laid the delph and jug on the table before her. 'Look, I don't mean to cast aspersions on the police. But occasionally things do go missing. It's been known to happen.'

She looked intrigued, her expression bidding me continue. I stood up and opened the drawer of the TV stand. The tenner, I'd already resolved, was going nowhere. So I took just a fist of change.

'There was this money lying out in the open,' I said, and I poured it into her cupped hands.

She shook her head wistfully. 'Not a lot to show for a life, is it? Even a life like his.'

'There's more,' I told her, and now emerged with the table lighter and the small Claddagh ring.

Her face creased in recognition. 'I've been down below for the past hour, taking stock. And I missed these, I swear to you, I did. Now, I wasn't surprised that this was gone,' and she held me up the lighter. 'In fact, I'm amazed he's not hocked it over the years. But this? Never ever, not for the world, would he have parted with the ring. That belonged to Ellie, y'see.'

'To . . . to who?'

'Oh, it's a long, long story. You don't want to hear it.'

'Please,' I said. 'I very much do.' I did think about adding 'if you feel up to it'. But I wanted to give her no way out. I *had* to know.

'My uncle wasn't always the pitiful, deranged old man you found sprawled on the carpet yesterday. As a youngster over in Mayo, he was top of his class – a gifted child, I believe. But his people were poor, so he got very little in the way of formal schooling. Instead he went to England, to go working on the buildings. Like damn near every other lad his age in the West of Ireland back then. And by the time he was just twenty-seven years old, he was foreman on this massive building site, and considered outstanding at his job. This was a presentation from a very appreciative employer.'

She turned the lighter upside down for me to see. There, engraved in the cut glass, was '*From the Lancon Construction Company. To Andy Whitty. Luton '77*'.

'He was earning good money, living with a lovely Donegal girl, by all accounts. But this summer – 1977 – he got involved with her younger sister, Ellie.'

'The girl in the phot—' I blurted before I could help myself.

Carla heard. She nodded. 'You noticed? Pretty, wasn't she?'

'Christ, yeah.'

'The kind that'd turn any man's head. But just fifteen years of age.'

'Only fifteen?' I gasped, but by now my surprise wasn't total.

'My uncle should've ended it before it began. But he didn't. He wouldn't. And his whole world caved in around his ears. He lost his friends, his job, his family here in Ireland, naturally enough. They disowned him on the spot. Only under the threat of prison would he agree to finish with her. And even then he couldn't tell her to her face. So he wrote her a letter, breaking it off for good and all, left it where she'd find it, then packed up and walked out. But a mile down the road he changed his mind and came back, fully intending to stay with her and to Hell with the consequences.' She stopped, lifted her teacup, held it a moment near her lips, then put it back. 'He was too late. She'd found the letter, read it, and . . . had taken her own life. Straight away, he tried to do the same – he got the knife and slashed both his wrists. But a friend of his happened on the scene, kicked the door in – got him just in time.'

Each word, each fresh revelation was like a punch to the stomach. But I continued to try to feign amazement and said, 'Wow. That's a helluva story. Helluva friend, too.'

'Poor oul' Shafty, God be good to him,' she muttered, under her breath.

'Well, whoever he was, he saved your uncle's life.'

She looked up and sighed. 'No . . . no he didn't. That day in Luton twenty years ago, my uncle's life ended. Just as surely as if he'd been allowed bleed to death, it ended.' She tailed away, her eyes now fixed somewhere on the carpet by my feet.

And I'd found a spot of my own in the middle distance as I, too, contemplated an ending, an absolute conclusion. Whitty's book was a life story, autobiography barely disguised. He himself was Ned, Ellie stayed Ellie, Shafty stayed Shafty, that's how thin the varnish was in places. To think that it had been my intention to put my name below the title and fob it off as pure fiction – my considered and sober intention, what's more! In a way, I had reason to be grateful. At least it was getting the kybosh before I'd wasted any time, energy or printers' ink. Through the tears in my mind's eye, I could already see the *Evening Herald* classifieds, the situations-vacant column, the fucking fitters-wanted ads. Meanwhile, she took the teacup in both hands and went on, 'From that day, my uncle wasn't living, he was . . . existing. In and out of mental asylums, his back turned on the world, just trying to run down the clock any way he could. Which usually involved staying as drunk as possible for as long as possible. And with not another soul on this earth speaking his name. Apart from myself, of course. I may not be much, but I was all that he had.'

I nearly told her that her uncle did entertain a second occasional caller. But what was the point? She seemed somehow honoured to have been his one and only. Instead I said, 'So why've I not seen you around before? Y'know, if you and he were close.'

'I was here once, three or four years back, I think, when he was down with a bad dose of flu. But even then, he made it plain I wasn't terribly welcome. That little room was his domain, whatever went on there was private. And absolutely nobody else's business. It's like you said, he very much kept himself to himself. And woe betide anyone who tried to intrude.'

I knew this better than most. So I nodded and asked, 'How'd you keep in touch, then?'

'With difficulty, but I managed. Tuesday was his dole day, he signed on in James's Street, right across from the hospital. I'd wait for him there, and take him for a burger and chips to the Roma café. You can imagine how chuffed the management used to be to see us coming.'

'I'll bet.'

'Actually, it wasn't too bad. They knew me, so they kinda tolerated him. Which, by the way, is more than his own flesh and blood did. I grew up listening to my dad ranting that this man was "a disgrace to the family name,

and should be left in disgrace". One brother to another
– who'd ever believe it?'

She looked into her cup, swirled the contents, looked
up again. 'So now, Brendan. That's my late uncle's story
in a nutshell.'

It was a bit pushy, but I pushed on regardless. 'And
what's the story with the typewriter?'

'Oh, you spotted the typewriter?'

'I did.'

She lowered her gaze again and snorted a sad little
laugh. 'The typewriter,' she whispered. 'The famous
typewriter.'

I sat myself upright, now all ears.

'When his girl committed suicide he blamed himself,
of course, but more specifically, he blamed that letter
he'd left her. If he'd not written it, she'd not have read it,
she'd still be alive. And, overnight, he lost the ability to
write.'

'He did what?'

'True as God. Even when he was well enough to be
released from the institution, he still couldn't. Every time
he picked up a pen, his hands shook so badly that no one
but himself could read the scrawl. Now, under normal
circumstances, that wouldn't have been such a terrible
handicap. But he'd locked himself away from civiliza-
tion. He wouldn't browse in a supermarket or an off-
licence. Where he could help it, he wouldn't even speak
with the landlord or the social-welfare people. Instead,
he'd write letters. Or leave notes. Or hand in shopping
lists. Trouble was, they were completely illegible.'

'Bit of a drawback,' I agreed.

'You might say. Anyway, with my first month's wages, I bought that typewriter for the poor sod. A Sharp, it was. Dead snazzy back then, and he thought he was the bee's knees with it. Mind you, he'd have been better off with a basic, manual model.'

'Oh? Why's that?'

'With the old-fashioned ones, you stuck a ribbon in and you were set for life. But the electronic uses ribbon *cartridges*. Disposables.'

'Disposables?'

'Yeah, use them once, then throw them away. And pricy enough they were, what's more. Though in all honesty, that was a bit of a Godsend when birthdays or Christmases came round. I'd get him a supply of these – perfect excuse not to have to give him money. 'Cos we all knew what he did with his money. You probably saw the bag of cider bottles down there too.'

I nodded. She emptied her teacup. 'Brendan, thank you very much for everything you've done. I'm sure the man himself, wherever he may be, is thankful too.' And with that she began to gather her things, making ready to go.

I'd not yet asked what I'd lured her here specifically to discover, and by now there seemed no point. But, I allowed, no real harm either. 'Tell me, Carla. Did your uncle ever try write a book?'

She faced away, inwardly replayed the question a time or two, faced back and mouthed, '*What?*'

'A . . . a book. Did he ever . . . I dunno . . . write one?'

Her laughter was swollen with disbelief. 'No! Jesus Christ, no! What makes you ask?'

'Ah . . . nothing.'

She now turned her full bewilderment on me. 'No, c'mon, tell me. That's no question from out of the blue, there must be a reason. So, why d'you ask?'

I shrugged idiotically and spluttered, 'No reason at all, really.' But still she sat, her glare unflinching. 'I . . . ah, y'know how it is. Even with a pair of tin ears, if someone gives you a guitar, you're going to try learn a chord or two, aren't you?'

She still was far from happy. I went on, 'I just thought he might've. I know I did when I got mine,' and as I said this, I indicated my PC in the corner.

Immediately, her suspicions seemed to soften. 'Good for you. Any luck?'

'No.'

'You mean no, not yet.'

'I mean no, full stop.'

'Oh, don't be like that! You've just been dealing with the wrong . . . company? Publisher?'

'Well, I have been disgracefully treated, that's true to say. But it could be argued, too, that I've never quite delivered on my potential. Look, no false modesty, okay? My forte is my writing style. I've got a way with words that's absolutely phenomenal. At times, it takes even *my* breath away. The problem's been finding a suitable plot to weave those words around. Y'know, coming up with that one story – something raw, something powerful, something original . . . maybe even something based in fact—' I stopped.

A look of panic had crossed her face as she fumbled the old man's leavings into jacket pockets. 'I should be going. I've got . . . things to do.'

And in the next split second, I could tell the cause of her great haste, could see just what it was she was fleeing.

'Hang on a minute, won't you?' I said softly.

'N . . . no,' she flustered, now all a-tizzy. 'I really must . . .'

We both knew the question that was hanging. She winced as I steeled myself, took aim and said grimly, 'What about it, Carla?'

She stood. She swallowed. 'About . . . what?'

'Let me write your uncle's story. As a novel. As fiction.'

'Mr Stokes, you've been very kind. But I have to go now, honest I do.'

'I'd change names, places and all that, obviously.'

She rushed to the door and began foosthering with the catch.

'I can do it anyway, y'know. And I will, with or without your blessing.'

Her arms dropped to her sides. Slowly, she turned. 'No,' she whispered. 'Please. I'd prefer you didn't.'

'Why?'

'You know the end my uncle came to. D'you seriously think I'd want that immortalized in print?'

'But isn't that all the more reason? People around here only saw your uncle in his latter days. They couldn't even begin to imagine how he really lived, or what a tale he had to tell. How could they? And how can they ever, if no one ever puts them wise?'

Her mouth tightened. I'd got her thinking.

'No,' she said, but not decisively. 'No . . . unless . . .'

'Unless what?'

'Unless you agree to end the story the way he wanted.'

'You mean . . . ?'

'Yeah. With a double suicide. Let him die beside the girl he loved. If he couldn't have it in reality, then at least he can have it in your book.'

'Of course!' I shrieked, scarcely able to believe this stroke of good fortune. 'Brilliant! What an ending that would be!' Riding my luck even further, I went on: 'His best friend follows him to the house, kicks the door in, but . . .' I could ignore it no longer. 'But there's something you're still not happy about, isn't there?'

'Yes!' She scowled. 'Yes. Too bloody right there is.'

Easy does it, I thought. Nothing too rash when the big fish is this close to being landed. 'Okay, Carla. You just tell me what.'

The lips pursed tighter yet, the breath drawn hard through the nostrils. When she spoke, it came even, measured and final. 'For years now, I'm the one person on this planet, the only one, who's cared about that old man, about his well-being, or about his good name. And that isn't going to change just because he's passed on.'

'Well, naturally,' I said, not quite following. 'Why would it?'

'What I'm getting at, Mr Stok—'

'Please, it's Brendan.'

'Mr Stokes, is – can I trust you?'

'Eh?'

'You've just admitted to being pretty desperate for your big break. That's what *you* care about, not my uncle's memory. So how can I be sure that you won't take the piss, and go for your cheap laughs at his expense, making him out to be—'

'Carla, d'you think you could find your way here again? On your own? To this flat, I mean?'

'Sure, yeah.'

'Well, girl, you're welcome to call at any hour of the day or night to keep tabs on me. And if you ever see anything you don't approve of, you just say the word. I'll take it out, rewrite it, rewrite it again if needs be, until you're completely satisfied. You have my oath on that. And I can't say fairer.'

She continued to look me over a while, to size me up, top to toe. Gradually, the frown turned first to neutral, then to an easy smile.

'And you've got to promise you'll give Shafty a fair crack of the whip too.'

'Sorry?'

'Shafty. That's what his best buddy was called. Y'know, the guy who kicked the door in. Shafty McDermott, by God! You hear a name like that, you don't easily forget it.'

'There can't be too many of those knocking around, right enough,' I concurred, remembering that the cop had seen the name in my possession one whole day earlier, and deciding there and then that when the name-changing started, this'd be the very first to go.

'By the way, in case you're worried about getting Shafty's permission, don't be. He's long, long past making trouble for you. Or for anyone else.'

'You're absolutely sure – I mean, is that a fact?'

'Aye. It's a lot of years ago now I heard my uncle say how he never did make it home again. Pity, that. I think I'd like to have met him.'

I mumbled something.

'Anyway, Mr Sto – beg your pardon, *Brendan*, I really should be leaving.' There was warmth in her tone as she added, 'Good luck with the story. Don't forget, I reserve the right to drop in here from time to time to check on its progress.'

'As you wish.'

'You're sure you don't mind?'

'Mind? I damn well insist upon it!'

We shook hands, firm and sincere, then she was gone.

Without even waiting for her to clear the building, I raced to my seat at the PC, my fingers trembling, my head in a twist. I'd done it, I'd won the rights. Now it was a simple matter of getting it done, getting it dusted, and getting it away. But getting it started proved more difficult than I'd bargained for. Such was my exhilaration that I could neither think nor see straight, and it was taking me whole seconds to locate each successive letter key. It soon became obvious that, for the time being, I'd best hold my fire. That in my current state, there was no way I could do the thing justice. And after the lengths I'd gone to securing it, my best was the least it deserved.

But, Christ, I had to do something. In the next room, I heard my young son wake. I snatched him up and together we went to the payphone in the lobby. First the money. Then the Kilkenny prefix. Then the number, old and familiar, though not dialled in an age.

'Dad?'

'That's right – Brendan! Howya?'

'Grand. Dad, I've good news.'

'Yeah?'

70

'Yeah. It's been accepted.'

'The book?'

'The book.'

'About Barron's farm?'

'N . . . no. I've had to put that on the back burner for the time being. This is a different one entirely. It's still at a very early stage, mind, it'll need a rewrite. But they've said yes. It's happened, Dad. My foot's in the door.'

'Son, the blessings of God on you! Didn't I tell you to stick with it, that they couldn't turn you away for ever?'

'You did.'

'Well, fair play. You're a topper.'

'Thanks, Dad. I've got to go, I must try to get this thing start— I mean, get on with it.'

'No problem, boy, no problem. Hey, is that young Robert I hear there with you?'

'Oh, who else would it be?'

'Give him a hug from his grandad, won't you?'

After I hung up, I did just that. Then I raised the toddler high above my head and said, 'This old man of yours will *not* be kept down, little fella. He's going to be famous in spite of them all!'

He gurgled in reply.

'I hope you make the most of the situation, bucko,' I told him, 'because, have no fear, I bloody well intend to.'

CHAPTER FOUR

Of all evenings, my wife would choose that one to come home early. Feeling a little under the weather, she claimed. And in the mood for a quiet, not to say rare, night in. At about ten, her mobile rang. She took the call in the bedroom, where she had an hour-long conversation, often heated, with 'nobody'. We retired shortly after and made love, I remember. Not that the sex was in any way memorable, only the fact that we had it at all.

When she'd fallen asleep, I got up and got to it. For writing, there's no time like that quiet time of the morning. My first act was to take old Whitty's manuscript and bung it into the furthest corner of the hot press, making access most difficult. Leave it lying at hand and I'd only be tempted to refer, to ape, to plagiarize. The story might have been another's, but the style would be all my own. Otherwise, what was the point?

In those wee small hours before Dublin began to stir, I worked like a man possessed. As dawn broke, I'd put in place the modern-day setting, the first-person narrative, and done all in trademark fashion: droll here, moving there, readable everywhere. One quick review of the night's work, and in very good heart, I slid between the sheets again before I was missed.

At seven-thirty, Angie's alarm sounded. Never one to stand on ceremony, she was up and gone in minutes. And I was right behind her, back at my desk, back on the job. With only the occasional time-out when my son or I needed feeding, I worked straight to, and through, the church clock chiming midday.

It was then that Alan Bradshaw came calling. And looking, I thought, oddly furtive.

'Can I come in?'

'Come on.'

He shuffled by, then waited on eggshells till invited to sit.

'It'll have to be tea or coffee, Alan. I'd offer you a beer, but—'

'No . . . no thanks. This isn't a social call.'

'Oh,' I said, seating myself opposite. 'What is it, then?'

His eyes widened, his face a passport photograph. As if the conversation had already started inside his head. 'No offence now, Coops, okay?'

I shrugged.

'Y'know how your missus and Ger McEvoy were . . . were an item before you came on the scene?'

''Course. Doesn't everybody?'

'Well, they . . . ahem . . . they are again.'

Ah. So it was McEvoy who'd been latest in line. Disappointing, that. I really thought she'd have traded higher up the market.

'Coops? Did you hear what I just—'

'Yeah . . . yeah. Fuck me. How long's this been going on?'

'I don't know for sure.'

'Well, when did you learn about it?'

'Just last night.'

'Just last night? How?'

'Okay, here's the story. Like I say, I don't know how long he's been seeing her, but it must be a while 'cos it's got pretty fucking serious. Lately, it seems, he's been trying to pressure her into leaving you. The whole thing came to a head in The Black Lion two nights ago. He said he wanted an answer. She said she wanted more time. He told her she could waste someone else's time in that case, called her all the whores and prickteases, and he stormed out. Then last night he rang, couldn't apologize enough, but she refused to see him. Said she still needed time to think things through. So he got absolutely twisted, took a cab over to my place and, well, that's when he told me.'

Hmmmm, I thought. That clears up a thing or two. Where she's stayed on her nights away. Why she's been here and up for sex these past couple—

'Coops! For fuck's sake, your wife is contemplating running off with another bloke!'

'Jesus, yeah. Bit of a choker, right enough.'

'*Bit of a choker*? And, like, what are you going to do about it?'

'What can I do? What more? I married the woman, didn't I? And even that hasn't been enough to discourage McEvoy. So, short of killing him, and don't worry, I'm not going to kill him . . . Now her, on the other hand . . .'

The jaw fell, the eyebrows arched.

'A joke, Alan. Although if I did, there's not a man in this country who'd blame me.'

With a snort, his breathing restarted. Then he looked from me to the baby on the floor by his feet, then back: an unspoken reminder that I ought to be taking the matter a good deal more seriously than I appeared to be. But when I made no further comment, he said at last, 'You're not mad at me, are you, for being the one to pass this on?'

'Not at all,' I told him. 'It's always best to find out.'

'Yeah, well, if ever you're asked, you didn't find it out from me, okay?' He touched the side of his nose twice. 'I mean, Angie and Ger, it's not like I've got anything against either, but . . . look, I'm still going to have to work with them both.'

'Not to worry, I understand.'

'And speaking of work, if I don't head back there this instant, I'll be in some serious shit.' He stood and made for the door.

'Alan, thanks. I really appreciate it. If there are any further developments, you will let me know?'

'I will.'

'And even if there aren't, you'll still pay me the odd visit, for old times' sake?'

'Sure thing. Coops, I just wish there was more I could do. But keep th'oul' chin up, eh? And if you need anything, anything at all, you only have to holler. I know how this must make you feel.'

I doubt you do, I remember thinking. I very much doubt it. Because, at that moment, I wasn't rightly sure myself. The news hadn't shocked me. Hadn't hurt me. Hadn't even inconvenienced me to any great degree. In truth, all it had succeeded in doing was to wreck my concentration to smithereens.

Twice, three times after he'd gone I returned to my writing, attempting to pick up where I'd left off. But the focus wasn't there, nor could I locate it, try though I might. However, before frustration could take hold entirely, I was pleased to recall an errand that, in any case, did need running. So I loaded up my child's pushchair and off we set for the labour exchange. It was dole day.

As I was returning past the great gates of St James's Hospital, I heard my name being called. There, by the security hut and waving furiously, was Carla Whitty. With her stood a young man in jeans and cloth jacket. He, too, offered a wave, small and a touch embarrassed. I waved back, but I could tell that something more was expected. So I wheeled the buggy round and approached the pair.

'Brendan!' she gushed. 'We meet again. This is—'

'I know who he is. How're things, Garda Cambridge?'

'It's Denis. I'm off duty.' He looked a little less goofy out of uniform, but not a whole pile. 'And things are just fine. Hey, Robert!' he said, as he squatted down. 'My main man!'

Goofy or not, his memory was impressive.

'Did . . .' and she pointed from one of us to the other. 'Did you two meet just yesterday too?'

'No,' he told her, without standing. 'We're old friends.'

I said, 'That's right, we go back all the way to the day before.'

She groaned. 'I just called you over to tell you that my uncle's removal is this evening at half-seven.'

'To St Michael's Church, yeah?'

'Aye, to Michael's.'

'Sound enough, I'll try to make it. Garda?'

''Fraid not,' he said, as he came to his feet. 'I'll be out on the beat by then. There's an odd one of us who has to do a bit of work around here.'

'Will you go to blazes!' she said, mock indignant. 'I've been running around those wards like a blue-arsed fly the whole bloody night. You guys don't have the first idea what work *is*.'

I knew they'd just seen me come out of the social welfare centre, and became a little defensive. 'Well, for your information, Miss, I've spent the best part of the past twelve hours sweating over a hot keyboard.'

'Really?' Then, to the policeman, 'Brendan's a writer.'

'I know,' he said. 'And a damn good one at that. I read a sample of his work the other day when we met. And, this is no palaver, I swear, every time I thought about it last evening, I laughed out loud. Remember? What yer man said about the boss that sacked him . . . you remember, yer man . . . what was he called again?'

Like upon the throw of a switch, my face fell, my blood ran to ice and my heart stopped, restarting with explosion after explosion in my eardrums. As he stood there, features contorted and fingers clicking impatiently, I was one word, just a single name, from absolute catastrophe. I dared not breathe for fear of prompting him.

'Oh Jesus . . . this'll annoy me now . . . what the hell was his name?'

'Sorry, I don't remember.'

'Sure you do! You made him up, for Christ's sake . . . Sh . . . Shirty, was it?' I gulped audibly. Where would the next bomb land? 'Not Shirty, but something like it . . . Shorty? Not that either . . . oh, what *was* it?'

'Y'know,' I smiled desperately. 'Since then, I've written about fifty pages. And several new characters.'

'Fifty pages?' Carla exclaimed. 'Of you-know-what?'

I nodded.

'Good God, that was quick work. Hey, is that offer still open? Y'know, to come and see how it's progressing?'

'Any time you like.'

'How about now, then?'

'Fine,' I said. 'Why not?'

Stage left, the policeman cleared his throat. 'I guess we're taking a raincheck on that cup of coffee?'

She sighed. She frowned. Then, 'D'you mind awfully, Denis? It's, well, I gave this . . . this *genius* an idea for a story just yesterday, and I'm dying to see what he's made of it.' As she said this, she took my left arm in both of hers and snuggled close. Cambridge forced, really forced, a smile. 'Sure. No problem at all.'

'Denis! Why don't you come with us? You'd like to see it too, I'll bet. Brendan, that'd be okay, wouldn't it?'

After some ready reckoning, I calculated that it would be okay. Just about.

'No, that's all right,' Cambridge said, eyes now watering in the grimace. 'Go ahead, you two – sorry, go ahead you *two-and-a-half*. We'll have that coffee some other time, maybe.'

'Promise. And thanks for being so good about this. You're a real sweetheart.'

We bade him goodbye and headed off down Mount Brown Hill.

'Why did I not meet this young gentleman yesterday?'

'He slept right through your visit. He's an absolute angel like that, is Robert.'

'How old is he?'

'He's just gone one. And this oul' buggy'll be gone to the charity shop any day now – won't it, Tiger?' He chirruped as I tousled his hair. And then again as Carla did the same.

'He doesn't look a bit like you, lucky little sod.'

I said nothing.

'I mean he's— he's handsome too, but in a different sort of way. Y'know what, though, I must say I'm surprised to learn you have a wife and child. I take it you do have a wife?'

'Yeah. She works. In the textile mill.'

'Really? So she's apart from her baby all day?'

'Uh-huh.'

'And it doesn't bother her?'

'What bothers her or what does not is of no interest to me whatsoever these days.'

'Ooh, things like that, are they? Sorry, sorry. None of my business. Forget I spoke.'

We walked a while in silence. Then, 'Don't take this the wrong way, Brendan. But when I was in your flat yesterday, I thought it looked small and a wee bit, well, grotty. And that was when I was under the impression that you were a single bloke. Now you tell me it's home to a family of three. No offence, but . . . with even one wage-earner in the household, how *have* you wound up in this situation?'

She herself was so very forthright that I thought about

telling her everything, thought about starting with my dismissal from the factory and the circumstances that surrounded it. Then I thought again. It was all a bit complex, that version, all a bit involved. And she did have the appearance of one who'd struggle to comprehend properly. Easier for both of us, I reckoned, to make up something she might better be able to follow. Something a tad more black and white. I began, 'We got married in a bit of a rush, without thinking things through properly—'

I saw her look with significance at the baby I was pushing.

'Oh, no,' I told her. 'It wasn't him that forced our hand, he didn't come along till later. No, after we got hitched we decided that, soon as we could get the shillings together, we'd buy a place of our own. So we moved into Easton Terrace. It was a shithole, but it was a cheap shithole.'

'Your wife's not a local, is she?'

'She is, Chapelizod.'

'Well, why'd you not just bunk down with the in-laws? When couples are saving for their first place, it's quite common.'

'Let's just say we don't get on, me and the in-laws.'

'That's quite common too, I suppose.'

'Anyway, Easton Terrace gave us our independence. And a bit of privacy.'

'And, as you say, it was cheap.'

'For half nothing. But you've seen the kip – even at that it was overpriced.'

She laughed. 'Still, it allowed you put aside a good chunk of your wages each week, yeah?'

'It did that. Unfortunately we landed smack in the middle of Dublin's great property boom. Prices were rising far, far quicker than we could raise the few bob. And you can guess the rest.'

'By the time you'd saved any decent-sized nest egg . . .'

'The kind of house we wanted was out of our league. Exactly. And the longer we spent scrimping and scraping, the further away it went.'

'If it's any consolation, you weren't the only ones caught in that trap.'

'The *only* ones? D'you remember, for a while, everywhere you looked, there were brand new cars whizzing about? People were borrowing for house deposits, then discovering they couldn't afford anything on the market, and blowing the money elsewhere.'

'So what did you do with yours?'

'Well, there weren't many options. We could've bought a car, which we didn't need. We could've bought a house in one of the ghettos, and been stuck there for all time 'cos it'd be impossible to sell on.'

'You could've rented somewhere that was a bit more . . . fit for human habitation.'

'Yeah, but it'd still amount to no more than a roof over our heads. And we'd be watching our savings going to stuff some fat-cat landlord's mattress. Though, to tell the truth, I was all in favour. It seemed the best of a bad lot.'

'So, why didn't you?'

'It was the wife's idea. She knew what I was capable of, and she knew what an awful waste of talent it was to have someone like me working somewhere like Kilmainham Textiles.'

'You worked there too?'

'That's where we met. She was a machinist, I was a fitter. Anyway, we weren't spliced a wet day before she started nagging me, begging me, hounding me till eventually, I handed in my notice and took a stab at writing full-time. The way she'd got it figured, what we had in the bank would tide us over until I came up trumps. Then, when we were in the big bucks, we'd buy big. Nothing done by halves, no expense spared – at least, that's how the plan went.'

Carla pulled at an earlobe, seeming to weigh up the sense of this. Then, 'Well, hats off to your missus. That's quite a bit of faith she's shown in you.'

I nodded. As I did, I tried to look suitably appreciative. But something in my expression must've given me away, because she winked archly and went on, 'Though why do I get the feeling that you really didn't take all that much persuasion? That you wanted out?'

'I did,' I admitted. 'For a long time I'd been deeply unhappy there.'

'Was it the job? The money? The workmates?'

'The job was a piece of piss, the money was adequate, the lads – well, they weren't Mensa candidates, but I could relate to them on a certain level. By and large, we got on.'

'So what was it, then?'

'It wasn't any one thing, it was everything. It was the whole package I was signing up to. It was looking thirty years down the line and seeing only an older, greyer, more embittered version of the drudge I was fast becoming.'

'But you . . . sorry, you've lost me.'

Just as I thought I might. Gently, I continued, 'Carla, my dad's an old man now. He never got much of an education, but he could read and write and he was honest. A fair day's work for a fair day's pay – if I heard him say it once, I heard it a thousand times. And in the fifty-odd years he spent labouring on farms the length and breadth of South Kilkenny, I would swear that nobody ever had less from him than that fair day's work. You want to know where it's got him today? He's over seventy, he suffers from arthritis, and he barely owns the clothes he stands up in. Don't you see? It's a choice we each get to make. Be somebody, or be somebody's lackey. And, Carla girl, I was not put on this earth to take orders from anyone.'

'But we *don't* get that choice, Brendan. We've all got to answer to a higher authority. Look around you: it's the way the world works, it's what keeps the wheels turning. We may not always like it, but what's the alternative?'

'Rise above authority, of course! Make your mark, then you can make your own rules. And, very important, leave behind a legacy, a monument to your memory, so that even when you die your name never will.'

'What about this?' She pointed towards the pushchair. 'Doesn't this keep your name alive? Doesn't it count for anything at all?'

'What? Passing on my DNA? Well, it's nice, but it's not nearly enough. For fuck's sake, rabbits procreate every couple of months, but the last time I saw one of them, he wasn't on the cover of *Newsweek*. He was crossways in a terrier's mouth with half his head missing.

Any fool can have a child and, whether or not you've noticed, the vast majority of them do sooner or later. But if you've been blessed by the Almighty to accomplish something more, then how can you even *contemplate* settling for less?'

'And to accomplish this, whatever it is, you've been prepared to stay in that fleapit for the past . . . how long?'

'Two, almost two and a half years.'

'You're kidding! *That* long? And how much longer? I mean, how far are you prepared to go to succeed in this game?'

'This game's like this life, honey. You do what you have to do. Whatever it takes.'

She shook her head, dizzy with admiration.'Y'know, I have never, ever met anybody so . . . so single-minded. But I can't help wondering, what does your wife feel about it all, these days?'

'I couldn't possibly care less. I'm only waiting for the day when *Fair Eleanore* goes down that slipway and gives me complete financial independence, so I can turf that bitch out—'

She stopped abruptly and stepped away.

'*Fair Eleanore*? Is that what you're calling it?' I drew a long, quivering breath. I'd said too much. 'Not *Remember Me, Fair Eleanore* . . . are you?'

'It's a working title. Y'know, one possibility I'm kicking around at present.'

Suddenly, her face grew dark, just a little.

'You knew my uncle better than you're letting on!'

'N . . . no, I never . . . no way!' Then, mercifully, it struck me to ask, 'Why would you think I did?'

Her expression lightened nothing as she said, 'Of all the names you could've picked, why that one?'

'Well, like, why not? I mean, the girl in the story has fair hair and she's . . . em . . . called Ellie.'

'Yeah, but you go straight for Eleanore? Not a more common one like Ellen? Or Elizabeth, for God's sake!'

'Eleanore,' I told her solemnly, 'is my mother's name.' And I made a mental note that henceforth, in discussions with this young lady, it had better continue being my mother's name.

Carla looked me up and down a while, put her hands on her hips and began laughing to the ground. 'Christ, this is bizarre!'

'What is?'

'That just happened to be his favourite song.'

'Get away!'

'Honest to God, as long as I knew him. Every time we met, he'd be singing it. Or trying to, at any rate.'

I scratched my shaking head at the wonder of it all.

She went on, 'I guess it's understandable enough. When the song was fresh, he was young then too. And, in the years after . . . well, there were other reasons why it would've struck a chord. Whatever the case, that was his song. Y'know, I can still hear him now. Probably will till the longest day I li—'

But the last of the words died in her throat. As they did, I saw that one corner of her eye had just begun to glaze. After a long moment of very awkward hesitation I leant over, took a firm hold of her arm and announced, 'Carla, I'll do it. You've made my mind up for me.'

'Do what?'

'The book. It's *Remember Me, Fair Eleanore*, or it's nothing at all. Upon my word, I won't even consider calling it anything else.'

'Really?'

'I've gotta, don't I? For him. For old Andy.'

Now closer to tears than ever, she said, 'You're a good guy, you know that? It's just what my uncle would've wanted.' Suddenly, out of nowhere, in not the worst voice I've heard, she softly began, '"When your hopes and your dreams come apart at the seams, when you've hoped and you've dreamed all in vain."' She paused, then whispered, 'C'mon. Won't you join me in a few bars? To his memory.'

By the grace of God, I did happen to know it; at least, well enough to warble along in patches. And again she linked my arm as off we set in step, in harmony of sorts:

'"When your hopes and your dreams come apart
    at the seams, when you've hoped and you've
    dreamed all in vain,
When your bridges are burned and there's
    nowhere to turn,
When you're down and your star's on the wane,
When the passing years tear at the heart of you,
And time's not a friend any more,
When it feels like your God has deserted you,
    then remember me, fair Eleanore."'

There exists a second verse of which, to this day, I don't have one single word. But my luck was holding on that day: neither did she.

So we ended up dissolving in a great fit of the giggles, which upset her not at all. On the contrary, she nestled even snugger and said, 'Tell me, d'you believe in fate? In karma? That some things are just meant to be? And that no matter . . . Hey! What's that?'

Easton Terrace had just come into view. There before us was what looked like a large bundle of rags, piled on the pavement by our gatepost. Only as we drew nearer could I identify it as human. A type of person. Mr Whitty's tramp, to be exact. Looking very much alive, despite the policeman's prediction to the contrary. Slumped on the path, a stream of his urine running to the gutter, and rattling a Styrofoam cup at those going by.

'Any few coppers there?' he called as we passed, his words surprisingly clear. I had no loose change, certainly none I cared to share with him, so I quickened my step. But Carla had already disentangled herself and was making towards him. I pressed on a few yards further where I stooped and began attending to the baby.

'Hi, you!' came the call behind me. Determinedly, I ignored it.

'Hi – *you*,' louder this time.

'Er, Brendan? I think he wants . . .' I straightened myself and turned to face him.

'Is he dead?'

'He is,' I said.

'When?'

'Couple of days ago.'

He began to nod, to grumble, to lose himself in far-off thoughts of his own. Before he got completely out of range I said, 'There's no one here for you any more. So

87

clear off about your business.' Still nodding, still grumbling, he strained to his feet and shambled away.

Carla came again to my side. 'What was all that about?' she asked, a mite suspiciously.

'I don't know if they were what you'd call friends,' I told her, 'but he called round occasionally. Your uncle, I think, was good to him.'

She rolled her eyes and said, 'That'd be par for the course, I suppose. Birds of a feather and all that.'

'He obviously recognized me just now. But I didn't want to give him money, or any encouragement, for that matter. This place is doss-house enough without his kind straggling around.'

She helped me unharness Robert, took his hand in hers and walked him up the front steps, then up the two flights of stairs indoors; I followed, lugging the buggy behind them. Back in the flat, he was well ready for his nap, so I thought I'd put him down a while. But before I did I sat Carla at the desk, then on screen I accessed the story from the opening paragraph.

It was some minutes before I got the baby sleeping and could join her at the PC. I wasn't expecting plaudits, exactly, but I surely hoped she'd have got further than the two pages she'd read. Just a little peeved at her clear lack of enthusiasm, I said, 'You don't like it.'

'Oh, no, no, no!' she blustered, protesting too much. 'It's . . . brilliant. Really. And, hey, you do know some big words. "Bibulous"? What's that mean?'

'It means overfond of the drink. A pisshead.'

'Aw, yeah, right. I see now how it fits.' She read on a little. Then, 'I don't mean to be impertinent or anything, but why d'you not just say "pisshead"? Y'know, use ordinary language. Then anyone could read it – anyone could understand it.'

'And anyone could write it too. Any bloody Tom, Dick or Harry.' As she nodded, pretending she accepted this, I went on, 'So that, mainly, is what you've got against it, yeah? The words are too big?'

'Oh, Lord, I've nothing against it,' she argued, no more convincingly. 'In fact, I love it. I'm just . . . not used to reading from computer screens.'

'I could print it out for you.'

'That'd be great. But why don't I wait till you've got a bit more done? That way, I'll get a better idea of how it's really taking shape.'

'Whatever you like.'

'You're sure I'm not imposing?'

'Don't be silly, you're always welcome.'

'I wouldn't be interrupting your work, would I?'

'Well, you might, but I might be glad of it. There are times when I feel myself going ga-ga, stuck here all day long with nobody for company except that little bundle of wind and water in the next room.'

She laughed, then chided, 'A nice way to talk about your son, I must say! You're horrible, you know that?'

'I'm horrible? What about you? You hardly know that poor Garda twenty-four hours, and already you're standing him up, breaking dates, and God knows what else.'

She blushed. I pressed on, 'Carla girl, you've won yourself a fan there. Made a big impression.'

'Aw, shut up, will ya?'

'I'm not joking, he has the hots for you. Thinks you're cute, he does.'

She blushed some more, laughed some more, then from the bottom of the deck, 'And what do you think?'

I wasn't prepared for her to be this forward, this upfront. By reflex, I squirmed away from the question, pretending I'd misinterpreted. 'What do I think? I think you could do a lot worse. He seems like a sound chap.'

She looked away; close, I thought, to tears. Or to punching my lights out. Eventually she lifted her eyes, but not to meet mine. 'I'd best be getting ready for that funeral,' she faltered.

'Fine,' I said awkwardly. 'I might see you there.'

'If you like,' and she stood, still avoiding me, still stinging with humiliation.

'Seven o'clock, wasn't it? In St Mich—'

But she was already at the door, fumbling with the latch. Which meant I needed to act fast, but I couldn't think straight to act: I could scarcely think beyond the right good kicking I owed myself following this fiasco. Was I that badly out of practice I could pass up a goal so open, a legover so perfectly presentable and so fucking easy? Feverishly, I dredged for that line, for that sugared hook, for that one little white lie I knew might yet turn the tide my way.

'Carla?'

She didn't look round.

'Very, very beautiful.'

'Eh?'

'You asked what I thought of you – well, I'm trying to

tell you what I think. Or is "beautiful" too big a word as well?'

She froze. In the eternity it took her to turn, I wondered if maybe my original reading was correct, and only *now* had I taken the wrong end of the stick and made a complete arsehole of myself. But in an instant we were together, grasping frantically, kissing longer and harder than I'd done for many a day. From there, we sank to the floor, to a carpet that hadn't seen brush nor Hoover for some considerable time.

Heavy though the going was underneath, I never suggested we adjourn to the bedroom: it didn't seem right, not with the baby lying in the cot alongside. Even if there was the possibility that that same baby was the result of just such an encounter.

CHAPTER FIVE

The months that followed went by in a blur. My wife soon resumed her hectic social whirl, her drunken nights out, her questionable acquaintances, her mysterious phone calls at all hours. Occasionally, we slept together. More frequently, she harangued me about desisting from this nonsense and getting myself a job. Once in a while, she even presented me with an ultimatum, threatening to leave and take Robert with her if no action was forthcoming. No action of the sort ever was, of course, but by then she'd have forgotten both the deadline and the displeasure. And have continued on her merry way.

Carla called round for sex a couple of times each week, sometimes more often if her working hours suited. Though I could never get her actually to read anything, or to take a printout with her, she did insist on hearing of all headway made, all ground gained. And, in return, she'd fill me in on my son's growth and development. He might have been coming on fine and dandy in the playpen just yards from my work desk, but I scarcely noticed. I was vaguely aware that he no longer needed the playpen bars – or, indeed, anything at all – for support, and was walking with a fair degree of independence. I thought I could also hear some of his gibbering begin to take form, to sound like words I almost recognized. And he came into possession of at least a dozen teeth: Carla pointed them out to me one day, and there they were.

Carla was also on the plot, doing what she generally came to do, when Alan Bradshaw next called. As soon as he realized what he'd stumbled upon he coughed an apology and beat a bewildered retreat, saying he'd talk to me another time. I leapt into some trousers and followed, catching him up at the front door. There, I attempted no excuse, no defence; this was how it was, exactly how it looked. Thinking I sensed a certain disapproval, I reminded him that I was not the one who'd strayed first. Indeed, that I was not the only one straying even now. He just laughed, saying it was none of his business. But saying also that, with the two sides equally at fault, it wasn't right asking him to spy on one for the other. This, I accepted, was fair enough. And we parted company, both pledging to keep in touch. Though he'd not be making any more spur-of-the-moment visits to my flat, he warned. Not after the scene that greeted him today. This too I accepted.

But these diversions aside, my life over those weeks ran on a single narrow track. I worked night and day, every available waking hour on *Remember Me, Fair Eleanore*. Not once did I consult the original: it lay buried in the nether corner of the hot press where I'd stashed it before even the first line was typed. The time setting I made modern. The location, Luton, I had no choice but to leave. To all characters, I gave completely new aliases, save for Ellie. I allowed her hang on to her Christian name: I needed it for the book's title. And though I'd have liked to retain Shafty among the cast list, he too had to go – the copper and his goddamn inquisitiveness had seen to that. So my narrator now became one Whacker McGrane. Not a patch on the original, I conceded. But it ensured that in no way, shape or form did Shafty McDermott continue to exist. Every trace of him and of his memory was stricken from the record. It was safer that way.

Fourteen chapters, plus epilogue, all written and righted. Now came the most important name change – my own. For no company regarded, or respected, the first-time author like Monitor Press; nowhere else was the fledgling guaranteed as fair a shake. Despite our previous turbulence, I knew it represented my best, maybe my only chance. However, if 'Brendan Stokes' were to appear on the title page, I knew precisely what my chances would be. So, for the occasion, I became Bernard Swords. And for the return address, I risked omitting a flat number. Bernard Swords, 256 Easton Terrace – it was still close enough that all correspondence would find its way through to me. But just different enough, I reckoned, to throw the good Ms Rooney, Chief Commissioning Editor, well off the scent.

If the months of writing breezed by, then the days spent waiting for a reply were interminable. However, I don't believe that, as long as I live, I'll forget the somersault my heart turned when, there on the doormat one morning among the bills, flyers and junk, the name Bernard Swords was blazing up at me. Not attached to some great wodge of rumpled, rough-packaged discard, but to a small, dainty, brown envelope, franked with the logo of Monitor Press, Rathmines. As if in the throes of a great and protracted orgasm, I began ripping at the cover, aware I'd better not damage whatever lay therein, but unable to contain myself.

> Monitor Press, Publishers
> 1008 Rathmines Road
> Dublin 6
> 13th November 1996

Dear Mr Swords

I have just finished reading your manuscript, *Remember Me, Fair Eleanore*. Perhaps you could give me a call at the above number in order that we might discuss it. You can reach me any day between 1.30 and 5.00.

Yours sincerely
Aoife Lyons

Still light-headed and leery, I'd just begun trying to calculate who the Hell Aoife Lyons might be, and what all this meant exactly, when the doorbell rang.

'Things were quiet, they let me go early,' Carla said. 'Brendan? Is something wrong?'

Without a word, I pushed the letter to her. She took it and read at a mutter. 'Discuss it? Discuss what?'

'Discuss *what*? A contract, obviously! Jesus girl, what else?'

'A contract?' She looked up from the page, her eyes twinkling. 'Wow! So you reckon this is . . . ?'

'Well, I can't say for certain what it is. But I can tell

you for a sworn fact what it's not, it's not the thumbs-down. Believe me, I'm pretty familiar with those.'

'Past tense, buddy, you *used* to be,' and as I swept her into my arms she yelped, 'A published author! Mama, I've got it made, I'm shagging a published author!'

After I'd rolled out of bed and was dressing, it struck me as odd that she was making no move to do likewise. I went to the living room, fed and changed the child, then returned to find her as I'd left her: staring at the ceiling, deep in thought.

'You won't leave her now,' she said evenly, as if from a trance.

'Huh?'

'Your wife.' The tone was the same, just as flat, just as bloodless.

'What're you talking about?' I said, rightly taken unawares. For this was something we never, ever spoke of. It wasn't that I didn't intend leaving my wife, it's just that I didn't intend leaving her for Carla Whitty. Carla had her uses but she was strictly mistress material, middle-of-the-week fare and no better. Promising nothing, yet having her believe she was heir-apparent: up to now, I'd been judging this trick to a nicety.

'I may as well face it,' she sighed, as she turned on to her left elbow, 'I'll never have you to myself, will I? It'll be shiny, happy families here from now on. This just settles it.'

'And how, in God's name, d'you make *that* out?'

'Isn't this the final part of the master plan? The reward for all those sacrifices you both made? Isn't this your ticket to the suburbs, to your four-bed semi with the conservatory out the back and the second car in the drive?'

'Well, honey, I most certainly hope so. But not with that wife of mine in tow.'

'Really? So you'll be ditching her, then?'

'For Christ's sake, Carla, you must know that I've only stayed with her till now because I didn't have a choice in the matter. Financially, she had me over a barrel. And where the little fella was concerned, what court in this land would grant custody to an unemployed father? Jesus, girl, I stuck with that slapper because I couldn't afford not to.'

'And d'you reckon you can afford not to now? Because – you wrote that book while you and she were still married. In the event of a split, she's entitled to fifty per cent of everything it earns. Now and for ever. Have you thought of that?'

I hadn't. But no facts, figures or similar unpleasantries were going to put a crimp in my day. Certainly not this day. 'So? Let her have her pound of flesh. It's just one book, the first of many, many more to come. You wait and see – once I'm up and running everything will fall into place.'

'Oh, yeah? And what will you write about?'

'Sorry?'

'What will you write all these other blockbusters about? I mean, I gave you the idea for this one, only because you didn't have a single thought of your own.'

'Well, thank you for such a ringing vote of confidence! What is it you're suggesting, exactly? That I amn't up to the task? That I don't have what it takes? Just an ordinary, average, common Joe, yeah, and miles out of his depth here? Is this *your* considered opinion?'

'No. It's not my opinion. It's plain undisputed fact.'

'Carla, you'd better get dressed and get the fuck out before something is said that can't be mended.' And with that, I turned on my heel. It was gone one-thirty, I had a call to make.

I snatched up the letter from the kitchen table where it lay and descended to the lobby, to the payphone. I was fuming and with every step of the stairs, the more incensed I became. Where did she get the nerve to speak to me in that way? And who the Hell did she think she was to cast such aspersions? In a matter of minutes, I'd hear my ability acknowledged, my future prospects affirmed. In the space of this one single phone call. How dare she?

'Aoife Lyons? Bernard Swords here.'

'Bernard! Thanks for getting back to me so promptly.'

'No problem. You read my manuscript?'

'I certainly did. A very impressive piece of work.'

'Thought you might like it.'

'Well, there was plenty to like about it. Your first?'

'Yes, it is.'

'My God, you've really hit the ground running. Strong, strong, *strong* story. Marvellous potential.'

'Potential? You mean, as it is, you don't reckon it's good enough?'

'That's not for me to say, I'm afraid. I don't have the final word. I'm just one of several readers for the company. And we all answer to a lady named Kate Rooney.'

'Kate Rooney, right,' I said, attempting to sound as if this was news to me.

'She's the top dog, the buck stops with her. Now, I'd love to pass your manuscript on to her, but there'd be absolutely no point. I know she'd turn it down.'

'H . . . how? How d'you know?'

'Trust me, this is what I do for a living. I've had you ring me so that we can discuss what's wrong with your book, and what we can do to put it right.'

At that very moment, Carla came ambling down the stairs. I turned my back to her, allowing her to pass without even a glance exchanged.

'Now, let's establish one thing. Are you the kind who's fiercely precious about his writing?'

'What?'

'I mean, if I recommend some cuts or changes, are you likely to be stubborn and fight me every word of the way? 'Cos if you are—'

'Oh, no, no, not at all! I want to be published. That's the bottom line. In fact, that's the only line.'

'Excellent. Then I'm sure we can work something. So, let me cut to the chase, to the book's biggest flaw, in my view. It's a first-person account.'

'So?' I shot back, probably too belligerently. Then, 'That is . . . You think it shouldn't be?'

'Good God, no! No way, never. Your narrator, Whacker, is a gas man, but he's peripheral to much of the action. Take the book's ending – by far its most powerful passage. The girl, Ellie, sees she's getting the elbow, so she cashes her chips in. Your hero finds her, decides that life without her isn't worth the grief, so he does the same. At least I *think* that's what's happened, but because Whacker doesn't get there till it's all over, we're never told for sure how it went down.'

'Yeah, but—'

'Bernard! You want to be a writer? Well, here's a scene crying out to be . . . to be *written*. And you've ducked it! You've let all the action, the feeling, the emotion happen off page. Take it from me, this needs a straight bat. Just put it down as you imagine it happened.'

I quickly calculated that such a rewrite would be no great imposition. After all, Whitty's original was a third-person telling.

'Another thing, there are parts, small parts, where events don't quite mesh. Like as if there's a scene, or a twist, or a piece of information missing. I'm not going to go through it with you blow by blow. I'd just advise you to look it over carefully, and try to put yourself in the place of a person who's reading it for the first time, and who doesn't already have the story in their head like you do.'

I had no idea what she could possibly be talking about. But, eagerly as I could, I said, 'I'll do that, it sounds like good advice. In fact, everything you've advised makes sense.'

'Wonderful! It's refreshing to run into someone who's so keen to learn. And to improve.'

'Ms Lyons, it's like I told you earlier. I'm willing to do what it takes.'

'Well, do what I've suggested for starters. There isn't all that much the matter with your story, so get the head down, get busy, and we'll expect to hear from you before too long.'

'You can count on it,' I assured her. And I hung up, feeling it could've gone better, knowing it could've gone a whole lot worse.

At once I set about a thorough review, a line-by-line deconstruction. Not of my own effort, of course – there was no earthly purpose to be served by that. Instead, I exhumed the master copy and began. Truth to tell, there *was* something to be said for placing the narrator completely outside the story. And I did find an instance or two where Whitty's idiot-standard recounting was perhaps that bit clearer, where my version might've proved too sophisticated for the great unwashed. Mostly insignificant details, none requiring major surgery. This rewrite would be a doddle.

I'd only just started when my wife arrived home. It was almost nine, so I wasn't expecting her to put an appearance in that night. Inevitably, she smelt of liquor.

'Who was that woman?' she began.

'What woman?' I asked, without facing round.

'The woman who called here today. A little on the heavy side. Brown hair.'

I shook my head.

'Myself and one of the vanmen had to go to the stockist's around twelve, and she was at the door as we were passing. Then, when we were coming back some time before two, she was on her way out . . . No? Odd that. Because you were the one who let her in.'

Now I had to give the dialogue some attention. 'That was Carla Whitty. Nice, friendly girl. She's a niece of the old man who died in the flat downstairs six months back.'

'But that flat's been relet this long time.'

'I know. I suppose she was . . . look, I don't fucking know what she wanted. And I didn't ask.'

'I haven't chanced upon anything here, have I? Because, frankly, she doesn't look your type.'

'Really. And what's my type?'

'Well, tall, slim, dark. A bit like your wife.'

'Maybe my tastes run to several different types. A bit like my wife.'

She sighed, 'Oh, Christ, if I'd known you were in one of your moods, I'd not have come home.'

'Nobody's stopping you going out again.'

'Thank you. I just might . . . hey, what's this?'

She'd found the letter from Monitor. '. . . call . . . discuss it . . .' She looked up. 'Is this what I think it is?'

I shrugged. 'Could be.'

'Did you make the call?'

'Yeah.'

'And?'

'And they want me to redo certain bits. Which is what I was trying to get started, until you—'

She lunged at me, threw her arms around and planted a great, sopping, drunken kiss on my lips. I shook her free and said, 'I thought you were going out.'

'I am,' she cooed. 'But I'll be back!'

She returned in minutes with what looked, and later tasted, like a bottle of the vilest cheap champagne and a carrier bag straining with tins of lager – and with a certain look in her eye. All of which put paid to any notions of progress for that particular night.

But it was strictly a temporary delay. This new draft proved every bit as easy as I'd envisaged. I wrapped it up in jigtime, despite the several phone calls I had to make coaxing Carla back. And the two or three interludes each week when, normal service resumed, she'd call in the quiet of the midday. I also had to contend with the mothering and smothering my wife now visited upon me. Bradshaw never said, but my guess was that she'd abruptly ended things with her fancyman, concluding that I was the better bet after all. It was more hindrance than help: I worked far more effectively when we barely spoke. And while it'd be nice to say that at least she meant well, I knew for a fact that she did not. Her motives were anything but honourable.

Added to that lot, there was the occasional phone call from my parents, demanding updates, lowdowns and good reasons why I hadn't come south to visit. There was little Robert, his feet now found in earnest, scurrying about opening cupboards, eating whatever fitted in his mouth, swinging from every flex and curtain within reach. All things considered, there were distractions a-plenty. But overriding everything was the belief, the *knowledge*, that the light at the tunnel's end was no illusion. For the first time in my life, I was working to order, writing at a publisher's commission. That commission, admittedly, was nudging me a little closer to the original, to another man's creation. Still, though, my conscience was clear. For what had begun life as an unholy mess was now a thing of order, of structure, of merit. It was I who'd supplied all three and then some. The manuscript in the registered envelope on its way to Monitor Press that March morning was mine. Distinctively, unmistakably mine. Nobody else's.

Walking away from Emmet Road post office in the chill spring sunshine, floating on the uplift of mission finally accomplished, I'd almost gone by Garda Denis Cambridge before realizing. There he was, in full regalia, standing by the gates of St Michael's, not doing very much.

'Mr Stokes!' he called cheerily.

'Oh, Garda. It's yourself,' I called back. 'Hard at it?'

'Ah, sure, struggling along.'

'This what they've got you doing now, policing St Michael's estate?'

'Or St Michael's Mistake, as some of the locals call it. And believe me, my friend, it does not police itself. Anyway, let's hear it. Is that book going to be tumbling off the presses any time soon?'

'Actually,' I said, 'I've just now come from sending away the manuscript.'

'What? Only now? I really don't know how you guys work, but I saw it . . . Christ, it must be near twelve months ago. And it looked pretty much ready then.'

'Yeah. It was. I sent it away shortly after, and the publishers showed an interest. But they wanted one or two things changed. That was the second draft today.'

'So it's been accepted? You've cracked it?'

'Er . . . yeah, I guess.'

'Well, good luck to you. Sooner or later, the cream will rise, eh? Mind you, I'm not surprised. I've still not forgotten that bit of it you let me read. Y'know the character who's resigned over a difference of opinion with his boss – the boss *doesn't* consider himself the biggest wanker in Europe. I just wish I could remember that character's name, though. Believe it or not, it's been bugging me ever since.'

I dread to think what colour I turned.

He went on, 'D'you remember? I asked you about it the last time we spoke. And I got the impression you didn't want to tell me because Carla Whitty happened to be there.' He looked at me, his expression open, prepared to wait.

I knew I'd better give him something, or he'd keep on trawling till he found. 'Oh, that guy? That's Whacker. Whacker McGrane.'

'N . . . no,' he said hesitantly. 'That'd never have slipped my mind. Y'see, I've got a brother they call Whacker.'

Oh, good Jesus, I thought. You *would* have. But I smiled my sunniest and said, 'Well, whoever he was then, he's Whacker now. I change names, characters and places all the time. I couldn't tell you what he started out as.'

He nodded, seemingly satisfied. 'Whacker, eh? Good a name as any, I suppose. Now what about that other man, the little lad – Richard?'

'Robert.'

'Robert. How's he?'

'Fine, thank God. A right wee hooligan.'

'Walking?'

'Running, Garda. Head first into every kind of devilment.'

'Where is he, by the way? 'Cos, like, I assume your wife is at work.'

'She is. Robert's being minded.'

'Oh, you've got a sitter, then?'

'Sort of, yeah.'

'Very good. And your missus, she's keeping well?'

'Never better. How've you been?'

'Ach, y'know. Getting on with things.'

'And how's the love life?' I asked, thinking he'd be glad to move on from work and family to something a bit more blokey.

But, immediately, he was examining his shoes, sucking air through his teeth as he did. 'Not great, to be honest. I run into Carla every once in a while, and I've asked her out a couple of times. But it seems she's involved with someone.'

I gulped loud enough to deafen us both. He suddenly looked up. 'Is it you?'

'I have seen her . . . once or twice.'

'And she's minding your child right now, yeah?'

'That's right, she is.'

His smile was very fixed, very strained. 'Some guys have all the luck. A book with the publishers and two birds on the go.'

I gave an uncomfortable little snort of laughter by way of reply.

'Women – there's no sense to them, is there? I mean, Carla Whitty is not a fool. She must see that she'll never have a future with you. And she can't possibly fail to notice that there are men out there – single men in good respectable jobs, who'd give their eyeteeth to . . . Oh, don't worry. I amn't going to confront her with this piece of logic or anything like that.' Now, looking as bitter as he sounded, he pressed on through my obvious unease. 'I'm very fond of that girl, Mr Stokes. I really am. And, no offence, but I have to question how much she could mean to you, if you're prepared to stay married to another woman. Y'know, I only upset myself by doing this, but I can't help thinking how different things might've been if I'd found her uncle's body and not you.' He paused a long while, waiting for me, for my line.

At last I obliged with, 'Why's that?'

''Cos then I could've swiped the old man's stuff, handed it back to her the next day, and that might've made me the great fellow.' He stood bold and unblinking, daring me to rise to the bait.

'D'you have some proof for what you've just accused me of?' I enquired calmly, reasonably.

He smirked, eyebrows raised. 'I don't remember accusing you of anything.'

'Good. In that case, I'll be on my way. I've got things to attend to.'

'I'll bet you do,' he said sourly. 'I'll bloody bet you do.'

And I walked away, knowing I'd surely exchanged my last civil greeting with Garda Denis Cambridge. From now on it'd be business, strictly business, or nothing at all.

The next reply, when it arrived, was still a little way short of what I'd been hoping. Mercifully, it wasn't 'Manuscript Returned, Better Luck Elsewhere'. Instead, another small, brown envelope, similarly franked, similarly sized to the first.

Monitor Press, Publishers.
1008 Rathmines Road,
Dublin 6
23rd March 1997

Dear Mr Swords

I've just now finished reading your manuscript, *Remember Me, Fair Eleanore*. Perhaps you could call to the above address some afternoon next week in order that I might discuss it with you.

Yours sincerely
Kate Rooney
Chief Commissioning Editor

Practically identical, then, to the one that came before – no contract, no deal, no firm indication of acceptance. More goddamn discussion. But at least that discussion had been upgraded to the face-to-face variety. And, evidently, I'd reached the top of the food chain: an audience with Kate Rooney, Chief Commissioning Editor, my great nemesis of old.

And so with my best foot forward, with a Sunday suit that had seen several Sundays too many, and with a bellyful of butterflies, I made my way to the Rathmines office of Monitor Press on the very next working day. 'Bernard Swords,' I lied to the mousy receptionist. 'I think Ms Rooney's expecting me.'

Without replying, she put through a brief, internal phone call.

Almost at once, the door at her back swung open.

'Bernard! Glad you could make it. Come on through. Kate Rooney,' she said, as she extended her hand. She was short, scrawny and wretched, a puckered death's-head under skeins of wispy white hair. Every inch the crone I'd been expecting. 'Have a seat,' she said grandly, then walked round the desk and retook her own. 'Now. *Remember Me, Fair Eleanore.*' She rolled each word round before releasing it like a smoke ring. 'Your first, I believe?'

'That's right.'

'And I also understand from Aoife – the girl who passed it on to me – that this is a second draft. A pretty fundamental rewrite, in fact, of the original.'

'I did change it round quite a bit, yeah.'

'Aoife's told me the alternatives she recommended, and I do think that all were beneficial. Because what we've got here now is an impressive piece of work. Quite impressive. With definite potential.'

Oh, for Christ's sake! I thought. Not more of this *potential* bollox.

She must've seen how my face fell, sensed how my heart sank.

'Everything all right, Bernard?'

'Erm . . . yeah. I mean, well, the book. Is there still something wrong?'

'I'm afraid, Bernard, there's a good deal wrong. A good deal right about it too, of course. But before we could even consider publishing, there are several adjustments needed.'

I shook my head, far from amused. 'Like what?'

'First, foremost and most obviously, the time setting is completely askew.'

'In what way?'

'Okay. It's England, the building trade, bang up to the minute. And you write very well, very sympathetically about the Lump. Y'know, the system whereby the navvies assemble at the kerbside, the foremen arrive in the vans and snap up the biggest and the burliest. Leaving the same puny weaklings behind morning after morning.'

'And?'

'Bernard, in the construction industry, 1997 vintage, the balance has shifted the other way entirely. These day labourers are just not to be had any more. Sites are so desperate, they'll employ anybody. It doesn't matter if you look like Emily Bishop from *Coronation Street* - you want work, you're hired.' She paused, allowing me the opportunity to account for this gaffe. When I didn't, when I couldn't, she went on, 'And that isn't all. It's littered with anomalies. For example, the Manchester United manager is sacked for having an affair with the physio's wife. And the boys on the site enjoy a field day, joking about how he's playing in the hole, scoring away from home, et cetera, et cetera, et cetera. Now . . . can you explain that to me?'

'Well . . . I'm not really much of a sports fan—'

'Oh, believe me,' she scoffed, 'that wasn't the bit I wanted explained. I mean, what made you include that in a present-day story?'

'I dunno, 'cos it's funny, I suppose.'

'Funny, maybe. But that's not how it happened.'

'S . . . so what?' I said, trying not to sound as indignant as I felt. As any self-respecting author would've felt at being pissed about like this. 'I mean, Jesus, is that really such a big deal? Aren't football managers sacked all the time?'

'Bernard, football is the most played game in the world, Manchester United its most famous club. Even *I* know that the incident you describe happened in 1977. A full twenty years ago. Put that in your story and you may as well chuck in . . . I dunno . . . Neil Armstrong's moonwalk. Kennedy's assassination. War with Germany declared. The Great Fire of London, even – imagine the adventures your characters could have as they set about rebuilding the city after the smoke has cleared.'

Inside my head, I began counting; only with great difficulty did I make it to ten. I'd had my bellyful of abuse from this woman. In the past, some small measure might have been justified. But now she was picking holes for the sake of picking holes, splitting hairs and then preening like she'd split atoms. A petty, contemptible old sneer, showing no more than her true colours. I perhaps wasn't about to tell her this in so many words, but I was poised to say something when she rabbit-punched me with, 'It's not actually your story at all, is it, Bernard?'

Instantly, I lost the power to blink or to move my lower jaw.

She laughed aloud. 'It's quite all right, young man, you needn't look so horrified! I don't care where it comes from. Maybe it's your father's, your big brother's – it's really not important. Somehow, you appropriated it. Here on in, it's your baby. But that doesn't mean it's got to be set in your era, when it so clearly belongs in another.'

I nodded, much chastened, much *much* relieved.

'So you'll see to that, yeah? Now, there's one other thing. Are you familiar with the term "overwriting"?'

'I think so. It means . . . kinda . . . saying too much. Going on a bit.'

'It means showing off a bit, too. And, Bernard, you have a tendency to overwrite. To use ten, twenty words, big ones, where one, or maybe none at all, is needed.' She sighed. 'Reading your book, I had to marvel at the number of four-syllable adjectives there are that can be applied to two men doing nothing more complicated than just getting drunk.'

I made a half-hearted attempt to laugh.

'Look,' she went on, now very earnestly. 'This is a question of natural style and flair. I do suspect that you can write. That under all that puff and padding, there's a real storyteller itching to be heard. Trouble is, Bernard, we'll soon be approaching a point where the jury's got to come back in on you and your ability. This is the third draft we'll be considering. Very, very rarely do we invest so much of our time in an unpublished debutant. Or in anybody at all, for that matter.'

So saying, she pushed the manuscript into a neat green folder and passed it to me across the table. We shook hands again and parted, amicably as could've been expected under the circumstances.

And so it was back, once again, to digging out Old Man Whitty's original. By now I was stomach-sick of the sight of it, and could've recited whole tracts of the thing, paragraphs where English seemed – at best – a second language. Still, if they wanted an authentic time setting, then an authentic time setting they would have. By its side on the desk was my own latest effort, waiting its turn to be scoured for outbreaks of this great and terrible overwriting. I knew – I *knew* – there was absolutely nothing wrong with the way I wrote. But, for whatever reason, it wasn't pleasing to that wizened little banshee over in Rathmines. And, after all, hers was the only opinion that mattered.

In any case, I made a start. Weary, demoralized, grudging, and glad to be interrupted by the phone from the hallway. Gladder still to hear Alan Bradhshaw's voice at the far end.

'Coops?'

'Uh-huh.'

'Now, first of all, you mustn't take this the wrong way—'

'What? What the fuck is it this time?'

'D'you fancy your old job back? It's yours here and now for the asking.'

'How come?'

'Ger's been sacked.'

'Eh? Just like that?'

'No, not just like that. Again, I don't mean to offend you, but you must have realized that your wife finished with him for good a while ago.'

'Yes,' I said. 'I had noticed.'

'He wasn't best pleased back then and, in the meantime, things didn't get any better. He began missing days. Lots of days. And when he did show up he'd always be late and so hungover that he wasn't much use to anybody. Y'know, he'd be fucking up, skiving off, generally pushing his luck. Plus, there was the atmosphere whenever himself and Angie came within an ass's roar of each other. Yesterday, he got called in and put on a final warning. If he was late again, or took another sickie without a doctor's cert, he'd be out. Anyway, he showed up this morning, on time, fair enough, but he really shouldn't have bothered. He wasn't hungover, he was still drunk. He went to replace a faulty knotter, took into the wrong machine and banjaxed two whole production lines. So he just downed tools, grabbed his coat and cleared off. Didn't even wait to hear his marching orders.'

'Jesus, that's quite a morning you've had.'

'Oh, never a dull moment. So, what about you? Interested? Now, I know from your missus how well things are going. Even my mother was telling me the other day that we're soon to have our first celebrity from the parish of Earlsgrove – I think your dad's been shooting his mouth off just a little. So I won't be at all miffed, or surprised, if you say no. But I thought I should keep you posted when anything arose.'

'Alan, I appreciate that. And I'll bear it in mind – maybe the day'll come when I'll be damn glad to have it. But not right now. I've got to stick with this thing.'

'I understand. You've done the work, now you might as well wait for the moolah . . . Anyway, I'd better go. Talk to you again.'

I'd only just hung up and returned to my post when suddenly, down below, the front door began to rattle as if in the grip of poltergeist activity. I hesitated: every instinct told me that it was trouble and best left on the outside. However, I had good reason to believe that the caller was for myself. That he'd not take an unopened door for an answer. And that if someone didn't let him in, and soon, the thing was coming clean off its hinges.

'I want a word with you!' Ger McEvoy garbled. His hair stood in tufts, his shirt hung out and his crotch sported a stain the size of a saucer.

'You'd better come in, then,' I said, from behind my bravest face, and walked ahead of him upstairs to the flat. He followed me inside and, swaying a little, looked about in mock wonder. 'So this is it, eh? This is where it all happens.'

'All what?'

'All the cutesy, lovey-dovey, till-death-do-us-part horseshit. This is where it goes on?'

'You sound surprised, Ger. I don't know why. I mean, you've been here before.'

'Yeah, I've been in Angie's. And she's been in my place. But she won't come any more. She says this is where she wants to be.'

'Probably because she lives here.'

'That's right, rub it in, you smug bastard. She should never have married you, that was a horrible fucking mistake. And it didn't take her all that long to realize, either. For years now she's been saying it – you're just not the man for her.'

'Really? And I suppose you are?'

'Yes!' he spat, taking a step towards me. 'I was there before you were. And I was going to be back there again, after she'd done with you once and for all. Christ, we were close,' and he held his thumb and forefinger a hair's breadth apart. '*Soooo* fucking close. She was walking out of this dive, out of this marriage, to be where she belongs. With me.'

Anybody else, and I'd have told him that if he'd only agree to leave peacefully, then he was welcome to her. I didn't much care for my wife. But I liked this guy a lot less. So I grinned, 'What can I say, Ger? She came to her senses in the nick of time.'

'Bollox! Twelve months ago, that was when she came to her senses. When she took up with me again.'

'So how come she's in my bed these nights while you're back to your true calling, back on the hand shandies round the clock?'

'You know, you fucker! You know what you did. You conned her, you fooled her again, you persuaded her that—' He spotted the typed pages on the desk where they lay. 'You lying piece of shit, you lured her back with *these*!' And, crying now with rage, he swept both manuscripts on to the floor, sending pages ticker-taping about the little room. In the next, wakened by the commotion, Robert began to holler.

I took a step forward till I could smell the stale porter on McEvoy's breath. 'Now listen, you ignorant grunt! If you think you can come in here, destroying my home, upsetting my child—'

'Huh? *Your* child? That's not your child!'

This stopped me in my tracks.

Emboldened, he puffed his chest out and crowed, 'Don't be codding yourself! That child's not yours.'

'Well, he's certainly not yours,' I lashed back, though a little unsure of my footing.

'But at least I might be able to give her a baby some day. 'Cos, mate, it's obvious that you're not capable, you fucking joke!'

At that, I grabbed hold of him, meaning to throw him down the stairs and out directly on to Inchicore Road. However, it was more than just the considerable weight advantage: here was a man whose everyday work was wont to be hard and physical. In almost three years, I'd done nothing more strenuous than punch a keyboard or, in due course, raise a toddler. Immediately he took the whip hand, hurling me into the far-off wall near the kitchen. He then picked up the chair from my desk and flung it after me. It made only glancing contact and I was quickly on my feet. McEvoy was well boozed up, which made him just that little bit easier to contain. Not that I was interested in defending myself, or indeed anything in the flat bar my writing equipment. Nothing else had any value, actual or sentimental. Meanwhile, behind the door, Robert's screams could be heard clearly, even above the mêlée.

The fight, I'd guess, lasted fifteen minutes, which, as anyone who's been involved in one will attest, is a second Stalingrad. And even after the quarter hour, McEvoy showed no signs of flagging. Instead, time was called by the entry of two uniformed policemen. With Carla Whitty just behind. 'That's him!' she fretted, and immediately they both fell upon the drunkard and bundled him out into the corridor.

Standing in the doorway, Carla burst into tears, came rushing forward and we hugged. She wiped a trickle of blood from my mouth, another from my left nostril as, unspeaking, we slowly surveyed the wreckage. It was a long moment before I thought to ask, 'How did you—'

'The downstairs door was wide open. Yours was too. I arrived about five minutes ago. Did you not see me stick my head around?'

'No. I was a wee bit distracted.'

'Well, whatever. I was going to pitch in alongside you, but then I remembered that the courthouse is right across the street beside the jail. And if you can't find a copper in a courthouse . . .'

'Good thinking,' I said. 'And a damn good job you thought of it. If you hadn't, I don't know how this might've ended.'

'Who is he, anyway?'

'His name is McEvoy. We worked together once.'

'And what did he want?'

'He's the guy who's . . . who used to be screwing my wife.'

'Oh. So that's him.' She considered the matter a second; I could almost *see* what she was thinking. And though it hurt a bit to laugh, I did and said, 'No, I dunno either why I was fighting him. Or it. Some things are just meant to be, and those two are only fucking *made* for each other.'

One of the policemen, a raw-looking recruit, was back in the open door. On seeing him, Carla whispered, 'I think I should make myself scarce.' Then, for all to hear, 'I'll go check on this little guy.' And she excused herself to attend to my son, who hadn't yet abandoned his attempts to roar the house down.

'Mr Stokes?' asked the Garda.

'That's right.'

'We've calmed him down a bit, and he's on his way to the station. How are you?'

'Okay,' I told him.

'It can't be very pleasant, having to put up with an assault like that. And in your own home, too. We'll want a statement, of course.'

'That's not necessary,' I said. 'I won't be pressing charges.'

'You won't?'

'No. Yer man, I know him.'

'He's a friend?'

'An acquaintance. But I'll not be taking things any further.'

'That's up to you. D'you mind me asking what this was all about?'

'It's . . . am . . . to do with my wife.'

He nodded towards the bedroom and asked, 'Herself?'

'No. My wife isn't here.'

'Oh!' he said, his indifference overdone. 'Well, however it started, it's ended in one godawful mess. Is there very much damage?'

'I think I've been lucky,' I told him, anxious to have the whole affair over and done with. 'My computer's escaped.'

His face opened into a broad beam. 'You're the writer bloke, aren't you? Dinny was saying—'

'Dinny?'

'Denis Cambridge. Another member of the force. He's been here – you do remember him?'

'Yeah, sort of.'

'Denis is a big buddy of mine. And he was telling me a while back that there was a novelist living in one of these flats. Very . . . taken he was, too, with something he read here.'

'That's nice,' I flustered, now more anxious than ever for him to go away and leave me alone.

Instead he very deliberately scanned the room, shaking his head in disgust. 'Will you look at the state of the place after that other thug . . . all your pages scattered about the floor. Here, let me give you a hand to straighten things up.'

'It's . . . it's all right. Honest. Don't bother.'

'No bother at all!' he said, then dropped to his knees and began to sift through the debris. 'Now, there's two different types of lettering here, so should there be two different bundles? I mean, d'you want these old-fashioned ones kept separate?' And he held me up a page from the late Andrew Whitty.

'Please, leave them!' I called, my panic ill-concealed. But already he was reading down the text, now with a smile, now a titter, now a hoarse cough of laughter. It wasn't my most subtle move, but I leant forward and snapped the leaf from his hold. 'Please! I can sort this myself.'

'You're sure?'

'I'm sure.'

'Fair enough,' and he got to his feet. 'But can I at least finish that bit I was reading?'

I smiled, reddened, and said, 'Look, I'd prefer—'

'Ah, g'on!'

'N . . . no,' and I held the page behind my back.

'G'on outa that! What're you ashamed of? It's bloody good!' And suddenly, full of the joys of spring, his arms were round me as he attempted to retrieve the paper.

For several seconds we performed this ridiculous tango, till my patience gave out. With a hand on his chest, I pushed him to arm's length. 'Look!' I snapped. 'I've told you, no. Now, would you please leave?'

He took another step away, head to one side, features tightening. 'Why d'you not want me to read it?'

'If you want to read it, go away and come back with a warrant. Then you can read to your heart's content.'

He laughed awkwardly. 'Ah, Mr Stokes, there's no need to be getting so sniffy.'

'I did try asking you nicely. But you seem to be still here.'

'Jesus, I can't think what I've done to piss you off. Most writers—'

'Goodbye, Garda.'

'Most writers would take this as a major compliment.'

'*Goodbye*, Garda.'

He shrugged. 'Fair enough. You're definitely not pressing charges?'

'I've already told you that. Now, if you wouldn't mind . . .'

With a deep sigh, I closed the door behind him. At once Carla emerged, my son's hand in hers. 'Good God, what was all that about?'

'Inquisitive bastard. Up to no good, I can tell you.'

'He seemed perfectly civil to me. And what's that I heard him say about there being two different letterings?'

'Nothing.'

121

'Hey, look, he's right!' she said, pointing. 'One's much smaller and fainter.'

'Yeah, I know. I did those years ago . . . listen, you'd better get out of here.'

'What? You're putting the run on me again? What've I done this time?'

'It's not you,' I told her, but told her no more as I uncoupled Robert and then guided her to the door.

When all was clear, I sat myself on the one chair left upright and tried to assess what harm, what *real* harm, had been done. Garda Denis Cambridge already harboured suspicions. Oh, nothing he could prove, of course, not much more than flimsy theory and lucky guesswork. But I'm certain it would've enlivened his grey little existence no end to believe that he was somehow on to me, that he'd got me running scared, watching my every step, sleeping with my back door unlocked, with a travel bag at the ready and with one eye open. Up to now, I'd found this risible; suddenly, it wasn't quite the laughing matter. For this big buddy of his had just stumbled upon something of potential significance, something that, if properly interpreted, lent undoubted support to Cambridge's hypotheses. How *would* it all pan out when the pair inevitably came together to compare notes?

CHAPTER SIX

But fretting about Garda Cambridge would profit me nothing. I had work to do. So, pushing him deep to the back of my mind, I got on with it. Yet another bloody rewrite. The third. And, I vowed, come what may, the last.

I'd been fairly churning it out since Angie had left for work and was due a breather. So when I heard some mail through the letter box, it seemed as good a time as any. I'd flipped through the assorted envelopes, found a thing or two of mine, and was halfway up the stairs again when I stopped.

It wasn't, was it?

It *couldn't* be.

I bolted back to the junk on the doormat and began a second riffle.

Small and brown it was, I knew the form. Addressed to Andrew Whitty, of 256 Easton Terrace, Kilmainham. With a return address printed neatly on the back in the event of non-delivery: Taurus Books, Publisher, 68 Baggot Crescent, Dublin 2.

If ever I'm diagnosed with anything terminal, and am given that diagnosis by post, then this is how I expect it will feel. The seams of my head strained, not with a riot of awful possibilities but with the one single stonewall certainty. The old man had made a copy, maybe *copies*, of the text. He'd dispersed it for consideration. Today was, or would've been, his lucky day. Taurus had bitten. Taurus were big, big fish.

I tried to focus on the rust-coloured rectangle. How very tiny it was, practically weightless, outwardly inoffensive. And yet nothing, not the hardest blow I'd ever been dealt, not the worst news I'd ever been handed, not the force of all my own rejections combined, could've caved the roof in so. A silver lining was hard to find among the rubble, but at least in the immediate future I'd not have much time to mope or to mull. With a collapse this total, this final, my work was well cut out. There'd be phone calls to make. Explanations to concoct. Reality to face. And the stench of yet one more failure to endure, a failure more bitter than any preceding, torn as it was from the very jaws of triumph.

Which was to say nothing of the here and now, of the radioactive waste I was holding in my hands. Should I leave it for Carla to find when next she came calling? And then wait for her to turn me in, as she most certainly would – as she had every right to? Or should I present it to her in person, along with the most abject apology? Then throw myself on her mercy. And grovel like fair hell. I could always destroy it. Wouldn't do me much good, of course. Wouldn't stop them sending another. Wouldn't alter the fact that copies of the manuscript were out there.

Or I could open it.

For sheer pointlessness, this topped the lot, managing

to make not a grain of sense. But when you're going down for the third time, not very much does. Gingerly, and for no reason I can even yet put in words, I slipped my little finger where the flap had come unstuck. Then, as if defusing an incendiary device, I eased open the envelope.

Before my eyes, the words swam.

Dear Mr Stokes,

Dear Mr Stokes? I blinked. I refocused. It was still there.

Dear Mr Stokes,
One day I'd dearly love to make detective, but the powers that be aren't optimistic. You see, they don't consider I have what it takes. They praise the hard work that's carried me this far, but keep reminding me that hard work will carry a bloke only so far. However, the fact that you're reading this, another person's letter, just goes to show that even a plodder like myself gets it right every once in a while.

From the start, Brendan, certain things didn't add up. In the dead man's flat, there was a typewriter, but not a sign of a typed page. In yours, on your computer stand, there was a large bundle of typing in a font that struck me as very old-fashioned for so modern a machine. Then, there was your unease as I began to read. And there was that character who gave me such a laugh but who, the very next day, had disappeared. Somehow you, his creator, had forgotten him to the point where you were claiming that he never existed. I admit, I was baffled. Until I spoke to a colleague, who told me what he chanced upon in your home the other day. There were, he said, typed pages in two very distinct letterings: one from your own PC, the other obviously from elsewhere. And there was yourself, jumpy as a hen on a hotplate, guilty as mortal sin.

I *know* you stole Andrew Whitty's manuscript, the one you're now passing off as your own. What's more, I know that the character, the one who mysteriously slipped your mind, plays a key role in all this. Which is why it galls me so much to admit that his name continues to escape me too. But it won't escape me for ever. Any more, Brendan, than you will.

Yours for as long as it takes,

Denis Cambridge.

I crumpled note and envelope into the same ball before barrelling upstairs and bolting the flat door behind me. I then rushed all about the place, pulling curtains, drawing blinds, closing shutters. Back in the living room, as the maelstrom in my head eased a little, I allowed that maybe this last precaution was scarcely necessary. But still I left all visual access blacked outside and switched on the lights. Taking an unsteady seat at my desk, I ironed out the letter and reread it.

First things first: I was getting shot of that goddamn manuscript. Twice it had come close to my undoing, and now this. In any case, I was so familiar with what it contained that keeping it under my roof for even another hour was a risk not worth taking. Unfortunately, I had no shredder. My open fire was long out of use. We were days from the next refuse collection but, if truth be told, I wasn't entirely comfortable with the thought of just leaving it for the binmen. And I could hardly burn it, sheet by sheet, in the kitchen sink as I'd done with the title page one year earlier.

Still, I had to dispose of it somehow, and I had to do it right away. That lett—

That letter. What, I gradually found myself wondering, had been its purpose exactly? To rattle me, no doubt, but – was that really the extent of it? Or was it also designed to provoke me? To goad a mistake from me? To panic me into coming out in the open and doing something stupid? Would Cambridge be watching? Was he watching this very minute? The bastard was so dogged, the possibility could not be discounted. And, anyway, what was the guy's beef? Why was he chasing down a crime not reported, the theft of an item he had no proof ever even existed? There had to be more to it than one fusty old manuscript. Carla Whitty was somewhere in the mix as well. Or, more precisely, his envy that I appeared to have taken his share of the cake along with my own. Did he honestly believe that if I were to be unmasked, or discredited, or just plain taken down a peg or two, he'd have a clear run on goal? If he did, he was every bit as gormless as he looked.

I took the manuscript and returned it to the far-off corner of my hot press. There it'd be perfectly safe, completely out of harm's way. I would destroy it, but not till the time was right. Not till this final draft was done, dusted and delivered. And not till that little old lady over Rathmines way had said her 'Yes'. In the meantime, I'd keep it well hidden. And keep my wits well about me.

In that same meantime, I decided, it'd be no bad thing to act natural around Garda Denis Cambridge if and when we met. I'd salute him, bid him the time of day, receive him like always, not as a friend but not as an enemy either. Wrongfoot him. Make it plain that his letter never did quite hit the spot. Whether because it was lost in the post, or delivered, then read, then rubbished. Or – what? Let him try figure out where his grand plan had gone awry. Let his be the hair scratched and torn.

Once that script is mailed away, everything's in the lap of the gods. Like the politician on election night, when the last of the votes has been cast, who knows that no amount of worry or soul-searching will now alter the result one iota. Never does a man feel so free of care, so at liberty to swing the lead without a single qualm of conscience. This state of limbo can last months, or the verdict might be returned in a week or two.

Either way, I was just days into my rest-break and was thinking about nothing in particular when, late one morning, I went to collect some post freshly fallen on the mat. Descending the stairs, I heard the doorbell chime. There was Carla, beaming from ear to ear, hands folded behind her back. 'Close your eyes!' she ordered, as she stepped inside.

'Eh?'

'G'on. Close 'em.'

I did.

'I've got something for you. The postman couldn't squeeze it through the letter box. And I just happened to be coming up the garden path. Okay, *Mr Bernard Swords*, you can look.' And she handed me an envelope. Heavy, bulky and brown. Returned. Rejected. In less than a week. 'Brendan? I saw the sticker that said Monitor Press – I thought you'd be . . .'

My eyes stung as I turned away and went trudging upstairs, my heart as heavy as my step.

'But, isn't this what you've been waiting for? And they've got back to you so quickly.'

I began to tear at the flap. To go clumsily through the motions.

'What's the matter. . . here, let me.' She briskly removed the contents and unclipped the note attached. Together we read:

Monitor Press, Publishers
1008 Rathmines Road
Dublin 6
8th July 1997

Dear Mr Swords,

I'm returning your manuscript for what I regret to inform you will be the last time.

When this first arrived at our office, we were quite hopeful: a good story, let down by writing that was overblown and indulgent. But no lost cause. Since then, it's had two separate overhauls.

Through each, the story has remained consistent, while the writing has become more pretentious and detestable. Plots come and plots go, but a writer's style is permanent. It can scarcely be changed, and can never be taught. It's inborn:, you've either got it or you don't. And, Mr Swords, you don't. Rarely have I been able to make an evaluation with such absolute certainty.

You seem like a pleasant, agreeable young man, and it's upsetting to think of you wasting the best years of your life in pursuit of a career that so obviously is not for you. Please take this advice as constructive and well intentioned. And good luck in whatever path you decide to follow here on in.

Yours sincerely
Kate Rooney
Chief Commissioning Editor

Carla slipped me the merest sidelong glance, then chewed her lip a while. These next words would be carefully chosen. 'Ah, that's just one person's opinion. And, anyway, what does she know?'

I made no answer.

'Pah! Monitor Press? Never heard of them. Who wants to deal with small fry like these? You're too good for them.'

Still I didn't respond. I didn't even look, for fear I might do her a mischief.

'Seriously, Brendan, why don't you send it off to one of the big boys? Like . . . I dunno . . . Puffin. Or Collins. Or Taurus.'

'Puffin? Collins? *Taurus*? Sweet Jesus, that'd be like applying to La Scala after getting booed out of the local on karaoke night! Until you know what you're talking about, why don't you shut the fuck up?'

'S . . . sorry.'

For a time there was nothing said, nothing heard bar my heavy breath and black, brooding rage. Then, fearfully, 'But there must be something . . . Couldn't you, y'know, pay to have it—'

'What? Published privately?' I seethed. 'That'd be an idea, if I had about eight grand to throw away! At the present time, I'd have trouble raising eight quid . . . Maybe Kate Rooney's right. Maybe I should get myself a job.'

Now, when I dearly wanted her to protest, she wouldn't even do that, afraid of the fresh ambush she might walk into.

'Well?' I said, no less belligerently. 'Any suggestions? Something not quite so foolish this time, or would that be asking too much?'

'I . . . erm . . . I did happen to hear the hospital might soon be looking for porters, and . . .'

I glared, daring her even to attempt finishing the sentence.

She went on, almost in a whimper, '. . . and it wouldn't pay all that great, but—'

'Christ Almighty, you reckon I'm fucking hospital porter material, do you? Eh? When you look at me in a certain light, is that what strikes you? Even if I never wrote another page, I'm a skilled tradesman, I'll have you know. A qualified fitter. And y'see this?' I picked up the letter and waved it like I was trying to stop it burning. 'I'm taking no more of this shit, because I don't have to.'

'I was only saying—'

'Only saying, my bollox! Look,' and I calmed a little, 'keep an eye on the young fella. I'm going to make a phone call.'

Alan Bradshaw arrived, almost out of puff, at the other end.

'All right, boss!' I said, my pride in my pocket, my heart in my boots, but my disappointment kept strictly to myself. 'I think I might take you up on that offer, after all.'

'Offer? What offer was that?'

'What offer? Ger McEvoy's job – what else?'

'God, Coops, that was a long time ago.'

'Yeah. But . . . I didn't hear Angie say you'd filled the vacancy.'

'Well, we haven't. But it seems we aren't going to now.'

'You're not? Why?'

'The word is that the whole operation here is being computerized in the next year or two. Skills like ours, oul' stock, are going to be obsolete. It's only a rumour at the moment but, like I say, they haven't replaced Ger.' He paused. 'I'm keeping an eye on the situations-vacant column myself, to be perfectly honest.'

As a kick in the teeth, this wasn't far behind the news I'd had earlier. That mill was my safety net, my last resort should all else fail. I didn't need to ask directions to know I was up shit creek.

'But hey!' Alan demanded. 'Why in God's name would you be enquiring about a job in this place?'

'Ah . . . I dunno. Keeping my options open, I suppose. Better being sure than being sorry.'

'Being silly, more like. I believe it's barely a week since you sent away the book—'

'Five days,' I said weakly.

'Five bloody days! A bit early to start panicking, wouldn't you say?'

I laughed, weaker still.

'Listen, mate, your reply will be along in its own good time. And when it comes, 'tisn't the phasing out of the poor fitters in Kilmainham Textiles that'll be bothering you.'

'Yeah . . . Please God you're right.'

'Sure I am.'

'Alan, Angie is to know nothing about this conversation, okay?'

'No problem. But you'll gimme a shout when you get the good word, yeah?'

I hung up and began pacing in small, demented circles, afraid that if I stood still, grim reality would finally catch me up. Next I returned to the flat, where I grabbed the manuscript from my desk. 'I won't be long,' I told Carla, by which it was understood that she was babysitting until further notice.

Once sat on the bus I was pleased to discover that I had enough money on me to cover the fare; less so to note that I still wore the bedroom slippers I'd donned earlier that morning.

In Rathmines Road, I waited till the main door was buzzed open for another, then slipped into the building. On the third floor, the reception area was manned by that mousy secretary, just like before. 'I'm sorry, you can't—' she spluttered.

'She's expecting me,' I replied, eyes front.

'No, she isn't.'

'Well, she fucking well should be!' And I swept directly through to the lair of the serpent. She seemed somewhat surprised to see me, but only somewhat. 'This isn't right!' I thundered.

She stood. As she did, I felt her underling at my shoulder. 'I'm sorry, Ms Rooney, I tried—'

'That's okay, Helen.'

Behind me, the door closed again.

'Now, Mr . . . ?'

She'd *forgotten* me!

'Swords,' I said. 'Bernard Swords.'

'Oh, dear lord, Mr Swords,' she said painedly. 'What can the matter be? And what exactly isn't right?'

I crashed the manuscript on to the table before her. 'You didn't even read it all. You couldn't have!'

'No,' she replied, perfectly matter-of-factly. 'I looked at maybe the first twenty-five pages.'

'Just twenty-five pages? What could you possibly tell from twenty-five pages?'

'I could tell it wasn't going to turn into Marcel Proust on page twenty-six, for one thing.'

'But if you'd—'

'Mr Swords! I tried to be forthright in my correspondence with you, and I really don't mean to labour the point here. But you – *you* – are just not a writer. You're not readable. You're not even bearable. Now, it's a shame, and I wish there was some way round this, because I can see how strong your desire is. But desire alone won't see you through, not in this business. Please try to meet me halfway here. I am doing my best to let you down gently.'

I stalled an instant, disbelieving, almost admiring. What effrontery, what sheer neck! It was as if she was expecting my gratitude for this bum's rush. I laughed to the floor, then parked myself defiantly on the chair that faced her. 'You can't do this to me.'

Her tone was curt. 'I'm afraid you'll find I can.'

'I'll tell you what you can do. You can open that fucking manuscript at page twenty-six, and you can start reading the rest of it. 'Cos I'm not leaving here till you do.'

She eyed me a moment, part amused, part amazed. Then, nonchalantly, she lifted her receiver. 'Helen? Security. Now, please.'

At once, I drew in my horns and sprang to my feet, first leaning across the table in an attempt to shush her, then standing well back, my open palms upraised. 'All right, all right,' I pleaded. 'I'm going.'

The receiver remained *in situ* by her ear.

'Honest, I'm on my way, nice and quiet, no hassle,' and I reversed another step. She looked me up and down, twigged the carpet slippers on my feet and must've concluded I posed no terrible threat. For whatever reason, she rested the handset on her chest and said pointedly, '*Goodbye,* Mr Swords. And take this thing off my desk, or I'll call the police and have you done for littering.'

Shamefacedly, I gathered up the pages and turned for

the door. With my hand on the knob, I faced back one last time and said, 'All the trouble you put me to, and now you discard me like this. Ms Rooney, you owe me better.'

She put the phone down and blustered, 'I beg your pardon?'

'I said, you owe me. And if you had any integrity, or even a scrap of conscience—'

'*I* owe *you*? I, this whole bloody company, has spent – has *wasted* - more time on you than on any unpublished author in our entire history.'

'You mean you had to read a few drafts? Well, what about me? What about the bloke who had to write them? I first approached your company almost a year ago, and you could've done the decent thing then. You could've told me "Sorry – not interested." But no. It was "Change this, redo that—"'

'Mr Swords, I never gave you any guarantees.'

'You saw how desperate I was. You saw you didn't need to.'

She sighed loudly and shrank, limp and lifeless, in her swivel chair. 'Okay, then, what are you proposing? And don't even suggest I wade through the rest of that. Under no circumstances will I even consider it.'

This rather narrowed the possible proposals down. 'How about . . .' I said, brain-racking furiously '. . . how about one more rewrite?'

'For Heaven's sake, Mr Swords, you've just now berated me for demanding rewrite after rewrite, and now you want to do another ?'

'If I did, would you promise to read it?'

'No! I absolutely would not. I've seen your style—'

'I'd change my style completely.'

'Impossible. Sorry, Mr Swords, I can make you no such promise.'

'Would you promise to read just twenty-five pages, then? That's not going to kill you. And you claim it's all you need to make a judgement.'

She looked at me, exasperated, and said quietly, 'I must be off my head.'

'Thanks a million!' I smiled. 'You won't regret it. And I swear you won't recognize it from before.'

'I'd better not. Because if I do, it'll go directly—' and she pointed to the wastepaper basket in the corner.

'If you do,' I told her, 'you can bin it with my compliments.'

I retook my seat on the bus, reasonably pleased with the bargain struck. It was an outrageous long shot, but I did have one last roll of the dice in me. Or, rather, in the bottom of my hot press back in Easton Terrace.

That very evening I began, Whitty's work at my left hand as I typed verbatim. Nothing altered but names and, where called for, spellings. No frills. Description kept to a bare minimum. Nothing intentionally well put or neatly phrased. No evidence whatsoever of craft or of technique. Untypical of anything I'd ever in my life written; indeed, untypical of any form of printed English I'd ever in my life seen. Still, something different she'd asked for. And just three weeks later, something very, very different was what I delivered.

August 19th, as I'm unlikely ever to forget. Early on

August 19th. Angie was pottering about prior to leaving for work, while Robert and I dozed on.

'Hey!' she hollered. 'Something's come for you. At least, something's come for a Bernard Swords, and I'm guessing that's you.' In a twinkling, I was clear of my stupor and on tenterhooks. 'Looks like it's from that book crowd.'

'What kind's the envelope?'

'Huh?'

'Is it big or small?'

'Oh. Am . . . big, kinda. Will I see what's in it?' and through the open doorway, I could hear she was already tearing. '"Dear Bernard, *mea culpa*." *Mea culpa?* Who's she?'

'Nobody! Will you just read what it says!'

'Okay. "Dear Bernard, *mea culpa*. After twenty-eight years in this business, I thought I'd seen everything. Apparently, I hadn't. Anyway, many congratulations. When you're happy with the contract, sign both copies and return one to me. I'll then forward your cheque . . ."'

But by now, I was grabbing the letter from her, struggling to read it for myself, what with the shake in my hand, the mist in my eye and the thunder in my heart. A contract. A book deal. Mine. At long, long last.

CHAPTER SEVEN

I spent most of that morning in my underwear, studying, ogling, drooling over that precious slip of paper, those words I'd dreamt of seeing for near half a lifetime. It was hours before I thought to take a gander at the contract I'd been offered. When I did, it seemed pretty standard, all much as I would've expected. Not that I was at my critical best, not while this frightfully important, impeccably drafted legal document went on referring to me as 'The Author', capital T, capital A. And if there's jam at all, it might as well be on both sides: there was also mention of an advance. A grand now, upon the signing of contracts. Another thousand when the book was published. Token amounts, of course, pocket money till the cash registers began jingling in earnest.

I was still in my night attire when Carla called round. And quickly out of it after I'd gone with her through the rights, the rates, the royalties, the whole new ball game. God, the sex that afternoon was good.

Before leaving, she asked if she might have a read of the winning final draft, a request that was easily met. I'd saved the text on the computer's hard drive, so it was only a matter of running her off a copy and sending her on her way. I don't remember doing a great deal that afternoon once she'd gone. I played a little catchball with Robert till it bored us both. I rang Alan Bradshaw: he'd had the gist of events from Angie, but looked forward to discussing it all in greater detail during the course of this most almighty bender he'd already begun planning. He further advised me not to inform my folks over the phone, that a parent was entitled to hear such news face to face. He'd take a spin down home to Earlsgrove the very next weekend he was free, he said. If I could contain myself till then, I could accompany him and deliver the glad tidings in person. The proper way.

It was later that evening, with my wife home from work and my muddle-headed euphoria clearing a little, that I remembered one order of business outstanding. Whitty's original was still surviving, still on my premises. All along, I'd pledged that if this great day should ever dawn, that manuscript would immediately find an unmarked grave. Now this dawn had broken; now the stakes were too high to trip on something small, something avoidable. Nobody – not my wife, not my child – must know that the manuscript existed. Must not even suspect that it ever had. As it happened, the next morning was bin morning. I'd been reluctant to leave anything incriminating to the care of the city's binmen, for fear some over-zealous copper might fancy a rummage. So I rose early, not long after sun-up, and waited for the truck to arrive. Only then did I appear down the steps with my refuse sack, and personally flung it aboard. I even stayed a moment to watch the huge mangles swallow it up, then chew till it was an indistinguishable part of the sodden, stinking cargo. There'd be no comebacks, I knew. Not from this source.

*

'Absolutely brilliant!' Carla gushed, a little disbelievingly. 'And not just because it's your book – it is genuinely bloody marvellous.'

'You're finished already?'

'It's been quiet on the wards these past two nights. But, anyway, it's . . .' she looked like she might be about to burst, '. . . it's just addictive. Once you start at all, you can't help yourself.'

'Thanks,' I smiled, and reached to accept it from her. But, smiling too, she drew it away.

'Would it be okay if I was to lend it to one of the other girls? She could hear me laughing, and—'

'Certainly not! Let her buy it when the time comes, like everyone else. I'm serious, give it here.'

Again she proffered it, but again she took it back and clasped it to her chest, arms crossed. 'You're joking, right?'

'Course I am. Lend it to who you like. Spread the gospel.'

'Thanks . . . erm . . . thanks . . . D'you mind if I ask you just one thing?'

'Ask away.'

'You know the bit about the bloke who sets fire to newspapers while people are reading them?'

'Uh-huh.'

'And for his other party piece, he takes the ham from his bread, blows his nose in it, puts it back, then goes ahead and devours the sandwich?'

'Yup.'

'How did you know that?'

'I'm sorry?'

'My uncle, God rest him, could be a right old rogue when he wanted. I've told you before how I'd meet him for a bite to eat most Tuesdays. And he'd always wait till the food came, and I'd made a start on mine, and then he'd launch into this great yarn about the character in Luton with the cooked ham. It turned me green around the gills every single time, and he thought this was just hilarious.'

'Yeah?'

'Yeah. Never failed to crease him up. But . . . how did you know it?'

'Well, I heard it from you, obviously enough.'

'You didn't. In fact, until this very minute, I've never brought myself to repeat it to anyone. Ever.'

'That so? . . . hmm . . . maybe he told me himself, then.'

'What? Brendan, when I first met you, the man was already dead. And you had no idea he'd ever worked on the buildings. Remember? You were actually surprised to find out that he'd ever worked at all. Anything you got on him, you got from me. But you did *not* get this.'

I felt myself redden. 'Jesus . . . I dunno. You're sure you didn't—'

'Certain.'

'God. I suppose I must've, y'know, just made it up, then.'

'You made it up?'

'Well, yeah. Carla, you only told me the bare bones of a story. There were lots of gaps I had to fill in, that I could only guess at.'

'So . . . you'd never heard of this guy. You knew nothing about him. And you just happened to create, to *guess at,* a character identical to—'

'For Christ's sake!' I snapped. 'Is it such a big deal? I mean, what's important here? That my book's to be published, or that there's one bloody bit-player in it that you, for some reason, are not entirely sure about? Listen, give me the fucking script, and I'll draw a line through what's-his-face, eh? You won't even know he was ever there. Would that make you happy, yeah?'

She opened her mouth to speak. But before there came a sound, there came a rap, sharp and urgent, on the door. We both stood, marble-made. There was nobody expected. There was no person who, at that moment, I was keen to admit. But there was no way of pretending that the flat was empty, not with the volume of the argument that had just been interrupted. Carla looked at me desperately for some, for any, guidance. I could do no better than shrug, and go answer.

Outside there stood a shortish man, probably about my own age but far, far better groomed and coiffed. He was close-shaven and deodorized, while the box-jacket suit screamed business before he opened either his mouth or his briefcase.

'Paul Gibbs, Taurus Books. If it's a bad time, I can—'

'As you mention now, it's not the greatest . . . Are you selling something?'

'Oh, certainly not,' he purred. 'Quite the opposite, Mr Swords – it is Mr Swords?'

'Ah . . . well . . . yeah,' I stammered. Rarely in my life have I been as mystified.

'Good. May I come in, then?'

Once inside, he introduced himself to an equally bewildered Carla, again as Paul Gibbs of Taurus Books. She responded with only her name, nothing more. It didn't seem to bother him any. His smile undimmed, he turned to me and said: 'Mr Swords, you've recently been offered a contract by a rival publishing house.'

'How'd you know—'

'That's not important. This contract, have you signed it yet?'

I searched his face for some clue as to what answer he was hoping for.

'Signed and returned? Yes? No?'

'N . . . no. Not yet.'

'Excellent. In that case, I've got a proposition you should hear. May I?' he asked, already finding himself a seat. From the back of the fireside chair, Carla picked up her coat, intending to take her leave. I bade her hold tight a while: I knew I might have need of someone stoutly on my side, someone to stop me doing, saying or signing anything rash.

'I'll be blunt, Mr Swords. You're about to make one big mistake. Those publishers are not right for you. And certainly not for the manuscript you've produced.'

'You've . . . you've read it?'

'We . . . I . . . have, yes. Again, how it came into our possession is not at all important. But what's critical is that you deal with a firm capable of doing justice to such an extraordinary piece of writing.'

'R . . . right. And, like, what's wrong with Monitor Press?' At once, I wondered if I ought to have mentioned that name, since he hadn't yet. But I was sure he knew it; he seemed to know everything else.

'Monitor are a fine little company at what they do. But their scope is too narrow, too limited. Your book has the potential for sales the world over, given the right publication, distribution and publicity. The kind that, frankly, Monitor is not in a position to provide.'

'No?'

'Doesn't even come close.'

'Oh. So what d'you have in mind, then?'

'We'd like you to let *us* publish *Remember Me, Fair Eleanore*. Given our imprints right across the globe, we can deliver the international hit that your work deserves. And I don't just mean in the English-speaking sector. Every year our company is strongly represented at the Frankfurt Book Fair – you're familiar with that, yes?'

'Oh, naturally,' I said, nodding sagely as I could at this double-Dutch.

'Then you won't need me to tell you how lucrative the foreign-language markets can prove. Every year, without fail, we sell a number of our titles for translation. And we've already earmarked yours, provisionally of course, for this year's convention.'

I nodded again, this time on the dawning of some little understanding.

'It's not just that aspect,' he continued. 'D'you honestly think that Monitor's commitment, that the belief they've shown in you, has been satisfactory?'

'I'm . . . not with you, I'm afraid.'

'Okay, how many of your books have they commissioned? Just the one?'

'I've only written the one.'

'For the moment, Mr Swords. But you aren't thinking of stopping now, are you?'

'No. I—'

'Here and now, we're offering a two-book deal. After which we would hope to sit down with you and negotiate terms for at least another two. Now, I've no idea whether you've experienced much rejection in your career, but whatever your experience, let me tell you; it's nice to know that everything you write in the next couple of years will be assured – *assured* – an outlet.'

He needed say no more – I was sold. How could I not be? What a carrot this was to dangle, what a prospect to hold out to a man so long in the wilderness. But before I could signal my acceptance, he went on, 'Even where finances are concerned – and I do apologize for being the one to bring up the filthy lucre – but even at the sharp end, Monitor don't really come up to the mark, do they? I mean, d'you mind if I ask what you've been offered by way of an advance?'

'I get a grand right away—'

'Pah! Mr Swords, you can multiply that sum many times over, if you come aboard with us.'

The question a-begging was left to Carla. I was already halfway up the gangplank.

'How many times, exactly?' she asked.

He clipped open the briefcase and removed a prepared contract, remarkably similar in appearance and dimension to the one I'd been sent two days earlier. 'There,' he said, indicating with his thumb a point near the bottom of the third page. 'You see? Seventy-five.'

I looked. Carla looked. Then we looked at each other, slack-jawed and bug-eyed.

'That's yours up front, in full, to keep no matter what. So, if I leave you a copy of this contract, and I'll be back—'

'Won't be necessary,' I said. 'If you've got a biro, I'm ready to sign.'

'Don't you want a chance to think it over?'

'No. And I don't want you to have that chance, either.'

He laughed as we went to my desk where he 'X'ed a blank line, then put the pen into my trembling hand. I'd only just bolted down the last letter of my surname when he cried, 'Beg your pardon?' He squinted low, then eyed me suspiciously. 'Who's . . . Brendan Stokes?'

Now I, too, had a squint. And saw that, in my haste, I'd forgotten to use my pseudonym. Immediately, I began to fear the worst, the nameless, shapeless worst.

'It does say "Brendan Stokes", doesn't it? Is that you?'

Now that fear took shape in earnest. This crowd had turned me down out of hand and on more than one occasion in the long ago. Indeed, if memory served correctly, our dealings had ended with a certain amount of rancour. There'd been a letter from me with a frank evaluation of their publishing house and everyone connected with it; there might have been phone calls involved as well. And I did not trust so excessively neat and officious a little man to have forgotten this entirely.

'Yeah,' I swallowed hard, 'it's me. My real name.'

'You write under an alias? For any reason I should know about?'

'No, no, good God, no!'

'Fine. Entirely your own business. But which handle would you prefer to see on the spine of your book?'

'This. I never really liked that other one. And, anyway, it's well served its purpose.'

Polite and indifferent, he watched as I applied the name with which I'd been baptized here and there about both copies of the document. 'Now,' he said, a little uneasily, 'You keep one of these. Have a good read through, study it closely. Er . . . when you do, you'll see that we expect your co-operation when it comes to promoting this book.'

'Sure, no problem.'

'Only that process is likely to start as early as next week. The thing is, when we pay an advance like this to a new author, we try to milk it for what free advertising we can. It's usually good for a column or two in the broadsheets with a photograph accompanying. I couldn't help noticing Kilmainham Gaol across the road – what a backdrop, and practically on your own doorstep. So, Mr Swor— *Mr Stokes*, you can look forward to featuring in the national press some time soon. Make the most of it. When the first royalty cheque comes, you'll be glad you did.'

'Sure,' I repeated. 'No problem.'

'Well, then, I'm happy. So if you're happy too . . .' and he began to set about gathering up his accoutrements. At his back, Carla was exultant. As I should've been. But from the mid-point of our negotiations, there'd been that stone under the door. They'd rejected me before. Rejecting me again, under our new agreement, would hardly be so straightforward. It might involve the returning of this advance. Maybe even a lawsuit.

'Mr Gibbs, what if you don't like my next book?'

'Sorry?'

'I've just signed up to write you a second one. What if you decide you don't like it?'

He shook his head, his bafflement seemingly genuine. 'You're . . . concerned it'll not be *good* enough?'

'I can guarantee it'll be more than good enough. I just can't guarantee it'll be quite to your taste.'

'Mr Stokes,' he gleamed, 'I've read you, personally. I know this game, I know how it works. I'm very rarely wrong when it comes to picking winners. You just enjoy your success, enjoy your windfall, keep doing what comes so naturally to you, and let me worry about the rest. Deal?'

I gleamed back in answer. Following this, he could never cry foul, never claim he hadn't been warned.

'Oh, one other thing,' he said, turning back in the doorway. 'Monitor Press will need to be informed that you're taking your business elsewhere. I'll be happy to convey—'

'That's quite all right' I told him. 'I think I ought to break this to them myself.'

It was a different man altogether who now went whistling by that pale little secretary on the third floor of Monitor Press, Rathmines Road. I threw open the inner door and was not at all put out to find that the Grand High Witch already had company.

'What? Bernard!'

'I needed to see you,' I said chirpily.

'Sure. Why? Dropping back the contract, was it?'

149

'In a manner of speaking.'

'Oh, I beg your pardon. This is . . .' and she stated a name that didn't even go in one ear. The man in the chair stood and extended his hand as she went on '. . . and this is our latest, most-promising discovery, Bernard Swords.'

I ignored the handshake on offer and whispered, 'No, it isn't.'

'Excuse me?'

'Bernard Swords isn't the name. It's Brendan Stokes.'

She didn't know what this was building to, she couldn't know. But some instinct clearly told her that it would not be pleasant. The merry face was agonized as she choked, 'Really?'

'Yes!' And from an inside pocket I removed the letter, unfolded it from its quarters and smoothed it flat on the desk before her. '*That* Brendan Stokes.'

She began to read. There was a great darkening of the countenance and much gulping as she worked her way down the page. Once she'd done, she fixed that rictus again and said, 'You've got me. I am suitably embarrassed.'

'Suitably embarrassed?' and I snapped the letter back. ' "Dear Mr Stokes . . ." ' I scanned for a juicy bit. ' "You don't know when to quit, but there seems to be so much more besides you don't know." ' I smiled, nodded solemnly and scanned on. ' "Your books are turgid, boring and utterly pointless . . ." ' Wait, wait a sec, you've not heard the best bit. "You're not a writer and you never will be. If another manuscript bearing your name should arrive on my desk, it will be dispatched at once, not to my out-tray but to my shredder."' I folded the letter, saying nothing, watching her stew. Then: 'And you reckon you're embarrassed. Because it was written by you. Now, if it had been written *about* you, as it was about me, how d'you think that'd make you feel?'

She blushed, she paled, then she whimpered, 'I was only doing my job.'

'Your job? "Commercially speaking, it would be of interest to nobody, save those one or two misfortunates on whom this drivel is based. And even then there'd be no guarantee of book sales, as I would have grave doubts as to whether any of those people can actually read. Indeed, illiteracy, at its varying levels, may well be endemic down your neck of the woods." Christ, can't you just hear the gusto, the sheer thrill of putting your boot in good and proper? This was no chore for you, Ms Rooney. This was a labour of love, if ever I saw one.'

Her eyes found a spot on the floor between her feet. Meanwhile, I glanced at the other man there present who was standing open-mouthed, utterly bamboozled by all this. And then I winked at him, which seemed to perplex him even more.

'Did you ever once stop to think of the hurt and the humiliation you caused with that poisoned pen of yours?'

Still she said nothing, refuted nothing, denied nothing.

'Or did you ever once stop to think that, somewhere down the line, one of these so-fucking-funny hatchet jobs might have repercussions?'

'Repercussions?'

'You were right, I have come to drop back the contract. Now,' I said, drawing it from my pocket,

151

turning it over, 'you'll notice that I've left it completely blank. You can use the space to work on your material, to write some brand new put-downs and general-purpose insults. Alternatively, you can stick it up your hole. Because I've signed for Taurus Books.'

'For . . . *Taurus*?'

'Oh, you've heard of them, then? Funny, I don't believe they've ever heard of you. Or your Mickey Mouse firm, for that matter.'

Out the door I went, down the steps and into Rathmines Road at full stride. I'd have to reconsider, I decided. I could no longer remain so confirmed an atheist. There might just be a God above after all.

CHAPTER EIGHT

The press duly arrived and asked a few harmless questions, between incredulous glances around my living quarters. They then photographed me standing by the main gate of Kilmainham Gaol, once a fully functional prison, now a museum and sometimes movie set. When the piece was run a few days later, I wasn't thrilled with the picture. I thought it made me look dishevelled, even gaunt. Though it was possible I'd lately become dishevelled, even gaunt. And whatever my misgivings, that snapshot could not have better supported the accompanying text: 'Wannabe author, impoverished, turned down more often than your average bedspread, finally hits big time', or words to that effect. My new employers were quoted as being tremendously excited by their capture: '*Remember Me, Fair Eleanore*, a tragicomedy, set a generation ago in Luton, Bedfordshire, among the muck and the madness of the Irish navvying fraternity.' As saying that my sparse yet fluid style gave rise to inevitable comparison with no less a scribe than Cormac McCarthy. As predicting that an advance like theirs for raw talent like mine would prove to be one of the bargains of recent publishing history. Just seventy-five grand? For that kind of money, I was practically giving it away.

After the newspaper article, that trip to Earlsgrove couldn't be postponed much longer. Alan collected Angie, Robert and me early on the next Saturday morning and we all headed south. My wife, being city-raised, detested countryside, countryfolk, and everything that went with them. She'd only been to my family home once, shortly after we'd first got engaged, and even then it was under protest. However, given the circumstances, she was prepared to endure a second visit.

My mother, daft and unpredictable as ever, made barely a mention of the deal I'd struck. She was far too busy admiring Robert, her only grandson, remarking on how he'd grown since last she'd seen him, further remarking that it had been so long since last she'd seen him, she'd half expected him to be shaving. She'd not seen Angie in just as long, but was far less put out over that. However, the two women did kick the odd word between them, and meagre though the dialogue was, both managed to agree that the nipper must definitely be a Forrister – my wife's maiden name – because he looked nothing much like anyone from our side.

My dad, meanwhile, was exactly as I'd expected him to be, feigning high indignation that 'the papers, the bloody dogs in the street' should have had the story before he did. Grousing, bellyaching, wondering aloud if it wasn't 'little enough' for me to have let him know right away. But his act was as transparent as it was dire: the very first chance he got, the old fraud was on the phone to one crony after another, alerting them to the fact that I was in town, ensuring they'd all be in Shem Murray's later that night for a pint.

To kill time till pub time, I took Robert on a tour of some farm buildings nearby. My parents owned nothing: even the house I was born and brought up in was council property, my dad having spent his working life as a poorly paid agricultural labourer. Next door, however, were the Freynes. Big people, but good neighbours nonetheless, who would come rambling into our place as we rambled into theirs – without need of invitation or permission.

Strange how it can take a whole new surrounding, or an outsider's perspective. Walking now from sty to stable to byre, his little hand in mine but his little feet determinedly leading the way, I could see precisely what had impressed my mother so. Not only was the child growing like an anthill, his speech and vocabulary were improving beyond recognition. Wherever we went, I was invited to 'Look, Daddy, big cow,' or 'Look, Daddy, chicken.' The big cows, the chickens, the sheep he was captivated with. He wasn't even deterred by the bull, not at all. But the very young calves, frisking about in the corner shed, petrified him. He seemed to take them for enormous dogs and damn near lost his reason. I tried explaining. When that got us nowhere, I picked up an old hay fork that was lying close by and pledged to stab the first one that so much as looked crooked in his direction. But far from helping, this prospect only freaked him more and set him screeching till half the parish resounded to the echo. Seeing his hysterics, and considering the harmless little creatures that had put him in such a passion, I couldn't help but laugh. Much less amusing, however, was that other observation of my mother's. He didn't look like me. Or like anybody belonging to me. Not as much as I once imagined. And certainly not as much as he should've.

Later on, and to my wife's great disgust, the pub was men only, a lads' night out. And a healthy session it was: my dad had done well, rounding up all his old sparring partners. Alan Bradshaw, too, was there, but he wasn't saying much. Indeed, Alan was hardly permitted to speak at all as everything – *everything* - was directed to, through or about me. This was something I'd have to get used to, some small appetizer for the fruits of the fame-game to come: I found it exhilarating. I wasn't quite so thrilled with the antics of my father as he sat alongside vying for the limelight, primping, preening, rephrasing questions, embellishing answers. Like his was top name on this bill; like anyone gave a fuck what he had to say. And then, to blacken my humour still further, a man named Cathal Ó Domhnaill entered the premises just on closing time. From his place at the counter I saw him note me, then advance on our corner with purpose. A thundering pillock, Ó Domhnaill was the local historian, *Gaeilgeoir* and culture buff, self-appointed elder of the community, authority on practically everything. And, displaying the boorishness that often accompanies these notions of intellectual superiority, he leant in across several of our company and shook my hand. 'Well done, young man,' he grandly announced.

'Thanks, Cathal,' I squirmed.

'Well done. You're a credit to the little village. Everyone is proud of you.'

'Nice of you to say so,' I squirmed some more.

'And you're just the man I want to see.'

Round and about me there were funny glances, with the odd snigger into a pint or up a sleeve.

'You know what year it is, young man?'

'Y . . . yes.'

'Well, then, you'll know we've got a pretty big anniversary looming.'

'We have?'

He rolled his eyes, hamming it up dreadfully for the others' benefit. 'Doesn't the name Theobald Wolfe Tone mean anything to you?'

'Oh, yes,' I said. 'Of course.'

'Yes, of course. The bicentenary of the '98 Rebellion. Two hundred years since Tone and Father John Murphy and all the brave men of Wexford gave their lives to end British tyranny in this land of ours.'

'That's right.'

'Damn sure it is. And I feel we ought to do something to mark that. Because South Kilkenny's contribution to the struggle for independence is often overlooked. Not just nationally, but among its natives too.'

As far as this native was aware, we in South Kilkenny had made little or no contribution to the struggle for Irish independence. Not ever. But I nodded and asked, 'So, Cathal, what did you have in mind?'

'A public seminar on the subject. Some speeches, some questions and answers, you know the kind of thing I mean. I'd say a few words, of course, and I've arranged for D. S. MacAongusa, the history teacher from Waterpark College, to give a bit of a lecture as well. I'm trying to persuade a man by the name of Jamesie

Loughran from West Waterford – he's not exactly the full shilling, God help us, but he's a direct descendant of the great Thomas Francis Meagher. Y'know, "Meagher of the Sword".'

Good Jesus, I thought. What a prospect that sounds.

'So, what d'you think?'

'Sounds excellent. But where do I come in?'

'Ah, well, y'see, we'd want a big name to chair the meeting. I mean, who's going to come hear an eejit like myself?' and he laughed raucously around each of the gathering.

'Me? A big name? I wouldn't say that yet.'

'Maybe not, but you're the biggest name we could get for nothing. Did I explain that there'd be no payment involved?'

At this, there came another eruption of mirth from around the table. When at last it quietened, I said, 'Okay, then, but – how d'you mean, chair it?'

'Introduce the speakers. Then get a bit of a debate going afterwards. And generally keep order.'

On all sides, faces hung slack with expectation.

'Ah, you'll do it all right! 'Cos it's like I said, no one ever heard of myself or MacAongusa. And if they did hear of poor oul' Loughran, then 'twasn't as a public speaker, faith. But, God Almighty, they'll all want to see the local boy made good.'

'Yerra, go on!' my dad urged.

'Um . . . will I need to know anything about the topic up for discussion?'

'Well, it wouldn't hurt if you did. But sure I can fill you in all you want in the meantime. So, are you on?'

'When would you be hoping to have it?'

'I thought the Saturday of the June Bank Holiday. The following Monday is a day off, so nobody need be in too much of a rush away afterwards. We can make a right weekend of it.'

A right weekend indeed. As we slouched home from the pub, the serious reservations were hardening as to what I'd just let myself in for. June '98 was nine months away, and would find me up to my armpits in that second novel, the sequel to *Eleanore*. How could I give time or priority to Ó Domhnaill or to his lunacy? Well, I couldn't was the simple answer. So, in order not to disappoint, I'd show up for him. I'd wing it as best I could. And I'd do no more: there would my involvement start and end. Anyway, I didn't imagine this seminar was likely to prove much of a crowd-puller. Indeed, there was a reasonable chance that, even if I were to cock things up royally, I might just get away without any member of the outside public actually witnessing.

Before we left next day, the conversation came round again to the holiday home, this rustic retreat that my mother simply refused to let lie. I suppose that, never having had an acre of ground to call her own, her heart was set on seeing something, *anything*, of the locality registered in the family name. My father, I suspect, was just as keen. But it wouldn't be his way to say so. Instead he cut in crossly, berating my mum to have a jot of sense, and that a home for day-to-day living was more in our line. It was now, after eye-contact agreement, that Angie and I deemed the time right to tell. We'd bought. Or, at least, we'd put down a holding deposit. The property –

house and contents – had come on the market in Inchicore, just off the canal. Jamestown Square wasn't cheap but, in the context of Dublin prices, it wasn't fantastically expensive either. And being able to lop seventy-five grand off the bank loan needed was a helluva start, making the eventual mortgage repayments very, very affordable. The house itself was small – two bedroomed – but perfectly formed, end-of-terrace with tidy front and back gardens. Around the central courtyard, each residence was allocated a numbered parking space; ours, for now, sat empty, but surely would not sit so for long. Meanwhile, at the entrance to the estate there was a security barrier, preventing the unauthorized movement of traffic in either direction. It was impressive by anybody's reckoning; maybe just a little on the extravagant side, but we'd slummed it for long enough.

Not being part of any chain, we pushed the deal through surprisingly quickly. It seemed like no time before Alan Bradshaw was on our doorstep another Saturday morning, this time to ferry us to the new abode along with our entire worldly possessions. These amounted to one toddler plus accessories, a few stuffed carrier bags, an Intel Celeron and the desk whereon it sat. So little, in fact, that Alan estimated he could do the lot in a single run, if we were agreeable to walk the half mile from Easton Terrace to Jamestown Square, upmarket every step of the way.

So, leaving Angie at the kerbside to fit the small stuff on board, Bradshaw and I began inching the desk down the two flights of stairs. The thing itself was light but damn awkward, with shelves, legs and attachments protruding at all angles. It was as we stopped for a breather on the landing that I heard Angie's voice. And that of a man. She'd struck up conversation with some passing stranger.

'A writer? Serious?' went the deeper voice.

'Yeah. I don't mean to boast, but he's done really, really well. We wouldn't be making this move without him.'

'I see. And has he written anything I might ever have heard of?'

'Oh, no, this is his first.'

'First written, or first published?'

'First published. He's written loads.'

'Loads? And what became of all the others?'

'Nothing. Between ourselves, I don't think they were much good.'

The man laughed. 'But I suppose he made up for it with this one, eh? Rightly struck oil?'

'To the tune of – I don't want to say it too loud – of seventy-five grand.'

'Seventy-five grand?'

But the amazement in the voice sounded, to me, affected. Indeed, there was something about the entire dialogue that didn't quite ring true. I picked up my end of the desk, bade Bradshaw do the same and began down the remaining flight of steps.

'And is this going to be the first place you've owned?' asked the male.

'That's right.'

'Is there much that needs doing with it?'

Now on the ground floor, I stuck my head round the doorpost. There was Cambridge. And he saw me too. Angie twigged nothing, crowing on, 'That's the best part – everything's ready. The couple we bought from are emigrating, so we got it lock, stock and barrel.' Still perfectly oblivious, she smiled and said, 'Which means that someone else's done all the work. We've just got to move in and call it our own.'

'Yeah, that's pretty much your husband's style,' Cambridge announced, facing Angie, addressing one and all. Then, only to me, 'This is not over, pal. Not by a long chalk. So don't go thinking you've got away with anything.'

And off he stormed. With the others, I watched him go, aping their puzzlement, denying all knowledge or any understanding. The entire length of the walk to Jamestown Square, I repeated those denials, offering no better explanation than that the policeman had me confused with another. Either that or he was mad. The subject was abruptly dropped as we set foot in our new estate for the first time as people of property. By our front gate, Alan had already parked up and was unloading our possessions, and our child, on to the footpath. Before going to help him, I stood a while in the very centre of the courtyard and looked all around me. Home. Home at last. This was more like it. This was an address I'd never, ever be ashamed to own up to. And this was . . . *this was Ger McEvoy in the upstairs window of the house across the quadrant.* McEvoy! Big, brazen and utterly shameless, craning his neck one way and then the other, missing not a single detail. Even when our eyes met, he didn't have the good grace to look away. Instead, he only narrowed his squint, the better to survey the goings-on below. I hissed Angie to my side. 'What the fuck's he doing here?'

'Him? He lives here.'

'You knew that? What'm I saying? Of course you knew it!'

'Yeah, I did.'

'And why did you not tell me?'

''Cos there's nothing to tell. Not any more.'

'But you didn't even think it was worth mentioning?'

'Hey, you two!' Bradshaw called. 'Quit yer squabbling and come give me a hand.'

Angie looked daggers at me. 'Typical you,' she spat. 'Won't be happy till you've ruined our big day!' And she wheeled away, indignantly.

I followed, praying that this wasn't some kind of omen. Because, thus far, this big day of ours had ample room for improvement.

For all that, we moved in at once, settled in almost as quickly. Our dwelling was middle of the range, no better, but to folk like us it might've been Versailles. I would later learn that my wife was so very chuffed she'd even made clandestine approaches to her parents that they might come join us one night for dinner. Clandestine they were, and clandestine they needed be: I disliked the Forristers every bit as much as they disliked me. They were the kind who believed that, where their daughter was concerned, no man alive was good enough. Certainly not some ill-educated, rednecked factory hand with notions way above his station. And with an intellect that utterly dwarfed both of theirs combined. From the very first day Angie took me home, it was like a competition between us to see who could hate the other more. Still, to their credit, they weren't now for bandwagon-jumping. In fact, they resisted the invitation just as vehemently as I would've, had I known.

Naturally, we found ourselves with a better class of neighbour. Most were childless, double-incomed young professionals, the glaring exception being McEvoy and his mother at number 19. I frequently ran into him when I went every Thursday to sign on the dole. My own claims to welfare were by now highly dubious, but I reckoned his to be downright criminal. A couple of times each week, armed with his toolbox, I'd see him leave the square early, and not return till all hours. Moonlighting, obviously, and drawing benefit to which he was not entitled. More than once, I was sorely tempted to report him. But in view of my own circumstances, I didn't want the authorities crawling around our little enclave any more than he did.

As he kept to no regular routine, then, I could never say for certain if he was in or out, watching me or looking elsewhere. Which meant that Carla Whitty and I were forced to tread carefully. Because if that jealous bastard were ever to catch wind of our affair, he'd be hotfoot to my wife, squealing like a stuck pig. So our trysts were kept discreet and generally preceded by a phone call or two. I now had a landline all of my own, and was listed in the directory for the first time in my life. Further confirmation of my new-found status – although with me about to turn thirty-six next birthday, it was hardly a day before time.

What it did do was allow Taurus Books to maintain contact, to keep me abreast of developments. It was all pretty standard till the day when there came a request rather out of the ordinary. The London-based MD of Taurus International was in town. The visit was a flying one, but while here he hoped to meet as many of 'his' authors as possible, to put faces to names and novels. He would fit me into his schedule at seven-thirty, Wednesday evening, in the Clarence Hotel. As to whether this was convenient for me, no discussion was invited.

So, leaving Angie holding the baby – the invitation was for one, and quite specific about it – I presented my best foot forward at the Clarence on the following Wednesday evening, seven-thirty sharp. And it was there I was made to wait for the best part of an hour. At Reception, I stayed out of the bar, for fear of the impression it might create.

The party, when it did arrive, was led by Paul Gibbs, new-pin neat, not a hair out of place. He had with him a man in early middle age, in slacks, sports jacket and black polo neck, greying a little around the temples but looking well preserved and sprightly. Also in the company was a woman, heavily made up and dressed far too young for her years, which could've been anywhere between mine and twice mine.

I stood. Gibbs, scanning the foyer, sighted me and over they came. 'Brendan! Glad you could make it, sorry we're late. This is Martin Shipperly, Managing Director, Taurus Books. Martin, Brendan Stokes.'

'I expected somebody much older,' he said cordially, as we shook hands.

'And this is Rachel Kellett, a member of the Taurus board.'

She smiled like it hurt, then offered only the deadest fish of a handshake.

'Let's adjourn to the bar,' Shipperly decreed, and together we trooped under the archway and seated ourselves in a corner nook. At once, lounge service arrived. Shipperly handed over his room key and began, 'G and T, squeezed orange juice, still water and . . . Brendan?'

No sign of weakness, I'd already determined. No suggestion of a flaw. 'I'll have a still water too, please.'

'A still water!' the main man boomed. 'Well, by crikey, that novel of yours certainly isn't autobiographical in that case! I was expecting you to call for a great big pint of Guinness. Rather hoping you would, actually. I don't like to drink alone.'

'Thank you very much, but still water's fine.'

'If you're sure.' Then, when the lounge girl had departed, 'That novel, incidentally, I loved it.'

'Everyone who's read it has loved it,' Paul Gibbs cut in. 'It's like my wife said: *Romeo and Juliet* meets *Lolita* meets *Boys from the Blackstuff*. And what kind of reader could possibly be excluded by a recipe like that?'

'I'm just now thinking about that piece at the very end. When Whacker gets up from the grave, says goodbye to his old comrade, turns his collar to the wind and takes his first step on the road back to Luton. Ah . . .' He scrunched his features '. . . how does it go again?'

' "Back to the land of the living"?' Gibbs suggested.

'That's the bit! "Back to the land of the living. Back to

the grind." Now, Brendan, I consider myself a hardened old cynic, but you'd need to be made of stone to read those lines and not feel something.'

Across the table I heard a very tiny whimper, then I saw that it had come from the lady, Ms Kellett, who suddenly seemed in even greater discomfort than earlier.

'Oh, God, I'm sorry, my dear!' Shipperly laughed, placing his hand on hers. 'Rachel hasn't finished the book yet.'

'I've just reached the part where the family arrive from Ireland to snatch Ellie home,' she twittered.

'Rest assured, I've spoiled nothing for you. Brendan – why Luton? How've you come to know it so well?'

'How . . . em . . . what d'you mean?'

'You've obviously been there – lived there, I dare say.'

'Not as such. But I've known several guys who did. And, in the course of my research, many's the night I spent round the alehouse fire, listening to all their yarns.'

'Remarkable. Absolutely remarkable. You write about the place with such intimacy. Like you were born and bred there. And, young man, that's quite a compliment, coming from someone like myself, who actually was.'

Oh, sweet Jesus, I thought. What *were* the chances?

'Yes, indeed,' he went on. 'I'm a Lutonian. My family hails from Frederick Street, just a stone's throw from Hightown Road, where much of your action takes place. The singer, Paul Young, lived round there once upon a time as well. I'm sure you're aware of that too.'

I nodded, afraid to utter even a syllable.

'By coincidence, I happened to be a newly-wed in Luton right about the time you describe. In fact, my daughter was born there in 1977. And you got it pretty well correct about those mad Paddies – they were some scourge! Loud, rowdy and gagging for aggro when chucking-out time came. To make matters worse, it was the very height of the whole punk thing. So, every once in a while, a mob of drunken Irish would go looking for the safety-pin brigade where they hung out down around the train station. And, good Jesus, it was bedlam! I'm not ashamed to say, I used to be petrified; for myself, for my wife, but mostly for the young family I was trying to rear. And if anybody were to tell me that I'd *ever* enjoy being reminded of those days; that I'd actually finance a novel set there and then, well, I wouldn't have believed it. But life's strange like that, don't you think?'

I did not fancy being probed any further on my Lutonian connections, so I began the sidetrack. 'I suppose. Anyway, d'you do this kind of thing often? I mean, come to Ireland to meet authors?'

'Oh, not at all,' he said. 'Seldom. Practically never. In fact, I've not come here now to meet authors – not principally at any rate. That daughter I just mentioned has recently moved over, so I'm killing a number of birds with the one stone.'

'Over to Dublin?'

'That's right. She's started work in our Irish office – y'know, where we're based off Baggot Street.'

'And she likes it?'

'Amm,' he exhaled loudly, 'knuckling down to a job has never been a forte of hers, but so far, so good. She's even moved into a place of her own. That's got to be a healthy sign.'

'Course it is. What's she got?'

'A small apartment in Tudor Hall, just across the river. I had to go guarantor on the lease, naturally. Then I had to come visit and be suitably enchanted. It's what dads do.'

The drink arrived. At the break in conversation, he climbed back behind the wheel. 'Anyway, let's hear more about yourself. Married?'

'Yes.'

'Kids?'

'Just the one. A little boy.'

'That's nice. And this is your first published novel. So how have you kept the wolf from the door all these years?'

'I worked as a fitter in a textile mill up to a short time ago.'

He looked smugly at the other two. 'Didn't I say that? That his roots wouldn't be at all academic, but more on the rough and ready side? I could easily tell – it's there on every page of your book. F'rinstance, you're obviously a big footie fan.'

Inadvertently, my eyes widened.

'A United man, I'd guess, judging by the incredible minutiae of your writing on the Docherty debacle. Nobody who wasn't a Red-Till-Dead could be so vivid.'

I could recall transcribing a page or two, and several bawdy gags, about someone named Tommy Docherty. But, for the life of me, I couldn't now recall *anything* of the context.

'Don't follow Man U myself – I'm a lifelong Hatter. Still, I have to take my hat off to Ferguson. He's really left all the others scrapping for second. Anyway, cheers!'

Of that last entire spake, 'cheers' was the only bit I properly understood. Glad of the respite, I raised my glass. But the swine got his back down first and went on, 'So, d'you get across much to Old Trafford?'

Oh, for Christ's sake, I thought, now what's he on about? Clearly, something I was expected to be familiar with.

'Ah . . . no, Martin, I don't.'

'Never?'

'Very rarely.'

'What's the problem – tickets?'

'Er . . . that's it, yeah. Tickets.'

'I can get you tickets – I've got a friend who's well placed with the club's sponsors. Hey, how about we take in a match together, me and you? I usually have to watch my son play hockey on a Saturday. If you were to ring and say you wanted to see a game, it'd give me the perfect get-out. So, what d'you think?'

'Sounds great,' I said. 'I'll do that.'

'Marvellous! I look forward to it, I really do. Anyway, being a Busby Boy, what d'you make of your latest? This Baby-faced Assassin? This Angel of Death?'

'I'm sorry?'

'Ole Gunnar Solskjaer!'

While he spoke in English, I stood some chance. But now it seemed that, to talk football properly, I needed a proficiency in languages as well. Out of my blank and total incomprehension, there came a clear-headed decision. This conversation was like quicksand: the more I struggled to stay afloat, the deeper down I was sucked.

'Mr Shipperly, to be perfectly straight with you, I'm not—'

'You're late!' he chided, tapping his watch, looking out over my shoulder. I turned in my seat. There, sashaying through the foyer and towards us, was this absolute traffic-stopper. Blonde, bronzed and blue-eyed, pneumatically proportioned, wearing a dress that was black, tight, and cut both high and low.

'I'm sorry, Dad,' the vowels were effortlessly upper crust, 'one of the guys got engaged, so we all went to The Shelbourne.'

'I take it then, young lady, that you won't be joining us for dinner?'

'I've eaten. *And* I've had a few.'

'Well, you'll have another with us now.'

'No, thanks, Dad. Honest. I'm going to cry off early.'

'One more, then we can all call it a night. Southern Comfort, rocks, yeah? Oh, beg your pardon. Brendan, this is my daughter, Neve Shipperly. Neve, Brendan Stokes.'

We shook hands. Up this close, she wasn't quite the Maker's masterwork. Her nose was slightly long, her mouth narrow, her tan fake, while underneath the platinum mane, her dark eyebrows jarred like nails on a blackboard. Still, fine feathers do fine birds make. And a body like hers will always excuse a multitude. She smiled as she spoke. 'Brendan Stokes, *Remember Me, Fair Eleanore*? *That* Brendan Stokes?'

'You've read it too, then?'

'Have I ever! And,' she said, as she went to another table, took a stool and sat herself beside me, 'there's just one thing I want to know. When'll the next book be ready?'

'Give the man a chance, will you?' her father scolded. 'Let him catch his breath after the last one.'

And as the gathering laughed politely, Shipperly Senior got more drinks in. Neve took hers in hand and said, 'Okay then, no pressure. No-o-o pressure. But have you started your second?'

'I've written a few pages,' I lied.

'Tell me it's another love story.'

Martin Shipperly frowned at her. '*Another* love story? You'd call *Eleanore* a love story?'

'Of course, Dad. What else could it be?'

'Well, it's a good laugh. A bit of a tear-jerker in places. It's about guilt. And remorse. It takes a riotous look at Britain's construction industry in times past, at the human waste created almost as a by-product and almost all of it Irish. Plus it's got a nice bit of seventies football thrown in for the truly discerning reader.'

'Brendan?' she asked. 'It's a love story, right?'

Ever since this book's acceptance, I'd been analysing it, dissecting it, tearing it word from badly put word. Knowing it lacked any quality, charm or erudition, trying to discover what in the hell, then, it *did* have.

'Yes,' I said. 'It's a love story. It's a lot of other things too, Mr Shipperly. But without the boy-meets-girl, there's very little there worth telling.'

'Brendan, my old mate, love stories aren't ten a penny, they're worth nothing like as much. If *Eleanore* was just another love story, it wouldn't have got past the doorman at Taurus Books.'

172

'I don't want you to feel duped, Mr Shipperly, but that was part of the plan from line one. To take something straight from the pages of romantic melodrama, the kind of thing that never, ever happens in real life. Then dress it up – or rather, dress it down. *Really* dress it down. Make the clothes, the characters, the location all dowdy and dirty and common. Set the whole thing in a time that was naff and unmemorable. What I'm saying is, disguise it heavily enough, and even a hardbitten old cynic like yourself won't realize he's actually reading Mills and Boon.'

Around the table, there was a thoughtful silence. Gibbs and the woman were both scratching points on their lower faces. Shipperly grinned crookedly into his gin and tonic. And although I couldn't properly see, I could sense Neve gazing, open-mouthed.

'Hang on!' she blurted finally. 'D'you not believe that love, pure love, could drive a person to do what your hero did?'

'Sorry?'

'You just said, "The kind of thing that never happens in real life."'

Insanely, I felt a knot in my stomach. Another in my tongue. 'I . . . okay, maybe not *never*, then. But very, very rarely.'

'Well, there you go!' she crowed, her eyes a-sparkle.

I turned on my stool till I faced her, till our knees touched, and bluffed on: 'But, Ms Shipperly—'

'Please, it's Neve.'

'Neve, whatever about it happening in real life, if it happens as the central plot of a book, chances are that book will be a soppy load of old hogwash. Send it to a publisher, a good publisher—' I briefly acknowledged her father '—and it wouldn't get past the doorman. However, set it among rude foremen, drunken labourers, football hooligans, bad language, acres of bum cleavage, whole oceans of beer, then end it all with a gory double suicide, and you hardly notice you've been following a kind of fairy tale.' Breathless and triumphant, I knocked back my water with one huge draught.

It was several seconds after I'd done so before Neve averted her gaze, downward and into her Southern Comfort. Only then she saw, and said, 'They forgot the ice. Back in a sec.'

Once she'd cleared the alcove, Old Man Shipperly leant across the table, chin on open palm. 'That must happen quite a bit.'

'What must?'

'The ladies being rather . . . bedazzled when they first meet you. Happens quite a bit, I'd guess?'

'Not as often as I'd like, Martin.' I cackled, then quickly became aware I was the only one laughing.

'Yeah . . . she's young, y'know. And quite impressionable. In any case, she has a boyfriend.'

'I'm not surprised, Martin. She's a lovely-looking girl. A credit to you.'

'Whatever . . . she's young.'

And back she came. As she retook her seat her father rose from his, made only the sourest, most grudging attempt at a smile and said, 'Brendan, I could listen to you all night, and that's the truth. I don't mean to flatter you, but I've never before had such an insight into the inner workings of a, well, a craftsman.'

I wasn't sorry the interview had come to an end. That Luton thing was close, that football thing closer yet. Anyway, I'd run fresh out of inner workings and insights, my dazzling all done for this night at least. Better to quit while I was ahead.

'Our table awaits, Brendan. So . . .' we shook hands '. . . goodbye, take care, and keep doing your stuff. Neve,' he said, facing away, 'I know you're bunched and all that, but could you come to the dining room with us for maybe ten minutes? There's something I need to talk to you about, something important that's just come up to do with your lease.'

'Sorry, Dad,' and she downed her bourbon in a single shot, then clinked the glass of ice to the table. 'Important or not, it'll have to wait. Talk to you tomorrow.'

I didn't stop to note the expression on her father's face as we went our separate ways, they to the dining room, the young girl and I to the exit.

'How're you travelling?' she asked.

'I'll get a cab. You?'

'It's just across the river. I'll walk.'

'Let me walk with you. It's not safe for a young girl this time of night.'

'How very gallant,' she said, as off we set. 'Y'know, there's a great pub near my apartment building. It's called the Croppy Acre. Can I persuade you to join me? Maybe even coax you into trying one of their pints.'

'I don't think so, Neve. I ought to be getting along.'

'Just the one. My treat.'

The devil came to my shoulder. 'Oh, just the one, then. But I'd better ring my missus. Y'know, tell her I won't be long.' Neve handed me her mobile. 'Or . . . should I, maybe, tell her I won't be home?'

'Yeah. Probably better you do that.'

CHAPTER NINE

There would be no binding ties, none asked, none offered. Which arrangement suited us both to the ground. I already had complications a-plenty on my plate, while she'd not gone to the bother of finding a place of her own to suddenly become monogamous or exclusive. And so, though the affair did continue, it advanced hardly any from that very first night we met. Things were kept just as casual, just as superficial and just as secret, more a succession of chance, cheery one-offs than a relationship that was going anywhere. However, although we'd established no emotional bond, or indeed any common ground at all, something told me that this was a pie I'd do well to keep a finger in. Pretty soon there'd be book readings, book signings, premieres, award ceremonies and various other gala occasions that I could not as yet even guess at. Just over half my age and looking like she did, Neve Shipperly was precisely the kind of eye-candy I wanted on my arm for when the flashbulbs would go a-popping. An adornment she'd be, pure and simple, but as adornments went, I could think of no better. That said, I could think of no earthly sequence of events that might ever bring this about or even make it a remote possibility. Still, how often does the truth prove stranger than fiction? How often is the greatest creation of the greatest wordsmith outdone by simple, wild reality?

So it was with a clear vision but no definite plan of action that I once – only once – chose to broach the subject. Neve had just remarked, quite innocently, what a lovely wee house I owned. Solemnly, I told her it was my sworn intention that she be installed, some day soon, as lady of this lovely wee house. That we maybe not marry as such, but certainly forsake all others and settle down together. The reaction shocked me. I was met by the hissy fit to end hissy fits, beaten back by an absolute firestorm. How dare I even suggest the like, she ranted, when damn near every impediment was on my side of the bargain? For starters, there was a wife. There was also another bit on the side, one she hadn't wanted to know about, but that I'd been fool enough to mention anyway. And to rightly queer the pitch, there was a child. When I'd rid myself of all three, then – and only then – might she be prepared to talk lasting commitment.

All things considered, then, she was setting me quite the conundrum. As if I wasn't coming up with problems enough of my own design. This sequel business, to begin with; progressing nicely, I'd claimed – in reality not as much as the dot of an *i*. I had made a start. I had made several. But the more I did, the more I felt like the young girl in Rumpelstiltskin, expected to spin gold from the straw that now seemed to be clogging my head solid. The problem stemmed not from myself, of course, but from the original. It had been done in a style that might most charitably have been termed distinctive. To avoid unnecessary suspicion, this follow-up needed to be set down in a similar vein. Put another way, I was now forced to subvert my nature, to suppress the talent and the flair I'd been born with, and write like a mental defective. Every theme, every ploy, every genre I tried, every possible variation. The only thing consistent about these efforts was their quality: they all stank.

But compared with my over-ripened private life, they smelt like lilies of the valley. The irony, of course, wasn't lost on me. Having gone so long with barely a sight of the ball, I now found myself juggling three. *None* of whom I could safely kick to touch. My wife was the mother of my child – *my* child – and would beat me out of sight in any custody battle. She'd be entitled to half the proceeds of what writing I'd done while we were together. Which, if my current attempts were anything to go by, might amount to half my entire career earnings. Carla Whitty, for her part, had given me the story. She'd been the first civilian to read the manuscript after its acceptance. And she was, so far, the only person who could take that text and underline several serious anomalies. Things she'd never told me, that I shouldn't – *couldn't* – have known, but that appeared there nonetheless. Things that, if they were to reach the wrong pair of ears, would leave me with some heavy-duty explaining to do. Never forgetting, of course, that Carla could, at any time, present my wife with the ammunition to take me to the divorce court and from there directly to the cleaners. I didn't feel comfortable even contemplating the kind of ruin that a disgruntled Carla Whitty could bring down on my head.

Finally, there was Neve Shipperly to consider. And not for one moment did I consider giving up on her.

It had been a hectic one, that last Friday in November. Carla rang mid-morning, having had early release from the graveyard shift, asking if the coast was clear. Some hours later, as we said our goodbyes at the front door, McEvoy appeared, returning. He had with him his box of tricks, so it was likely he'd been on a nixer. Seeing what he saw, he smiled greasily in my direction, then took an age fumbling for his latchkey, the better to assess Carla as she went by him towards the exit. All the way to the traffic barrier, his gaze followed. But as she and it rounded the corner his face fell, and even across the courtyard the gasp was audible. I feared: I feared with good reason. Neve Shipperly had chosen this, of all moments, to make an unheralded house call. McEvoy stopped rummaging; stopped even pretending to. He could do no more than look on, bug-eyed, as she went flouncing by, making a direct line to the open doorway where I stood. Then, to his utter disbelief, and barely pausing to announce herself, she slipped past me and inside. Nothing; no long, lingering embrace, no brazen kiss at the garden gate, could've been more familiar, more conclusive, more damning. When at last he'd forced his mouth shut, he gave me an arched eyebrow before we closed our front doors in synch.

Immediately, I knew damage had been done. With the next heartbeat, I should've started work on a denial I could later plead. Or on some plausible lie to account for this daft, but wholly innocent misunderstanding, and for the ease with which the wrong impression might've been taken by certain onlookers. But no, nothing so rational. Instead, I began to imagine how I might possibly get scot-free away with it all; some divine intervention, some miraculous set of circumstances that would make McEvoy hold his tongue on everything he'd witnessed. Desperately, I thought. All the while Neve was in the house, I thought. The same when she'd gone. And when my wife came home. And right through the evening meal. And as we readied Robert for bed. And after. And still I could not come up with one crumb of comfort, a single reason why that bloated yob might keep his trap shut. Then, shortly before nine, the doorbell rang. I was up and to it like I'd been shot from a rifle.

But it wasn't McEvoy. It wasn't anything remotely like him. Instead, my porchlight illuminated a small, ragged figure, bald and whiskered, laminated in grime, his coffee-coloured pate shining under the halogen glow. A derelict. But, my double-take revealed, not just any derelict. It was the same one who'd frequented the Easton Terrace tenement when I lived there. When old Whitty helped him hold body and soul together.

He looked at me crazily and, crazier still, asked, 'Can I come in?'

I had no idea how I should handle this, whether I should sweet-talk him away or maybe try something more direct. Still undecided, I stepped down from the door, on to the path, forcing him back a pace. Up this close, the smell was eye-watering. It was coming partly from the man himself, partly from the bags he carried. It was his custom, I knew, to spend the day scavenging in skips and in kerbside bins for anything that was edible, smokable or combustible.

'Can I come in?' he repeated, but more coherently.

I swallowed. I'd spent the last seconds breathing only through my mouth. I swallowed again. 'No. I'm afraid you can't.'

'I just need a quick word.'

'I've told you, no.'

'It won't take five minutes.'

'You may bet it won't, because you're not coming in,' and I closed the door in his face. Through the frosted glass, I watched him stand a moment. Then slowly, deliberately, his hand relocated the bell. Again it rang. And again. And again.

My wife appeared, wild-eyed, in the hallway.

'What the—'

'It's that fucking tramp from Easton Terrace.'

'What's he want?'

'What d'you think? What do his kind always want?'

'Well, you'd better do something.'

'I'm not giving him money. If I do, we'll never see the end of him.'

Another chime. And another. And—

'For Christ's sake, Brendan, get rid of him, will you, before he wakes the child.'

I flung open the door and, with a lunging, double-handed push, sent him sprawling back the path. He groaned long and low, then rolled on to his side and began creaking to his feet. Stooped now on all fours, he was perfectly teed up for a running kick to the stomach.

But I held back. The path and garden were in plain view of every front window in the estate.

'Now, look, you – get this one thing through your fucking head. Your old friend isn't home. He's dead. There's nothing for you here, you've no business anywhere near this house. So get the Hell off my property or I'll call the police.'

He adjusted his stance till he faced me full and fair. Then he cocked his head defiantly. 'You do that. Tell them there's a man at your door who won't go away. You can even give them the name. It's McDermott. Shafty McDermott.'

My mouth fell open, twitched a little, but nothing came. I couldn't think to form words. For an instant, I'd forgotten how to draw breath.

'Ha! That's softened your cough. Now, we'll waste no more time out here gabbing,' and that leather, hobgoblin face became very, very businesslike.

Slowly, I regained some little brain function, enough to blab, 'I was told you were de— I mean, I was under the impression . . .'

He ignored me as, head lowered, he shuffled towards the doorway. Instinctively, I stepped into his path.

'Huh? You don't want to talk this over? Fair enough, I'll find someone who's interested to hear what I've to say. And see what I've to show.'

'To show?'

'Last time I'll ask, Mr Stokes. Are you letting me in or not?'

I stepped aside and he hobbled by. As I closed the door behind, Angie re-emerged. She stared a moment, like a goat watching thunder, then screeched, '*What?*' but at so high a pitch as to be barely audible.

'It's okay,' I told her, aside. 'You just go straight on, Mr McDermott.' When I'd steered the tramp through to the living room, I turned again to my wife. 'Honestly, Ange. Relax. It's okay.'

'Okay?' she wheezed. 'How can it be okay?'

I took her hands in mine. 'Calm down, love. It's just the beggar from the old place.'

'I know who he is!' and she tore herself from my hold. 'What I'd like to know is, what the fuck's he doing in my house?'

'A little bit of unfinished business, that's all. Leave it to me, I'll have him out of here in a jiffy. Why don't you go check on Robert? Leave everything to me.'

'Eh? You're telling me you've somehow got mixed up with – with Johnny Fortycoats in the sitting room, but I shouldn't ask what the Hell is going on? I shouldn't at least be concerned?'

'I swear, there's nothing for you to concern yourself about.'

'Nothing to con— Jesus Christ, he – *that* – is under my roof, about to conduct *business* with my husband. Business, if you don't mind. It's—' She stopped short and threw open the living-room door.

'In!' She pointed. 'Get in before me. If you think I'm going to be kept in the dark, old son, then you can think again.'

Inside, McDermott was sat uneasily in an armchair. I seated myself opposite, at no greater ease. Angie stormed in, teeth bared, eyes and nostrils flaring. She straightened herself in the middle of the room and lit upon the now-petrified tramp.

'Angie, love, there really is no need—'

'Shut it, eh?' she faced round fiercely. 'I'm well capable of getting to the bottom of this without any prompting from you!' She faced away again. 'Right, whoever you are, start talking.'

'God, Ma'am,' he quivered, 'first and foremost, I didn't come here to cause trouble.'

'Well, Mister, in that case, you came to the wrong house. Now, quickly as you know how, tell me what you're doing here.'

He studied himself a while. It was as if he'd memorized something, and was now deciding where best to begin the recitation. 'All right, then, Ma'am. It's like this. Andy Whitty was a friend of mine. We grew up together, we left Ireland together and, across the water, we settled and found work in the same town. But things didn't wind up the best for either one of us. With him, 'twas woman trouble. His girl committed suicide, and he got some class of a nervous breakdown, so he left England and came back here. With myself, 'twas a lot of things, but mainly the drink, to be honest.'

'Well, how about that?' she huffed. 'Imagine my surprise!'

'Aye, Ma'am. I used to find it hard holding on to a job, and then I'd have no money, and often times the rent wouldn't get paid. 'Tis a long story, but I let myself slip till I finished up sleeping rough in and around Luton. And afraid that wasn't bad enough, I got jumped this night by a gang of skinheads – y'know, these National

Front boyos. For no reason at all, Ma'am, I never done them any harm, but they put me in intensive care for a couple of months. Punctured a lung, broke three ribs. 'Twas only the mercy of God I pulled through at all.'

She folded her arms across her chest, eyes unblinking, face lined with yet greater contempt, and, 'Yes. God does work in mysterious ways betimes.'

'Whatever about that, Ma'am. There was this dog I used to have, a terrier, a little brown lad, Rolo. They hanged him off the tall railings around the park.'

'It must all have been very upsetting for you,' she sighed, heavy, long-suffering and bored. 'But is this saga actually leading somewhere? Like, does it have anything to do with you being here at this moment?'

Disregarding her sarcasm, her scorn, he once more picked up the thread of his rehearsed narrative. 'They let me out of hospital, and I was after recovering fairly well, thank God, but sure I couldn't go back to living like beforehand. 'Twasn't safe any more, not in that bloody country. So a crowd of my friends got the few bob together and bought me a boat ticket – one way – to Ireland. And let me tell you, I did not need asking twice. I'm home now, Ma'am. Home to stay. Home till I die.'

'Really? Well, you'll find things have changed around here while you've been away. Nowadays, Irish people tend to sleep indoors. Mostly in places that have facilities for washing. Even showering occasionally.'

'I know that, Ma'am. And when I arrived back, I tried a couple out. But . . .' he shrugged, '. . . nah. Not for me. They wouldn't let me be, always telling me make the bed, tidy the room, pick this up, put that there, be in by such a time, be gone by such a time. Nah. I took to the streets again. 'Twasn't as comfortable, maybe, but 'twas what suited me best.'

'Quite right, too. I mean, what matter if it had Kilmainham looking like downtown Calcutta, so long as you were happy?'

'Happy as Larry, Ma'am. And then one day, strolling past the courthouse, who should I see but my old pal Whitty. I couldn't believe it, 'cos I thought for sure that the man was gone to his eternal reward. And, bedad, if he didn't think the same thing about myself!' He laughed.

She joined in with a mocking guffaw, then turned to me, jerked her head towards the door and mouthed, 'Get rid of him!'

But away he went again. 'Sure then the job was right! I'd call round to his little *tigín* every once in a while. And we'd smoke a couple of fags, and drink th'odd drop of cider. And we'd talk about days gone by.' He paused. His voice slowed and softened. 'And he'd read me bits of this book he was writing all about it.'

Angie lowered herself to the arm of the sofa and leant forward intently. I tried my damnedest to catch her eye, to signal that this should be taken with a great grain of salt. But all of a sudden, she only had eyes for the tramp.

'I'd listen, and I'd laugh, and say 'twas great. But, to tell the truth, I thought the guy was cracked. Still, it kept him amused. And it kept him busy. He filled notebook after notebook and then, when he was finished, he wrote out the whole thing on this fancy typewriter he had – I think 'twas the niece bought it for him one time. I was there, in the flat, the night he done the last page. He was delighted with himself, but he knew something was wrong, 'cos he was getting these oul' pains in his chest, and he couldn't catch his breath right. Anyway, he told me his plan. He was going to get a few copies made of the book, and send them off to these publishers. But this copying business, it seems, costs money, and 'twas hard for him put any few bob together. Y'know . . . 'twould take a while. Now, he knew he wasn't a well man, and he was afraid that if he took bad at all in the meantime, the flat would be cleared out and everything he wrote, every word of it, would finish up on the dump in Ballyfermot. So here's what he did. He gathered all the old notebooks, the ones he wrote by hand, and he gave them to me. In case anything did happen. And if the book ever made a pound or two, and he wasn't around to spend it, then that was to be mine as well. Sure I said to myself again that the poor misfortunate was off his head, but I thanked him all the same, and swore that I'd mind his stuff for him, come hell or high water. 'Twas a good job I did. 'Cos the next time I called round, he wasn't there. He was dead.'

She sat herself further forward still, hanging now on his every word.

'Shortly after, they gutted the flat completely. And when I heard no more of the famous book, I thought no more *of* it. I reckoned it must have gone to that dump in Ballyfermot, just like Andy was afraid it would. Then one night lately, I took some old newspapers out of a bin near the Black Lion, and I was making a fire with them under a tree in the Phoenix Park. But, God, didn't I spot something! An article about this book called *Remember Me, Fair Eleanore*. "Hang on," says I, "wasn't that what Whitty's book was called too?" So I read another bit. And it seems this book is all about a bloke on the buildings in Luton twenty years ago. Just like Whitty's. Cripes, I thought, that's a good one now. Then I sees the picture: Kilmainham Gaol, right across the road from where Whitty used live. Then I looked at the man in the picture and, by God, I recognized him.' He pointed. ''Twas yourself. So I takes another look at this article. And it seems you got seventy-five grand for that book, Mr Stokes. But that book is not yours, it's Andy's. And that money is not yours either. It's mine.'

Angie studied the old man a moment longer, then turned towards me, her face dark and furrowed.

'Rubbish!' I said emphatically. 'Absolute bollox. Not a word of truth in it.'

'But . . . your story. It's identical to the one this man's just told us.'

'So?'

'So? Can you honestly expect me to believe—'

'My side of the argument, when there's another side on offer? No, I wouldn't dare expect that. But I'll tell you anyway. That girl – heavy-set, brown hair, you've seen her here once or twice? Well, that's Carla Whitty. Niece of the late Andrew. When she heard I was a novelist, she told me all about her uncle's life and times, start to finish, the works. And she asked me – *she* asked *me*, mark you – if I'd write it as a book. Now, naturally, I don't anticipate you'll take my word for that, but give me a minute and

I'll get you Carla's phone number. You can check things out with her.' I knew the number by heart, but I rose to my feet and made a great show of rummaging on the mantelpiece for my address book.

'And while you're at it, Angie, you can enquire after her uncle, and his literary prowess. Ask if he ever wrote a book. Ask if he ever even fucking read one. I guarantee you, she'll be able to clear this up in an act. The number isn't here. Hang on, she'll be in the directory,' and I started out of the room.

'Look, why don't you just leave it?' my wife said meekly.

'What d'you mean, leave it?'

'Just forget it, okay? It doesn't matter.'

It wasn't the most ringing endorsement I'd had, but it was something to work on. From where I stood in the doorway I crossed the floor, fell to my knees before her and took her hands in mine.

'Come with me, please. We'll make this call, you can speak to Carla yourself. She'll confirm everything, I swear to you she will.'

Briefly she faced me, then faced away again.

'Angie, how can you doubt me?' and I squeezed on her hands tighter yet. 'You were there. You saw the hours, the effort, the sweat I put in. The rejection and the ridicule I put up with. You witnessed it all – *everything*, first hand. Ange, how can you even entertain someone walking in off the street, accusing me of just stealing it?'

With a weak, sheepish smile, and with a tiny tear welling, she mumbled, 'I'm sorry.'

I knelt upright till my face was just an inch from hers. 'You know your problem, Mrs Stokes? You're too good natured. And far, far too unsuspecting. 'Cos in this world, girl, you can't just go taking everyone you meet on blind trust. This fucking chancer . . .' I poked a thumb over my right shoulder, '. . . sees me in the paper, reads about my bit of good luck, realizes he's actually part of the story that's making *somebody* a small fortune. So he comes snivelling around to nose out anything that might be in it for him. Well, he's going to get something right now. The door. And a size nine up the arse to make sure he doesn't ever come back!'

She spluttered a laugh, then gulped hard as that tear threatened to roll.

'I'm no chancer,' came the voice at my back. 'And I have more than just a story. I brought proof.'

'Oh, yeah?' I said, rising, taking a swagger in his direction. 'Let's see your proof, then.'

He bent low, rummaging in the plastic bag between his feet. At last he dredged out a string-tied package: thirty, maybe forty jotters, the kind schoolchildren do homework in. These he planted on his lap and began to fumble with the knot, muttering to himself as he did. But the fingers, gnarled and knobbled, made little headway, and the growling increased along with his frustration. My wife lost patience even quicker, jumped from her seat and said, 'Wait up, for Christ's sake, I'll get you something.'

He didn't seem to hear her, didn't notice she'd gone till she returned with a black-handled carving knife. 'God bless you,' I think was what he said as he snipped off the twine, then laid the knife by his side on the floor.

'Now, Mr Stokes,' he said, offering me a sample from

the top of the pile. 'Take a good look at that. And then tell me who the chancer is.'

I forced a sneer as I flicked over the damp, musty cover. I looked a while, then raised up the page and had a squint. Angie, at my shoulder, was peering just as closely. On no given signal, we edged to the room's corner, where a table lamp glowed and the light was better. It made no difference. The contents were illegible, absolutely indecipherable.

Daring to feel a little confident again, I laughed. 'What's this?"

But he wasn't to be easily cowed. 'It's your book. Or, at least, the same book you're claiming is yours.'

'The same book!' I snorted. 'It's not even the same bloody alphabet!' With a flourish of high amusement, I tilted the jotter towards my wife. 'What d'you reckon? Does it look like written English to you?'

'I can just about make out the odd word here and there.'

'Well, good on you. Because that's as much as any person alive could do!'

I held out the jotter like it was badly soiled underwear, then skimmed it across the room to where the old man sat. It fluttered into his face before coming to rest on his lap with the others.

'Nice try,' I said breezily. 'But no cigar. So tidy up that shit, get it and yourself out of my house – now!'

He wrapped his arms round the precious bundle, clasping it to his midriff. 'You'll be sorry!' He trembled. 'I'll take them – I'll take them to an expert!'

'Oh, you will, will you? D'you really think that any

qualified man is going to waste time or energy on you or your fucking garbage? If you do, the best of luck to you. I only hope you remember that these guys don't work for nothing.'

I had him hands down, and was landing my punches at will.

'Well?' I blustered. 'About ninety quid an hour is the going rate, I'd imagine. You've got that kind of money, yeah?'

'Maybe not,' he whispered, now bunging notebooks by the handful into his bag. 'Maybe I don't. But I've got this,' and from a coat pocket he produced a slip of paper, well worn and not much bigger than a shop till receipt.

Something in the way he waved it about told me I wasn't clear of the woods just yet. 'Wh . . . what is it?'

'Well, for starters, 'tis typed, so there'll be no dispute about what's on it,' he said, and he flashed it in my direction. ' "To whom it concerns, I , Andrew Whitty, do hereby bequeath to my good friend, James Shafty McDermott, the original draft of the novel *Remember Me, Fair Eleanore*, of which I am sole author. In the event of my death, all royalties accruing from said novel should also go to said Mr McDermott. Dated this April 2nd, 1996. Signed, Andy Whitty." ' Again he flashed me the written side. 'And there'll be no disputing that signature either. It's hard to read, I grant you, but it's what he signed every Tuesday in the labour exchange when he drew his dole.'

'Let me see that!' I said, stepping towards him. But before I'd advanced even a pace, he was out of his chair and had grabbed the knife from the floor.

193

'Fuck off!' he frothed. 'Get the fuck away!' And he stuffed the little typed slip deep into the pocket he'd fished it from. Then, crouching but keeping me all the while at the point of his blade, he began to gather the rest of his worldly possessions. 'No, you smart bastard. No, I haven't that kind of money. But when I go to the cops in Kilmainham with all this lot, I think *they* might be happy to stump it up.'

The world had so turned upside down, I hadn't noticed Angie pick up the cordless phone at my back. Hadn't even heard her dial, though each press of the keypad made a small tone.

'You won't have to go to the bloody cops in Kilmainham!' she quaked. 'They'll be coming here for you— Hello? The police, please, and hurry. It's number—'

I spun round and snatched the receiver. Her distress became open-mouthed bemusement when I pressed the Talk/Off button, then tossed the handset on to the couch.

'Brendan? I almost had—'

'It's okay,' I said, easing her behind me to the background. 'Right, McDermott, put that down and we'll talk.'

'You're joking!' He cackled. 'You must be fucking joking!'

'Brendan, he's got a knife! I don't care, I'm getting the guards,' and again she began with the phone.

Again I ripped it from her. 'Be quiet, I told you! Fair enough, McDermott, your call. What d'you want?'

'What're you doing, Brendan?'

194

'Shut up, will you, for fuck's sake! C'mon, then, pal, name your price.'

'But it's like you said, isn't it? He's lying, he's chancing his arm, he's—'

'Good Jesus, will you shut your fucking mouth! Let's hear it, McDermott. I'm sure we can do a deal.'

'I want what I'm entitled to.'

'Eh? The whole lot? The seventy-five grand? Not a hope!'

'That's what the will says.'

'The will?' I laughed desperately. 'In the first place, that isn't a will you've got. And in the second, I don't care what it says, that much money just isn't possible.'

My heart pounded, my breath quickened. Time, along with everything else, was running badly against me. If he walked out that door with what he'd got, the game was up.

Still, he wasn't flinching.

'C'mon,' I pleaded. 'We can settle this, but only if you're prepared to be reasonable.'

He thought a while. 'Okay, then. Fifty.'

'Ten.'

'Forty.'

'I can go to twenty, twenty-five, but—'

'Hold on!' Angie jumped in among the haggling. 'Hold on a sec. So you did steal it?'

'Stay out of this!' I barked.

'You stole another man's work! All this time you've been—'

'Christ Almighty, I said stay out of this!'

'You're not a writer, you're a robber! How could I—'

195

I struck her, right across the jaw, open-palmed and hard as I could. First time I'd done it and long, long overdue. She went sprawling on to the sofa and there she lay, whimpering, unmoving, but winning not an ounce of my sympathy or my remorse. 'I warned you to mind your own fucking business! I warned you not to as much as set foot in this room. But, no, your goddamn nose got the better of you, like always.'

'I only want what's fair,' the tramp said, embarrassed, apologetic, rattled.

I calmed as best I could and said, 'Yes, Mr McDermott. And we're close enough to agreeing what's fair.'

'I'm holding out for forty, Mr Stokes.'

'Then you'll just have to take me to court. You might win, you might not. But even if you do, the legal fees will eat up most of any money you might be awarded. I'm offering you twenty-five here and now. You give me what you've got, I'll give you the money. It's all I can afford, and it's a good price. I mean, just think what you could do if you had—'

'I'll give you forty, Mr McDermott.'

Though the handkerchief she held to the corner of her mouth slightly muffled her words, they still were quite easily discernible. And, for just an instant, I wondered if I'd caused brain damage. But she repeated, 'Forty, Mr McDermott. What d'you say?'

The tramp seemed even more disoriented than I. His eyes darted from me to her and back again, the knife point following his line of vision. 'Is this some kind of trick?' he growled.

Staring straight ahead, she replied, 'No trick. It's a genuine offer.'

'Angie, what in God's name are you on about? We can't afford—'

'We?' She lowered the tissue to reveal a trickle of drying blood. And a sneer. 'Brendan, my dear, this has nothing to do with you. It's between myself and the man with the merchandise.'

'What? And how d'you intend—'

'Oh, it won't be easy, but I'll raise it. There's plenty of equity in this house, more than enough. Mr McDermott, I'll have your money for you within the week.'

I searched her face for some clue as to what the ruse was. But still she avoided me. The tramp, meanwhile, could do no better than wave the carver about and parrot, 'I only want what's fair.'

'And that's what you'll get. In return, Mr McDermott, I'll take all that gear off your hands. And maybe then I can see about getting what *I'm* entitled to.'

Now at last she turned to me. Slowly. Ominously. 'Y'see, Mr McDermott, for nearly four years, I've been out – *on my own* – every morning, working myself to the bone, so that this piss-artist could stay home and play at being Roddy fucking Doyle. Four years, a long time to live on nothing but pie in the sky. Then, just a few months back, it seemed like it had all been worth it. My husband gets his big break – a book deal and a handsome advance. And I'm there thinking to myself, our troubles are over. Now he's in, this is just the start. There'll be many, many others. Except . . . well, there won't, Brendan, will there? This is as good as it's ever going to get. A second novel? Fat chance, when you couldn't even manage a first one.'

'I only want what's fair – d'ye hear me? I only want—'

'Yes, yes,' she smiled, her eyes never leaving mine. 'That's all settled. And tomorrow, Brendan, we're going to get one or two other things settled. We'll go to our solicitor, and draw up an agreement about how the royalties from this book are to be divided. I am going to look for ninety–ten in my favour. And you are not going to quibble. You're going to sign it away and look happy. Because if you don't . . . well, maybe this poor man won't shop you, but by Christ I will!'

'Just what's fair. That's all I want.'

'After that's been dealt with, Brendan, you'll pack your things, you'll get the hell out of my house and out of my life. Live horse and you'll get grass, eh! The years I've wasted on you, on this *farce* of a marriage. Still, maybe all's not lost. I'm young enough yet to start over. And, don't forget, I'll have a few quid under the mattress, won't I? A monied woman will never be short of admirers.'

'I didn't mean to cause all this trouble, I didn't. I only want what's fair.'

'Now, as regards Robert, we'll have to work out visiting rights and . . . ah, good God, what'm I saying? You've got even less claim on that child than you have on the book!'

It'd be easy, and perfectly plausible, to plead that I was driven to it, goaded beyond the endurance of any man. But, truth to tell, I was thinking as clearly as ever I'd done. 'I only want—' McDermott began again, but he never got to finish his mantra this time round. Because

I'd grabbed a marble-based candlestick from the table beside me and swung it like a lump hammer, catching him on a point midway between the ear and the eyebrow. The contact was clean as I could've wished, the thud dull, splodgy and immensely satisfying. His temple caved and down he went, as if struck by a humane killer. Dead as a doornail, blood oozing from every visible orifice.

My wife's jaw dropped, to scream, I thought, although I should've known she'd be too battle-hardened for any such theatrics. However, it was unlike her to misread the runes so badly, to make such a hash of predicting what was likely to happen next. Because, after a cursory check of the lifeless heap on the carpet, she railed at me with the same venom, the same contempt as before. 'Oh, that *was* clever. Damn bloody clever. What *do* you use for brains, you simpleton? A book was one thing, but a corpse on the middle of your living-room floor, how in the hell d'you propose to explain this away?'

Even as she watched me pull the sleeve of my jumper over my right hand and with it pick the knife up where it had fallen free, she would not be staunched. 'Well, Einstein, you're in this on your own. I'll have no part of it, y'hear? None! Don't ask me to help you cover it up and, by Jesus, don't you dare ask me to lie for you.'

Unchallenged, I advanced to within touching distance. My intention could hardly have been plainer. But still all she could do was rant.

'This is your problem. Entirely your own doing. Doesn't often happen, I know, that you manage *anything* all by yourself but—'

The blade, scalpel-sharp, went in and up through the left side of her ribcage. It was too easy: she didn't even register surprise, more a look of severe disappointment. Twice more I plunged the knife, deeply and in much the same area. Her knees buckled and she fell like a chimney stack.

Now the clock was ticking. All decisions would need to be instant, final and absolutely correct. So before dropping the knife, I had to consider whether I should stab some more, and give the impression of a frenzied attack. But I decided not. I'd done enough.

The living-room door had yawned open throughout; for the next while, it was critical that it be shut, that no heat be allowed escape. Next I turned my attention to the late Mr McDermott, and to the poison he'd brought to my house less than one hour before. I took all the handwritten copybooks and piled them by our open fire. There, using the lighter fuel that my wife had very considerately kept on the mantelpiece, I doused each jotter in turn before tossing it on to the flames. This didn't just rid me of evidence that was damning: it raised the room temperature till the little place sweltered. Hot enough to retard rigor mortis. Hot enough to accelerate decomposition. Hot enough to make exact times of death downright impossible to establish. I waited, watching till the last of the pages had burned to black ash, then poked every trace beneath the glowing embers. Only now did I make the 999 call. Ten, maybe fifteen minutes had elapsed: that lapse did not concern me. No one could ever say for certain who died when. Or, more importantly, who died first.

There was blood on my clothing, a little on my hands. Almost all was my wife's, though I may have caught a spatter of McDermott's as it sprayed. Not that it mattered, one way or another. Before the police arrived, I'd have ample time to well and truly contaminate the crime scene; once I'd done that, forensic findings wouldn't be worth a curse. Which meant I'd be left in the happy position of lone witness, with nothing or nobody ever to contradict my account. So I threw open the front door, then returned to assume my place in the tableau as it was rigged. And this was how the cops would find me: the grieving husband, cradling the body of his dearly beloved, soaked in her innocent blood.

The first policeman came storming into the house and through the hallway, but was fairly stopped in his tracks at the living-room door. It would be a long moment before he properly took in the sight that awaited him; by then, his nerve had returned. He picked his way through the mayhem and crouched beside me, laying a hand on my shoulder. 'Mr Stokes?'

'Yeah,' I gibbered. 'Where's . . . where's the . . .'

'The ambulance? It's on its way.'

'Oh, Christ, make it hurry up. She's . . . Angie! Ange, hang in there, it's on its way.'

At this point a second Garda, older and more senior, was present. From the corner of my eye, I saw the pair exchange very grave headshakes. Now the older man, too, hunkered down. 'Can you tell us what happened, Mr Stokes?'

'I . . . don't know. I swear, I don't know. I don't understand any of it. I left the room for a minute, no more than a minute, and I heard a – I came back and he'd done it. He'd stabbed her. I hit him. With the candlestick, that one there. And I'm not sorry I did . . . I only wish I could've hit the fucker twice as hard!' and burying my head in my late wife's neck, I found myself overcome by a most convincing display of grief. The older one straightened himself and stepped over to McDermott's body. There, he flattened two fingers on the tramp's jugular, again looked to his colleague, again shook his head heavily. 'Do you know this man, Mr Stokes?'

'No . . . well, yeah. Kinda. He was mates with a bloke who had a flat in our old block. A guy named Whitty. Whitty's dead, but yer man – well, he's a fucking loony, and he came here tonight looking for him. We took pity on him, the cold night, y'know . . . so we let him in. He had no reason in this world to – *I can't feel a pulse!* Ange! Ange! Garda, help me, I can't – I mean, I should be able to feel something, shouldn't I?'

'Here's the ambulance now, Mr Stokes. She'll be in the best of care.'

Two paramedics came racing through, the second bearing a stretcher. They, too, stalled a while at the door to gawp, to catch the breath. The grey-haired copper sidled between and muttered, 'Look after the woman – the other one's had it.'

Now, more grimly than ever and with more heartfelt cries, I hung on. It took both policemen to ease me away and to my feet. 'She'll be all right?' I fevered. 'She will, won't she?'

'Everything possible will be done for her,' soothed the

older man. 'Now we've got to get out of here. It's important to preserve the crime scene.'

With one linking each of my arms, they set about escorting me out of the room. All the while, I kept up the act, continued the sobbing, continued the hysterics, but continued also to rack my brains for anything I might've botched or overlooked. I was just yards from the police line: once across it, there'd be no going back. It was in the doorway they struck me – not a single fatal oversight, but *two*. Angie's blood was all over me. I also bore traces of the tramp's. But there was no blood of Angie's on the tramp, the man who I would claim had stabbed her. However, that was the least of the blunders: I'd also managed to forget the will! It was still in the dead man's pocket, still asserting that the novel was the invention of Andrew Whitty and none other, still awarding all proceeds to James McDermott.

I stopped. I turned to face the medics as they tended my wife.

'I heard that,' I wailed.

'Heard what?' said the one nearest me, looking up, looking panicked.

'She's dead, isn't she?'

'Well, ah, we'll get her to the hospital—'

'She's dead!' I screeched, and made as if to lurch forward. The policemen accompanying spread their arms across my path to prevent this; at once, I darted sideways and flung myself upon the body of McDermott. My hand went directly to the correct pocket, drew out the tiny slip of paper and stuffed it into my mouth. With it came fluff, grit and the Lord knows what else, but I chewed on regardless for all I was worth. As I did, I pressed myself to the corpse, threshing and wriggling so my blood-soaked clothes matted against his, all the while flurrying punches about his mottled head and snarling, 'Bastard, murdering bastard!' Seconds, whole crucial seconds, elapsed before they prised me off and lifted me, kicking and screaming, into the courtyard outside. There, the younger one sat me down on the low garden wall, offered me a cigarette and said, 'I know you're upset, Mr Stokes. And you have every reason to be. But try to understand, the forensics team has to go in there and examine the place.'

The older man tossed his head and harrumphed, 'For all the use that'll be now!'

But there was no accusation in his voice. So far, so good. Now, over the next few hours, it was just a matter of keeping the front up, keeping the story simple and consistent. All going well, the big brunt of this storm might well be weathered come morning.

I lifted my gaze from the ground and said, 'I don't drive – will it be okay to travel to the hospital in the ambulance?'

'Er . . .' the younger man checked with his colleague, 'we'll take you there in the squad car, no problem.'

'And then,' said the older, 'we may want you to come down to the station with us. To make a statement, answer a few questions, that sort of thing.'

'Sure. But I've already told you that when he went for me, I hit him. And that I'd do it again if I got the chance.'

'Yeah, it's just . . . Hello! Who's this little man?'

I spun round. There was Robert, dwarfed in the door-frame, lost in the oversized blue pyjamas, shivering in the chill November night. Determined as I was to think of everything, I'd never thought of him. I leapt to my feet, but as I came near he took a step away and howled, 'Daddy . . . Daddy stab—'

I rushed and swept him up in my arms. 'Daddy stab—' he began again. Desperately, I tried to muffle him, grabbing the back of his head, forcing his mouth against the hollow of my shoulder. In my chest, my heart hammered; in my head, every wire crossed and crackled. Had he seen? Had he, maybe, been disturbed by the early stages of the fracas, left his bed and hidden in the dark of the stairs, watched through the banisters, through the open living-room door, witnessed the whole thing? The two Gardaí were coming up the path towards me. As they did, the child began to cough. I was smothering him! With the coppers by my side, I had no choice but to relax my grip just a little. Immediately, Robert yanked his head free, gulped in a lungful, looked at me, horror-stricken, and screamed, 'Daddy sta—'.

'Yes, yes,' I cooed, bottling him up once again. 'Daddy will stay. Daddy will stay. Daddy's going nowhere.' Then loudly, drowning out all else, I went on, 'This is Robert. He's our son. He's two-and-a-half years of age, for God's sake. Two-and-a-half! And I do *not* want him seeing any of this.'

The pair nodded.

'Best leave him with a neighbour,' the older suggested.

'I don't really know anybody here, we've not long moved in.'

'Well, what about your mother, your father, the boy's grandparents?'

'They're miles away. In Kilkenny.'

'Your in-laws, then. Your wife's people.'

And have him repeat his 'Daddy stabbed' for those two, who'd only be itching for such rope to hang me with? I offered no good reason, just shook my head vehemently.

'Fair enough, if there really is nobody else, one of the Bangardaí can look after him. I'll call the station and have them send someone round.'

At the press of a button, his radio hissed to life. As it did, I was assailed by a vision of my son, sitting like the twelve-year-old Jesus among the temple's elders, describing to the assembled workforce of Kilmainham Garda Station how his father had earlier taken his mother's life.

'Noel, this is Sergeant Pownall. Request a second squad car for—'

'No!' I lurched. 'It's okay. I've just thought.'

'It's all right, Noel. Cancel it.' He removed his finger, the radio went dead. 'So, who d'you have in mind?'

I had no one in mind, nothing in mind other than to prevent my child getting into a cop car without me.

'Mr Stokes? Who d'you intend leaving the boy with?'

Nothing. Not from anywhere could I dredge a name: keeping my son's whimpers from turning into anything discernible was as much as I could do.

The policeman wrinkled his brow. 'Tell you what, I'll call that squad car. If you can come up with something before it gets here, well and good. If not . . .'

Again he pressed the button to repeat his request. At that very moment across the courtyard, a front door opened and a squat, paunchy figure stood silhouetted in the hall light. McEvoy – come, no doubt, on the off-chance that there was some gloating to be done. Ironic, then, that the sight of him should make me a timely connection. 'Alan Bradshaw!' I cried.

'Pardon me?' said the policeman.

'Alan Bradshaw, a friend of mine. He'll look after Robert.'

'Good. D'you know for sure that he's available?'

'Ah, yeah,' I bluffed. It was Friday night, and Bradshaw was a single man.

'You should ring him, just to confirm,' and from an inside pocket, he produced his mobile. I took it, then took it and Robert to the furthest wall of the garden. It meant the child was now out of the coppers' earshot. It also meant I could speak to Bradshaw with complete candour. 'I need you to come over,' I told him. 'It's an emergency. The guards are here.'

'The guards? But . . . I've been drinking. Like, how big an emergency is it?'

At a sidelong glance, I saw one of the ambulance men appear out the front door and beckon the older policeman, Sergeant Pownall, to him. There followed a whispered conversation, some shrugging, much grave, resigned nodding. And then Pownall turned and was directly back on his blower.

'Coops? C'mon, what kind's the emergency?'

'A pretty serious one,' I said, again facing away from the crowd.

'Well, I'm not going to risk driving if the rozzers are on the plot.'

'Okay. If I take Robert over there to you, will you look after him for a couple of hours?'

''Course. Is that him I hear, giving out in the background? He doesn't sound himself at all.'

'Yeah, he's . . . Hang on. Lads?' I called. 'It's sorted. I just need a lift as far as Crumlin.'

'No problem,' said the younger. 'In fact, we'll head off this min—'

His radio call complete, the sergeant had just stepped back into the porchlight with a look on his face to stun any conversation. Even he seemed struck dumb for a time. Then, 'Slight change of plan, Mr Stokes. We'll go first to the station, and from there to the hospital.'

'What's going on, Sergeant?'

'Nothing. Just a slight change of plan. It's . . .' he was grasping '. . . it's normal procedure. We like to . . .' he was really grasping '. . . to hear exactly what happened while it's still fresh in your mind.'

'Sergeant, I mean what's going on—' I pointed '—with that lot! My wife should be in surgery by now – instead, they haven't even moved her.'

'I promise you, they know what they're doing.'

'Yeah? Well, that's what I'd like to know too. What the fuck *are* they doing? What – is – going – on?'

He opened his mouth, but was never, *ever* going to tell me that he'd just summoned the scene-of-crime officers and the detectives. That the ambulance would be leaving Jamestown Square as empty as it had arrived. That the bodies would not be moved, could not be moved, not this night. That, in the last hour or so, they'd become mere pieces of evidence. Exhibits A and B. Nothing more.

'She's in the most qualified, capable hands,' he said finally. 'Now, let's get this little fella bedded down for the night, eh? And we can take it from there.'

By now, Robert had cried himself senseless, at no time in the back of the cop car did he even attempt to form words. Once in Crumlin, I handed him over to Alan, saying I'd be back for him some time later.

We then adjourned to Kilmainham Garda Station, where I waived my right to a solicitor and repeated my story, stark and simple. The tramp was known to us from a previous residence. Tonight he'd arrived at our door, in search of a man named Andrew Whitty, a former neighbour of ours and dead for a year or more. The night being so cold, he being so addled and pathetic, we'd invited him into the warmth. I'd left the room to use the toilet down the hallway, was gone no more than a couple of minutes, heard some commotion and came running. On returning, I found my wife in a heap on the floor, the tramp (I was still claiming not to know his name) standing over her, brandishing a bloodstained carving knife. I picked up the closest thing to hand, a candlestick, and struck him about the head: a single blow was enough to disable him. Then, once I'd checked on my wife and realized that she was in urgent need of professional help, I called the emergency services. No, I couldn't say what might've triggered such an attack. Yes, that carving knife was my wife's, had come from a set in her kitchen. No, I had no idea what it was doing in the living room. And no, I hadn't handled the knife, not knowingly, and certainly not after the tramp had.

Then in mid-session, the uniformed officers were replaced by a pair of burly men in street clothes. They introduced themselves – I remember only that both were detective sergeants – and then broke to me the news that my wife hadn't made it. That her assailant, too, was pronounced dead at the scene. My grief was great and most apparent; the men told me how sorry for my loss they were and, after a very gentle preamble, the interview began again. Questions no different, answers identical; the plainest of plain sailing – till one of my interrogators enquired, far, far too casually, after the state of my marriage. I wasn't expecting this. I knew full well that both McEvoy and Cambridge would have themselves heard in due course, I just hadn't thought either would've been so quick off the blocks. Still, it didn't ruffle me too disastrously; I replied that my marriage had been in perfect health, then in the next breath admitted to having a girlfriend. Someone I'd met near the end of my tether, at a time when my wife had all but deserted me. This was easily verifiable, I said – her former philanderings were common knowledge among her former workmates. However, equally common was the knowledge that, in recent times, she'd mended her ways and returned to being the devoted wife in a union that was happy and contented. With regard to my own little dalliance, it had seen me through the rocky patch and so served its purpose. As God was my judge, I'd been intending to end it all, but gently and when the moment was right. And so my intention remained.

I just hadn't yet managed to find that right moment.

Fair enough, they said, but what about the other one? This I was better prepared for, and began with a wrinkling of the brow, a scratch of the earlobe, a look of dense incomprehension. '*The blonde*,' they chorused. Oh, her, I said. She was just an employee of Taurus, my publisher. She called occasionally, but with Neve Shipperly it was strictly business. This, too, they were welcome to check out if they so wished.

By now the hour was late, the heads were heavy on both sides. They were reasonably satisfied, they declared, they didn't have the grounds to charge or to hold me. Keeping a bit on the side was no boast, but no crime either. Other than that, it seemed a clear enough case of self-defence, while the one single blow I'd inflicted would never support a prosecution for excessive use of force. I was free to go. However, depending on what their enquiries unearthed, or what the forensics boys had to say, they might just want to get in touch again. In the meantime, my home was still a crime scene. Sorry they were, and all that, but did I have somewhere I could go for a day or two? I told them not to worry, it was but a minor inconvenience and, yes, I was sorted for bed and board. So, after I'd given samples of my prints, along with blood, saliva and body hair for DNA comparison, the same squad car dropped me back to Crumlin village. To Alan Bradshaw's – emergency accommodation for me and mine.

His eyes glazed as he struggled for some understanding, some handle on the sheer insanity he'd just been hearing.

It was like sleeptalk as he muttered, 'Bad business. Christ Almighty, bad business.'

'Yeah, terrible,' I muttered back, and folded my fingers round the steaming coffee cup.

'What, in God's name, could've sparked him off? I mean, why?'

'Why? Alan, d'you think the likes of him would need a reason? We're talking about a man who was mentally ill, and who didn't play by the same rules as the rest of us. I know he's probably not to blame but . . . Jesus, I have to blame someone.'

'You could start with a health service that allows such a dangerous madman to remain at large among ordinary, decent people.'

I sipped at the coffee, then drew a long trembling breath.

'Poor Angie,' he continued. 'I'll miss her, y'know. We all will, down at the mill.' He paused, then, 'Things were okay between you, yeah?'

'Yeah, never better. New house, second income on the way, a few quid to spare for the first time in our married lives. Why wouldn't things be okay?'

'Well, I hope you don't mind me saying, but it wasn't always moonlight and roses with the pair of you.'

'If you mean Angie's little flings, they never bothered me much. And, anyway, there hadn't been one in an age. She'd got all that carry-on out of her system.'

'I was thinking more of your own little fling.'

I'd forgotten that Bradshaw knew. Or, at least, that he knew the half of it. 'Carla?' I said dismissively.

'Yeah, Carla. Is that still going on?'

'On and off. She means nothing to me, she's just . . . convenient.'

'She won't be moving in with you, then, any time soon?'

'You can rest assured of that,' I answered, in full truth.

He nodded slowly, pensively, then stared a while into the distance. At last he said, 'And there was definitely no bad blood – between yourself and Angie, I mean? You'd swear to that?'

'Yeah,' I said testily. 'I've already told you, Alan. I don't know why you have to keep on harping back.'

'Okay,' and he swallowed. 'I'll say this. If I don't, I won't sleep tonight. After you left with the cops earlier, I sat young Robert at this table and gave him a drink of milk. Now, I wasn't prying, honest I wasn't. And I know his speech isn't perfect. But there was no mistaking what he said. "Daddy stabbed Mammy. Daddy stabbed Mammy." He even got a knife and showed me how.'

Case rested, he sat nervous, unblinking.

'D'you think I did it?'

'I ju—'

'D'you seriously think I'd be capable of such a thing?'

'Look, if you say you didn't, that's good enough for me.'

'Alan, nobody knows better than you that my marriage wasn't always what you'd call idyllic. But not even you know how bad it got at times. When I think of the way she paraded all those affairs before me, and grigged me with each new notch on her bedpost. Or how she loved to belittle me in front of strangers, poking fun at what I was trying to do, telling the whole world about the knockbacks – you *do* know, you witnessed that for yourself.' Still not a flinch or a flicker. 'Once or twice, she even taunted me that Robert was another man's child – it's hard to credit, I grant you, but that's how she was sometimes. And through it all, I never raised a hand to her. Not even once. Alan, d'you really imagine I'd want to kill her now, just when our luck had turned and things seemed to be going our way at last?'

'So what's your kid talking about, then?'

'Okay, this is what I reckon. When the attack started, I was in the jax, and I came running. This must've disturbed him, so he got out of bed and came to the top landing. From there, there's no view into our living room. So even though the door is open, he can see nothing. But he can hear perfectly. And he hears me roar, "I'll fucking kill you," or whatever it was I said. Then there's a loud groan, and the sound of something – a body, maybe – crashing to the floor. Now, I'm guessing that he ventures down a step or two for a look. And what does he see? Not the tramp, 'cos the tramp's lying to the side of the doorway. But here's me, his dad, standing over his mother's body with a bloodstained knife on the floor alongside. So what's he supposed to think? And, Christ Almighty, how's he supposed to think at all at such a time? Have you any idea how traumatic this must be for a child his age?'

Bradshaw thought it over. 'Yeah. I see it now. Sorry I asked, but . . .'

'That's all right,' I said. 'I'd have asked you.'

He smiled. Then he sprang to his feet and, without a

word, went to a cupboard above the sink. From there, he produced a bottle of Jack Daniel's, almost full. I did consider it a moment, but then declined with an open palm upraised.

'You're right, it's late. Coops, I've only got the one spare room, and your young fella is in it already. I hope you don't mind bunking down beside him.'

'Not at all. And thanks for this. I owe you, big time.'

Just how big, I doubted that he'd ever appreciate.

Inside the spare bedroom, Robert was snoring softly, sound asleep. I should've left him. But this wouldn't wait till morning. It had to be now, before those images inside the little head had a chance to harden properly.

I knelt by the bedside and shook him gently awake. In the glow of the touch lamp, his tiny fists rubbed hard on his eyes, then a thumb went to the mouth and he snuggled into the pillow to sleep again. Again I shook him awake. 'Robert,' I whispered.

He looked at me warily.

'Robert, d'you remember when you sat on the stairs . . . in the dark, a little earlier on?'

He nodded.

'Robert, tell me what you saw.'

His bottom lip curled and he shrank away, more wary now than ever.

'Robert, d'you know where Mammy is?'

He shook his head.

'Mammy is in Heaven, Robert. Mammy went to Heaven tonight. She's up there now with God, and all the angels – she's really, really happy there. We can't see her, but she hasn't gone away. We can still talk to her any time we want, we just have to say a little prayer. She'll like that, won't she?'

He nodded, though I'm sure he had only a very vague understanding of what he was agreeing to.

'Robert, Mammy is listening right now. She's like Santa Claus – she can see you all the time. And she wants you to tell me something. Robert, did you get out of bed tonight when you shouldn't have?'

He nodded.

'Why did you do that?'

Again the bottom lip curled and quivered.

'That's okay, Robert. Daddy's not cross. Just tell me why you got out of bed.'

Still no response.

'Was it, maybe, a dream you had?'

'A dream,' he whispered.

'Ah. You had a bad dream. So you were frightened, and you got up. Now, d'you remember what that dream was about?'

Nothing registered, nothing but fear and confusion. Ideal conditions. I moved closer and put my arm round him.

'You don't remember, but I bet *I* know. It was about Mammy, wasn't it? You're a good boy, you'd be worried about your Mammy.'

He smiled a little.

'And you dreamt that you saw somebody hurting Mammy. Isn't that right?'

He smiled a little less.

'And d'you know who you thought it was? You thought it was Daddy! Didn't you? Didn't you, you, silly-billy?' and I tickled him under the chin. He chortled. 'You thought it was your Daddy!' and I went on tickling till he yelped with laughter. Then I gradually turned the colour down, 'Nah, that was just a dream. What was it?'

'A dream.'

'Daddy wouldn't hurt Mammy. Not for real. Would he, Robert? Would Daddy hurt Mammy?'

'No.'

'But somebody did hurt Mammy. For real. The bad man. The bad man hurt Mammy.'

'Bad man hurt Mammy.'

'That bad man stabbed Mammy.'

'Bad man stabbed Mammy.'

'Good boy. And where's poor Mammy now?'

'Poor Mammy in Heaven.'

'Poor Mammy in Heaven. But she's looking down at Robert. And she's looking down at Daddy. And some day, we'll go to Heaven too. And we'll meet Mammy again. And we'll play games, and we'll have fun just like we used to. I'd say you'd love that.'

Across the little face, a huge grin widened.

'Thing is, Robert, God doesn't like boys who go about saying silly things. Saying things that happened in their silly old dreams. If God hears that, He'll just say, "Oh-oh, no Heaven for that silly boy, and his silly-billy stories! Let him go somewhere else." And Mammy will be there waiting, lonely and sad, saying, "Where's my Robert? He should be here by now. We can't have all this fun without him." But God will just shake his head and he'll say, "Sorry, Mammy Stokes, I'm afraid Robert is not coming. Because he wouldn't tell people what really,

really happened."'

More fear, more confusion.

'But you're a good boy, aren't you? You do know what really happened.'

He nodded determinedly.

'So tell Daddy about the bad man.'

'Bad man stabbed Mammy.'

'Who did?'

'Bad man stabbed Mammy.'

'Robert Stokes, you're the best!'

On the bedside locker, I spied a black plastic comb. I handed it to the child and then sat him upright.

'Now, Robert, show Daddy how the bad man stabbed Mammy.'

After barely a second's hesitation, he pushed the comb lengthways against my chest. Not in a downward motion, as might've been expected, but straight from the shoulder, slightly underarm if anything. No question about it, he'd seen all right.

I put the comb where I'd found it and tucked the boy back into his bed. 'Goodnight, angel,' I said, laying a tiny kiss on the end of his nose, brushing the hair from his forehead. Hair that was more speckled red every time I dared take a close look. But on this night that was the least of my worries.

CHAPTER TEN

Next day was a long one. Shortly after first light, I rang Forristers'. Being a retired old couple, they were unused to taking phone calls at such an hour of the morning, and only groggily was the receiver lifted at their end. However, nothing brings folk to their senses like the news that a daughter has been slain in a brutal and motiveless attack. They were up, dressed and round to Alan's flat within the hour.

After that, I had to contact my own parents. They owned no car, and they detested public transport, but they, too, dropped everything and got themselves on the early bus to Dublin. Alan went in person to Kilmainham Textiles, where he passed the word on to some shop steward friend of my late wife. Leaving the union man to disseminate the news, Alan cried off for the day and returned to his home, which by now had become the very centre of the aftermath.

While he was gone, I rang in her death to two of the national newspapers. Unnecessarily, as it would turn out: the story was destined for next day's front pages rather than the classifieds. Then, shortly after he returned, the Forrister parents arrived, ashen-faced, on the scene. We saw them in, sat them down, made them tea, and then I trotted out the official account of the previous night's events. Verbatim with what I'd told the police, with what I'd told Bradshaw. I did notice him raise an eyebrow during this, the third word-for-word rehash, but he made no comment. Meanwhile, the whole effect was greatly enhanced by young Robert who flitted into the room from time to time to declare, "Poor Mammy in Heaven", or "Bad man stabbed Mammy", or even "I *hate* bad man that hurt my Mammy." This dramatic change of evidence, too, had Bradshaw's eyes stretching, but again he held his counsel. All through my telling, Brian Forrister's teeth ground audibly, while his wife simply blubbed and blubbed. Maybe I was concentrating too hard on sticking to the script, maybe I was remembering the disdain they'd shown me in days gone by, but at no stage did I feel even a morsel of sympathy for either one. In fact, the more he ground, the more she blubbed, the more satisfied I was that a type of justice had been done; that, like their daughter, they had something like this coming. The details learnt, Old Man Forrister got to his feet, ordered his wife to hers, and off they set for St James's Hospital mortuary. But before leaving he took my arm, led me to one side and in whispered, earnest tones, he thanked me. For avenging his girl. For 'giving that bastard what he so fucking well deserved, and not the slap on the wrist that some liberal, do-gooder judge might've recommended'. For standing up and being counted; for proving myself a man. He'd had reservations about me in the past, he said. He was hereby apologizing for a great error of judgement. Both his wife and he were proud to call me family. They would for ever be in my debt.

The Last Chapter

It was fortunate they'd left before the Stokeses arrived: my lot had held an even dimmer view of Angie than hers held of me. And my mother, in particular, wouldn't have possessed the mental capacity to conceal this. Indeed, after I'd gone over the main points yet one more time, she came immediately to where her real concerns lay. Had I been injured at all? Had it properly sunk in, what I'd seen, what I'd done? And was I going to be in any trouble over, y'know, yer man? She then went on to wonder aloud how all this might affect the little fella. 'Twould come against him, she mused, maybe not right away, but some day, nothing surer than it would. And matters wouldn't be improved any if I were fool enough to try bring him up on my own. Did I realize at all how important it was for a small boy to have *someone* he could call his mammy? Don't leave it too long, she warned me, before getting another woman around the house. And a nice country girl this time, I was to make certain. Alan had popped out for cigarettes – I was pleased he wasn't there to hear this. The more so when, with barely a pause for breath, she went on to lament her own cruel misfortune. Months – bloody *months* – she'd been threatening to come to Dublin and see the new house. Now she'd finally endured that odyssey, but what should she find? That the place was out of bounds, a closed crime scene. This all seemed to her an ill-wind that blew nobody any good.

In the late afternoon, Bradshaw answered his door to the Shipperlys, father and daughter. Even before she'd sympathized, Neve began by loudly introducing herself, then asking if by any chance I remembered her from that

221

one brief encounter we'd had in the Clarence some months earlier. As she did, my son toddled into the company and casually addressed her by name. Prior to this, I used to wonder if she'd told her Dad of our situation. From the dumbstruck look on his face, it was clear she hadn't; just as clear that she'd not now need to. However, he quickly put his shock, along with whatever disapproval he might have had, to one side and offered condolences of his own. Then, as soon as it was polite, the pair were gone again.

Night came early and raw, with it a succession of my wife's workmates. Some I recalled from my time at the mill, others I'd never before met, but Bradshaw, thankfully, knew them all. My parents left shortly before eight to catch the last southbound express of the day. They volunteered to return for the funeral; I thanked them but said they oughtn't bother, that they'd already done their share. Then, as the final knot of sympathizers was preparing to go, a policeman arrived. He told me the forensics were all gathered, that I was free to return home any time I pleased. That post mortems were being carried out on both of the deceased, that my wife's body would be released for burial in four to five days. When I asked, he told me it was outside his authority to pronounce on charges, but he didn't think them likely. There'd be an inquest – there was always an inquest. And maybe then, he said, I could begin to put the whole sorry affair behind me. I thanked him sincerely; and as the hour was near midnight and the mercury near freezing, Alan offered him a cup of tea, a shot of whiskey, whatever. He declined, saying he didn't want to delay as he had with him a colleague. One who, for reasons of his own, wasn't keen to come inside, and had been waiting in the car all this time. We both looked from the living-room window to the street below; I think I'd have been more surprised if it *wasn't* Garda Denis Cambridge behind the wheel.

'So how long's that been going on?' Alan asked, as he tossed me a Carlsberg.

'What?'

'You know, Blondie.'

'Was it that obvious?'

None too pleased, he cracked open his can. 'You'd have told me eventually, right?'

I smiled, ''Course I would. I just didn't think that now was the time to go public. In fact, Alan, I still don't. So d'you mind if I ask you to keep it under your hat? For the moment.'

He didn't answer. Instead he swigged hard on his beer and said, 'That other cop, the one in the squad car. Didn't he look familiar?'

'Dunno, did he?'

'He's the same bloke who had a go at you the day I was helping you to move house.'

'Nah,' I said. 'I don't think so.'

Bradshaw just stared, pale-eyed, expressionless.

'Well . . . it could've been, now that you mention it. Actually, I think it very likely was.'

Still his face showed not a glimmer.

'Coincidence, Alan. Honest, nothing more to it than that.'

At last he took a second, longer swallow, and seemed

to lighten somewhat. 'So, let me get this straight. There was Angie, God rest her. There was that brunette I caught you with the day in Easton Terrace. And now it turns out there was a third iron in the fire. I'll give you this, mate, you've been a busy boy.'

'Alan, it's not how it looks.'

'No,' he said quietly. 'I'm coming to the conclusion that it probably isn't.'

I wasn't at all sorry to be leaving *chez* Bradshaw next morning and ferrying Robert with me back to Jamestown Square. There, the police had taken what they'd come for, and had done a presentable job setting the place to rights again. A certain amount of straightening and scrubbing was still called for, but in just a day or two it was as if nothing had happened, like we'd never been away.

Angie's body was duly released for burial; a sizeable funeral did occur. And the last clods of earth had scarcely landed on the grave before my difficulties with Carla Whitty began in earnest.

One less player, maybe, but the game was no less fraught. Neve Shipperly would now show up on my doorstep out of the blue, at any hour the fancy took her, sometimes staying for days at a stretch. And Carla, in the dungeon-dark, could not understand why she was seeing *less* of me than before; indeed, she seemed at something of a loss as to why she hadn't been invited to move in, to cohabit. And I was forced to spend a ridiculous amount of each day parrying her phone calls, fobbing her off however I might. Saying it was too soon. Saying the child missed his mother and needed time. Saying the neighbours round about would be scandalized. Saying anything at all to keep her away from my house. If only I could've ditched her, ended things clean, simple and civilized, like couples the world over do every day of the year. But I didn't dare. Instead, I strung her along on those occasional weekends when Neve was away visiting her folks. When she'd left the country. And left the coast clear.

It was just such a Saturday, following just such a Friday night. Both of us hung-over, bored, not a lot to do, nowhere to go, nothing but sport on the TV, and she'd wheedled the conversation round to the burning issue: her impending change of address. She'd already fired the opening shots, describing slovenly flatmates, an unscrupulous landlord and a general neighbourhood that made the South Bronx look genteel. She'd got as far as remarking how roomy, how *deceptively* roomy, this house of mine was. Then, mercifully, the doorbell rang. I didn't care if it was Jehovah's Witnesses, they were coming in.

It was worse. It was Cambridge. Though looking somewhat uneasy.

'Mr Stokes,' he said.

'Garda.'

'I apologize for just turning up like this.'

'That's okay. What can I do for you?'

'First of all, can I say how sorry I am for your troubles?'

'Thank you.'

'I called to your friend's flat – where you were staying – the night after.'

'I know. I saw you outside.'

'I didn't come in . . . I reckoned I was probably the last person you'd want to see at such a time.'

I made no comment.

'Anyway, how've you been?'

'It's getting better. Slowly.'

'Good. And what about the little guy?'

'He'll be all right too.

'Glad to hear it.' He half-smiled, then shuffled his feet a little. 'Some of the forensic results are back from the lab.'

'Only some?'

'Practically all. All that matter. I can call another time if it isn't convenient.'

'No, come on ahead in.'

'I was afraid you might have company,' he said, as I ushered him through.

'I do, but it won't make a difference.'

Inside the living room, Carla got to her feet.

'Miss Whitty?'

'Garda Cambridge!'

'That's right,' he said, reddening. Then, glad of the diversion, 'And look, there's Robert. Howya, Robert?'

The boy put some fingers to his mouth, regarding him uncertainly.

'He doesn't remember me.'

'No,' I agreed. 'They don't be long forgetting at that age.'

He took a seat at my invitation, and Carla excused herself to make some tea.

Right, then,' I said. 'What've you got?'

'Nothing. That is, nothing we didn't expect. Nothing that doesn't corroborate your account to the last detail. One end of the knife was covered in your wife's blood, the other in McDermott's prints. The crime scene was pretty well messed about, but everything was more or less consistent with how you say it went down. All in all, we can draw a line, and file this under "case closed".'

'Well, that's a relief,' I said. 'But after what I've been through, Garda, I think it's the least I deserve.'

'I understand. And again, I'm sorry for your loss.'

However, when I saw him begin to fidget with a button on his tunic, I knew there was some small distance still to go before the 'case closed' stamp was applied.

'Just one or two other things. Minor points—'

'I thought you said the investigation was done?'

'Oh, it is. This is only personal . . . personal curiosity. If you don't mind, of course.' I shrugged. 'One of the neighbours tells me that you were visited earlier in the—'

He pulled up abruptly as Carla appeared with the tea tray. Like a stutterer stuck in mid-word, he waited a seeming eternity before he leant forward, picked up his hat and said, 'Look, maybe I will come back another time. It's—'

'No,' I snapped, impatient. 'Sit down and let's get this finished with.'

'It's . . . erm . . . a little bit delicate.'

'Oh, will you spit it out, for God's sake?'

He cleared his throat, shaped to speak, then looked again at Carla and aborted the attempt.

'Hey, it's okay. We've no secrets from each other. So

anything you've got to say to me, I'd like her to hear it too.'

'Fair enough, then,' he faltered. 'One of your neighbours says that on the day of . . . y'know, on *that* day, you were visited earlier on by . . . by two . . . two of your lady friends.'

Carla jerked her head from what she'd been doing and bore her gaze upon me. I never took my eyes off the policeman. 'That's correct. I've been through this already with a couple of your colleagues. I explained—'

'Two?' The shriek was directed at me.

But it was Cambridge who answered. 'Yes, two. There was a dark-haired girl – that'd probably be yourself, Miss Whitty.'

'Uh-huh,' I said calmly, reasonably. 'Carla was round that morning.'

'Then later on, this blonde was seen—'

'And that was Neve.'

'Who's Neve?' Carla growled, lips unmoving.

'Neve Shipperly. Daughter of Martin. As in Martin Shipperly, MD, Taurus Books. Who just happen to be publishing my novel. Neve works for the company, she called on company business. Nothing more.'

'Thing is,' the cop went on, not so reluctantly now, 'the witness claims she's been known to spend the night here.'

'Never!' I shot back, without an iota of hesitation. 'No way. She's stayed late, but she's never stayed over.'

'Our witness is pretty positive—'

'What? You mean he's waited up till morning, keeping some kind of vigil? Has he nothing better to do, this fucking witness of yours?'

'With respect, Mr Stokes, that's hardly the issue—'

'Look! There have been times when the work's dragged on – into the small hours, even, once or twice. But—'

'Work? What precisely does she do when she calls round?'

I breathed deeply, sighed long and loud. I'd humour him. Humour them both. And they were both to appreciate this.

'A manuscript might go through as many as twenty separate drafts – by that I mean rewrite after rewrite after rewrite, till the story is exactly as it ought to be. When they're happy, the publishers take it and produce a proof copy – that's a rough attempt to type the manuscript into book form. At every single stage, the text needs to be checked for errors, omissions, alterations – you must've heard the term "proof-reading"? Well, that's precisely what Ms Shipperly was doing here, going over some things that needed changing. Basically.'

'Okay . . . okay. My witness says she's been here quite a lot in the past few weeks.'

'And you can tell your witness that if he keeps his eye to the crack in the curtains, he'll catch her again in the coming few. Yeah, she's been here. And, yeah, she'll be back.'

I wasn't sure if I'd totally convinced either one, so I said, 'Gimme a minute.' I went to a drawer in the TV cabinet and there I came upon some past correspondence from Taurus, letterheaded with the phone and fax numbers of Martin Shipperly. I dropped the letter on to Cambridge's lap.

'There, don't just take my word for it. Give the bossman a call.'

'Oh, Mr Stokes . . . I'm sure that won't be necessary.'

'No? I'm sure you'll do it just the same, though. If you haven't done already.'

He smiled sheepishly but didn't return the letter, folding it instead into a top pocket. From the same pocket, he removed a small, hard-backed notebook, flicked it open and began to consult. Then, 'This witness also claims that yourself and McDermott had some kind of an altercation – a struggle – right there on your doorstep.'

'We didn't. I helped him up after he fell, that's all.'

'He fell, just like that?'

'Yes. Lost his balance and toppled over. The night was frosting hard, the path was slippery. And he'd been drinking – I smelt it on his breath.'

I hadn't, but thought it a pretty safe bet. The cop bit on his bottom lip. 'Right. The post mortem did find alcohol in his bloodstream. Not nearly enough to have him roaring drunk, but . . . it's just my witness is absolutely adamant about what he saw.'

'Your witness has been such a wanker for so many years now, I'm surprised he can see a hand in front of his face.'

This drew from Cambridge a grudging laugh. I went on, 'He was looking across a darkened courtyard through a freezing fog. And he saw me first fight McDermott on the doorstep – yeah? – then invite him into the house. Now, d'you think that's likely?'

'Point taken,' Cambridge said. 'Point taken. Now . . .

the knife. The knife. What was it doing in your living room?'

'I've no idea. I didn't put it there.'

'We know that. And it's improbable that McDermott did — I mean, if he suddenly flies into this murderous rage, he's not going to take the time to first locate your kitchen, then your knife block. He'll use the closest thing to hand. Just as you did later.'

'I suppose so.'

'Which leaves your wife. Mr Stokes, is it possible that the knife was *not* just lying there?'

'Eh?'

'What I'm driving at is that she went and got the knife while McDermott was in the house. Maybe even got it *for* him?'

'Why would she go get it for him?'

'Because forensics found a piece of string on the floor. It was wrapped this way and that, and then double-knotted. Y'know, like it had been used to tie up some parcel or other, and was then snipped open.'

'Had it been cut by the carving knife?' Carla asked, well intrigued.

'It had been freshly cut, but we couldn't say for one hundred per cent certain. However, we did lift finger-prints off the twine. Two sets. McDermott's and one other.'

I sat back a little easier and said, 'Well, those others weren't mine.'

'No. Nor your wife's. In fact, they don't belong to any-body we've got on our database. And, Jesus, trying to find a match outside that is like looking for a needle in a haystack. Except we don't even have a haystack to begin looking in.'

Now I sat back a whole lot easier.

'But then, Mr Stokes, I remembered reading in the newspaper how your upcoming . . . *masterpiece* is set in Luton, England. So, purely on a hunch, I sent the prints to Luton, England. And bingo! There they were. They belonged to a gentleman named Andrew Whitty. He'd been arrested there, oh, all of twenty years ago. Some business involving an underage girl. His dabs were still on file.'

'It must've come originally from my uncle's flat, then,' Carla deduced. 'Mind you, they were friends.'

'They were, Miss Whitty. So that bit's not significant. But what probably is – significant – I mean, is what was in the parcel. What *was* tied up in that string?'

'What? Your forensics whiz-kids couldn't tell you?' I said, perhaps a little too acidly.

'No, Mr Stokes. Whatever it was had disappeared before we got there. So all they found was rubbish, half-eaten burgers, cigarette butts, that kind of thing . . . I understand you had a most magnificent fire burning in your living room that night.'

'Is that meant to be somehow *significant* too?'

'Not as far as I'm aware – I'm only remarking on how pleased our lads were to find such a blaze on so cold a night. Mind you, the pathologist wasn't too thrilled. It threw a right spanner in his works.'

'Oh?' I frowned. 'How come?'

'Something to do with core body temperature. I'm sure you're already familiar with this. It regularly crops up in these American cop shows you get on daytime TV.'

'Really? Don't actually watch them myself.'

'What – never?'

'Never. That sort of thing just doesn't interest me.'

'It's all very technical. Anyway, the long and the short of it is, he couldn't accurately establish times of death—'

'That's unfortunate.' I tsked.

'But . . . why's it important?' Carla asked. "Cos, like, didn't Brendan tell you exactly when everything happened?'

'Of course, so he did. And we're extremely fortunate to have his account, it being the only one and all . . .'

I sat forward in readiness. Robert was next up. Robert, pyjamaed in the open doorway, accusing me for all the world to hear.

'Mr Stokes—'

'Yes?'

'There's something you should know,' and he began to flip through his pocket book. 'McDermott, the vagrant, had a strange condition. A sort of quirk, part physical, part mental. The doctors gave me a name for it . . .' He thumbed page after page with rising impatience, 'Ah, shit, it's in here somewhere . . .' Then he gave up and snapped the notebook shut. 'The gist of it is, McDermott couldn't stand the sight of blood. Stemming, apparently, from some trauma suffered in his younger days, when he personally discovered the body of a girl who'd just bled to death. Anyway, it made him queasy, nauseous – was even known to induce fainting fits.'

'Really!' I mocked. 'Well, he got over it in fine style that night, then, didn't he?'

'Remarkably so. Almost beyond belief. He'd never

been known to attack anybody with a knife. And after he'd stabbed your wife the first time, he's the one who should've been panned out on the carpet. But instead he does it twice more. And then goes on to confront you. Bit of a puzzler, wouldn't you say?'

I looked to the floor, forced a laugh, then stood. 'I'd say, Garda, that if that's the best you've got left, then we're done here.'

'There's just one more thing, Mr Stokes. Very last, I promise.'

I retook my seat.

'Our friend, McDermott. His Christian name was James. But it seems he went by a nickname.'

My heart began to pound as it was attempting to break through my ribcage.

'Shafty, they called him. Shafty McDermott.'

'Shafty McDermott!' Carla whooped. 'That man was Shafty McDermott?'

'You seem familiar with the name, Miss Whitty?'

'Yeah. I often heard my uncle mention him. Jesus! I thought he was dead!'

'Well, he is.'

'No, I mean long, long dead. For years, Uncle Andy was firmly convinced that he never made it home from Luton. Christ, Shafty McDermott!' Head shaking, she turned to me, flabbergasted. 'Y'know, all this time I've been hearing about this man, McDermott, my uncle's closest friend, and, would you believe, I never made the connection!'

'I did, Miss Whitty,' the cop whispered. 'I made it right away.'

'You did, Garda? But . . . what connection would you be making?'

'Best part of two years ago now, I happened to be in Mr Stokes's flat – the one in Easton Terrace. And on his writing desk, he had a typed manuscript. For no reason, I picked up a page and began to read. It was hilarious – there was this wise guy, mouthing off to foremen, barmen, any man at all who crossed him. Next day, I could remember the gags, but I could not for the life of me remember the character. His name was on the tip of my tongue, but I could bring it no further, not till I became involved in this case. Because, you see, the name of the character in Mr Stokes's manuscript was none other than Shafty McDermott.'

With a deep breath, I called up every drop of courage, every ounce of brass. 'So? In the novel's first draft, that was the name I used.'

'That's right, Gàrda,' Carla chimed in. 'It was me who gave Brendan the story. And when I did, I told him the same names my uncle had told me.'

'Except, Miss Whitty, early the following morning, after I'd seen what I'd seen, Mr Stokes arrived in Kilmainham Garda Station, saying he was holding some property that belonged to Andrew Whitty. And asking if the old man had any next-of-kin so he might pass that property on. It was then, and only then, that I arranged contact between you two. So you see, Miss Whitty, Mr Stokes here was in possession of a document describing the escapades of a Shafty McDermott – one full day before you ever met him.'

Carla's head again shook, this time from absolute bewilderment.

'You're mistaken,' I gulped.

'No, Mr Stokes, it's all here,' and he opened a page of his pocketbook towards me. 'May twelfth, nineteen ninety-six, four-fifteen p.m., there's me in your flat. May thirteenth, six-twenty-five a.m., here's you in the Garda Station, asking—'

'And where does it say anything about Shafty McDermott in those notes of yours?'

'It doesn't. I just know—'

'You're mistaken.'

'Not me, Mr Stokes. Now, if I may continue—'

'No, you may fucking not continue! I've just had my wife butchered, I've come within a whisker of going the same way myself, the heart's ripped out of my family, my little boy will grow up never knowing his mother, and all you want to do is sit here and argue over whether you read a joke on this day or the fucking day after!'

'There's a bit more to it than that, Mr Stokes.'

I jumped to my feet and flung open the door.

'Get out! Get the hell out of this house.'

He rose, slow and stately. 'Miss Whitty, it's been a pleasure. Mr Stokes, I *will* be in touch.'

'Not with me you won't, you mealy-mouthed creep! From now on, you can talk to my solicitor, or you get yourself a warrant. 'Cos this is fucking harassment, and I'll not—'

The front door slammed shut. I stood a while, trembling, my breathing short and shallow.

'Brendan?' came the apprehensive voice at my back.

'What?'

She swallowed, she swallowed again, and then, 'Look, I'm sure there's a perfectly reasonable explanation—'

'An explanation . . . for *what?*'

'For the Garda seeing, or maybe thinking he saw, y'know, on your desk that day . . .'

'I've already said twice, he's mistaken. Jesus Christ, you're not deaf, are you? Or fucking retarded? He's got his facts wrong and he's confused. What he's claiming is impossible. Ludicrous. Makes no sense in this wide earthly world.'

'Unless—'

She'd blurted it, and couldn't now call it back. I waited a moment, then glowered slowly round. 'Unless . . . *what?*!'

'Nothing. It doesn't matter.'

'You've got something on your mind, yeah? Well, let's hear it, then.'

'No, honest, I'm only—'

'This isn't the first time I've had to listen to you, picking over the carcass of my work, and then making your sly, smart-arsed little insinuations. "There's no way you could've known this", or "I don't remember telling you that", or "Only me and my precious fucking uncle ever spoke about the other"! You want to accuse me of something? Come on, then, what're you waiting for? Accuse me.'

A look of consternation came to her face, a quake to her voice. 'Accuse you? Brendan, I never, ever—'

'Well, in that case, hear this, and fucking well heed this: if there's another word about the goddamn manuscript, you'll go out my door along with that nosy bastard copper, and you will not come back. It's too late in the day for this bullshit – you make up your mind here and now whose side you're on.'

The silence that followed was long and unbearable, but at least it made plain her decision. However, I knew that silencing the policeman would be another matter entirely.

CHAPTER ELEVEN

Once a fortnight or so, there'd come the call from Paul Gibbs. Ostensibly social, but in fact to keep tabs on the progress of the second novel, this sequel I'd signed up to. I'd tell him how well it was taking shape, how close I was to a mind's-eye view of the finished article. He'd say what truly wonderful news that was; and then, invariably, would try to slip something under my guard. Like, when was it set. Or where. Or what was it about, in general terms. But I'd be waiting. And at the first mention of anything specific, I'd explain, with regret, that there were still some major issues within the story to be resolved. That until those were sorted, I'd be revealing nothing, breathing not a word. He wasn't to take this personally, of course, it was me. Superstitious, insanely so, by nature, I was fearful of putting a hex on the thing if I shot my mouth off prematurely. He'd then laugh sourly and say I was unique among authors he'd known. That nobody else, closing in on a piece so obviously ambitious, could in his experience manage to remain this tight-lipped.

The truth was that I had plenty to remain tight-lipped about. For I'd completed not one line, or made a single inroad. The only thing I had achieved was a level of frustration I'd never known, not even in the good old bad old days. *Eleanore* was manna in the desert, a gift-wrapped godsend, but *Eleanore* had put in place a style which, for safety's sake, I now was forced to ape. A wholly appropriate word choice, that, because in parts the book might well have passed for the work of a higher-order primate. Even its purple patches were crude, plodding, amateurish and, frankly, a long, long way beneath me. And further still beneath my contempt. Write like Whitty? Why, it was like asking a thoroughbred racehorse to step between the shafts of a rag-and-bone cart.

That said, I might still have pulled it off, and thereby presented pidgin English with its second novel of real importance. I probably would have, too, if only I could've found myself the odd hour's peace, just an occasional sixty minutes of concentration unbroken. But there was Robert. There was *always* Robert. Still a month or so short of his third birthday, but tameless as a cyclone, rowdy as a brass band and constantly, *constantly*, in demand of attention. It was, of course, just possible that he missed his mother. And, just as I had a definite preference as to her replacement, so too did he. Carla amused him, indulged him, thought the whole world of him. Neve regarded him like acne: something that would clear away in due course, but a frightful nuisance while it endured. In fact, she acknowledged him only to regularly point out certain of his features that didn't wholly add up. His hair, for instance, was partly red; mine was black as jet, black as Angie's had been. His nose was small and snub; mine was aquiline. His eyes were a greeny-blue; photographs about the house showed beyond question that his mother's eyes were a darker brown than even my own. It's possible Neve lacked the wit to join these dots and so form a reasonable deduction. It's just as likely she held back to allow me supply the QED, a conclusion that, with time, had become excruciatingly obvious. Robert Stokes was simply not my child. He'd been fathered by another. Outside of gender and skin tone, we shared no common trait. Everything about us clashed, right down to our respective taste in women. And had it been just a matter of taste or a question of appearance, I'd have been big enough to get past it and to get along. But it was more. It was sharing a roof with this living, growing affront to me and to my manhood. With this blatant interloper, this cuckoo's egg I'd been duped into hatching. How could I not be resentful? How could I merely look on as he rampaged through my home tearing this, upending that, defying all my efforts to keep the little place in some kind of order? Good for nothing, producing nothing; nothing, that is, but destruction, distraction and enough shite each day to warrant the concern of Greenpeace. Small wonder if I was less than ecstatic with the arrangement. Or if, more than once, I found myself contemplating a good-sized sack, a heavy stone and that canal at the other side of the garden wall. This situation could not be tolerated indefinitely.

Neve had stayed the night, a week night, and we were sleeping into a working day. Just before eight, the door-bell rang. At first, it failed to impact on any conscious level; it rang on till it did, till it woke me. I acknowledged it, then deliberately ignored it. The ringing continued and continued till it woke us both.

'Must be the postman,' Neve croaked, one corner of her mouth open just a sliver. 'Probably got a parcel for you. Or a registered letter. Oh, leave it, you can collect it later on in the sorting office.'

The sorting office was in Thomas Street. Thomas Street was a six-mile round trip. I was out of bed, into my old jeans and at the front door before the fade of the last chime.

Carla Whitty looked grim, and instantly brought me to the remainder of my senses. 'Hiya,' she said sombrely.

My lips moved, then stuck in gear.

'Sorry to get you out of bed like this, but I thought you'd want to be told in person. Brendan, it's bad news.'

I was half hearing her at best, as my ears cocked to the stairs behind me, to the bedroom above.

'D'you remember a man named Larry O'Neill? From the textile mill? Worked there since Adam was a lad, apparently, so he must've been around in your time. He was a kind of general dogsbody, I believe. Sorta jack-of-all-trades.'

If I nodded, it wasn't voluntarily. I was too busy calculating how I might induce her to continue the conversation in the garden, with the door firmly closed at our backs.

'Brendan, he was brought in last night. To A and E, I mean. He's dead.'

I had to get her off the doorstep, but to where? Not outside: I was naked to the waist and barefoot, the morning was raw mid-March. And on no account was she coming in.

'It seems he was inflating a spare tyre for one of the

delivery trucks. Now, whether he took his eye off the ball, or whether the pressure gauge was faulty, I don't know. But whatever the case, he overdid it completely and . . .' here I became vaguely aware of some kind of explosion being hand-mimed '. . . let's just say the funeral will be a closed-casket affair. The only consolation is, it was quick. He wouldn't have felt a thing.'

To that point, I don't believe I'd spoken.

'It's not the sort of news you want this hour of the morning. Hey, why don't I make us a cup of tea?'

'No! I mean . . . no, I don't want tea.'

'Well for God's sake, you can't just stand there like that. You'll catch your death.'

'I . . . ah . . . I'd prefer to be alone.'

'You would? Why . . . was he, like, a friend of yours?'

'Yeah . . . yeah he was . . . we were great mates, me and . . .' I couldn't remember his name '. . . and old . . .' she tilted her head, one eyebrow raised high '. . . and old . . . Squire. We christened him that,' I gushed, 'because that's what he called everyone. Y'know, "Am I right, Squire? I'm right, Squire."'

Now, there had been an employee at the mill who was known as the Squire for just such a reason. Though it would've been quite some coincidence if the dead man and he were one and the same.

Carla hesitated. Then the wrinkles about her nose and brow unfurrowed, and she smiled a little.

'Thanks,' I said. 'I'm very grateful to you for coming to tell me like this. But I really must—'

'I just thought that if I didn't let you know, then I wasn't sure who would. You being off the scene there for so long.'

'Carla,' I shivered theatrically. 'D'you mind if I go and put some clothes on? I'll call you later, okay?'

'Sure,' she said. 'Talk to you . . . whenever.'

And she began down the path, no more than thirty seconds from a clean, undramatic getaway. Then, above my head, a rustling, a window coming open. 'Well, what was it?'

Still walking, Carla looked up, high to left, high to right. Then, absentmindedly, she turned and, 'Wh . . . who are you?'

'Sorry?'

'I said, who the bloody hell are you?'

'I'm a frien— What's it to you? I don't see it's any of your business.'

'None of my business?' Carla frothed. 'Brendan! You bastard. Tell me that's a prostitute!'

But my mouth had again stalled in neutral.

'A prostitute?' came the shriek. 'Brendan? Who is this *person*. What's she want? What's she doing here?'

On all sides, the picture was rapidly coming into focus.

'Now, let me think,' Carla spat. 'You didn't want me staying over because . . . because Robert was traumatized, right? And because the neighbours would gossip? And it was too soon—'

'Brendan?' The tone from on high was utter disbelief. 'Am I to understand that there's something between you and her? *This* is the other woman?'

'—but it was none of those things, was it? It was you, banging some dirty slut with her caked-on war paint and her stuck-up English accent—'

'You what?' Neve leant a little further out the upstairs

window, the better to see her adversary. 'Hold on,' she called. 'Don't go away, don't you dare. I'm coming down.'

And now there was no cold, no chill, nothing but disaster impending. All I could offer was a desperate, craven appeal to better nature. 'Carla, please. You should go.'

'I should, shouldn't I? 'Cos if I stay, there'll only be a fight. And you, you maggot, you're not worth fighting over. I wouldn't toss a coin for you this minute.'

I nodded contritely, in wholehearted agreement. But despite what she'd said, Carla hadn't budged an inch before Neve's footsteps were heard on the staircase. She'd hastily thrown on my white bathrobe and stuck her feet in the high heels she'd arrived in the night before.

'Now!' she announced, attempting to wriggle past me in the doorframe. 'You were saying?'

'Nothing,' Carla whispered. 'Nothing at all. I apologize – I've got no quarrel with you. Your . . . your *boyfriend*, on the other hand—'

'Well, thank you for that.'

'Thank me for what?'

'For admitting it. That he *is* mine.'

'Oh. You're welcome. And congratulations, he's quite a catch now. He wasn't always, mind. Not very long ago, all he had was a bad marriage and a drawerful of rejection slips. That, by the way, is where I came in. That's how *I* found him, face down in the gutter, without a penny or a prospect to his name. But we soon put that right, didn't we, Brendan? I told the story, you wrote it down, next thing you know the publishers are talking telephone numbers! Oh, we were a real team then, you and me, working together for the day when we could *be* together. For our future: at least, that's what you always led me to believe. And, Christ, I *believed* you. Yeah, you're quite a catch now. But just remember this, Stokes. Before me, you never amounted to Jack Shit. And without me, you never would've.'

'Brendan? What *is* she talking about?'

'It's okay,' I said grimly. 'She's . . . Carla, this is doing nobody any good.'

'Hah! Says he, from the safety of his swish, fancy townhouse, with his massive book deal sitting pretty on the mantelpiece inside. It seems to have done you plenty of good, you fucking sleazeball! So d'you honestly expect me to just walk away empty-handed?'

'Not at all, we wouldn't hear of it. We'll call you a taxi,' Neve smirked.

Carla took a stride forward. 'That meant to be some kind of joke, yeah? I wonder if it'll be just as funny when your own turn comes.'

'Huh?'

'Smart an' all as you think you are, you just don't get it, do you? What we're dealing with here is a rat, pure and simple. He cheated on his wife with me, then he cheated on me with you – he can't help it, it's what he does. And, might I remind you, he's still unpublished, he hasn't even hit top gear yet. Just you wait till he starts doing the talk shows. Honey, first chance he gets, first new floozie that gives him the eye, and he won't be long trading in the old one. He'll scrape you off his shoe like the dirt you are.'

Neve's smile was pained, was stretched over clenched teeth. 'No, no, no . . . *honey*. It's you who don't get it. He didn't dump you because he's a cheat, he dumped you because you're fat. And you're pig ugly. And you're—'

That third reason went unstated as Carla's left fist shot over my shoulder and caught Neve flush in the mouth. Back she went, sprawling into a low hall table, sending the phoneset jangling. There, she ran the sleeve of her borrowed bathrobe across her teeth, and examined the traces of blood she'd swabbed. Stung by the sight, she yanked off one of her stilettos and, wielding it like a tomahawk, hurtled back into the thick of things.

I was doing what I could to keep Carla at bay, and had pinioned her arms by her sides when, again over my shoulder, the shoe heel came arcing. It caught her a glancing blow on the forehead, opening a neat little gash from hairline to eyebrow. At once she reached in, grabbed a fistful of Neve's mane and tumbled back on to the lawn, hauling both of us down with her. From there it was a blur, a welter of nails and teeth and elbows and poison. Eyes were gouged, earrings pulled, hair yanked out in tufts as we threshed about on the rain-drenched topsoil. How long it lasted, I couldn't say; long enough, though, for a squad car to pull up, for both of the occupants to get among us before we'd even realized. The same pair who'd called to Alan's flat that night after the killings, the decent one and Cambridge.

It was the latter who made the first significant contribution to ending hostilities: he took Carla round the midriff and physically lifted her out of the fray. By now, she resembled something that had just crawled from a tar pit, though I don't imagine any of us looked much better. Cambridge seemed not to notice as he shepherded her out the front gate and into the courtyard. There, beyond our earshot, he spoke to her, calmed her somewhat. Meanwhile, his colleague was on a similar errand, ushering Neve and I towards the door, towards the hallway. Soft-soaping, cajoling, saying how this, whatever it might be, wasn't worth getting arrested over. This I seconded absolutely; after all, I'd been peace-making from the off. Neve took a little more convincing, but she, too, saw the merit in the policeman's advice. Before long, her fire was extinguished, the entire situation, it seemed, pretty well defused. Then, suddenly, my gate was flung open and Cambridge came storming, wild-eyed and lunatic, up my path.

'Stokes!' he roared, then advanced till I could feel his breath, hot and quick. 'So this must be the publisher's daughter you were telling me about. The one who calls around from time to time, but strictly on business? Yeah . . . I can well believe that those are her working clothes.'

I'm sure the insult was intended. I'm equally sure he was trying to nettle me into taking a swing. I'd not give him the satisfaction. On the contrary, and recalling the old torch he carried, I saw the chance for some nettling of my own.

'Garda,' I said solemnly, 'I'd like to make a complaint. She – that woman—' and I pointed out the gate '—that woman's come here, uninvited . . .' I expected him to redden, but instead he was paling '. . . and without provocation, for no good reason, assaulted my girlfriend – my new girlfriend, that is. Now, I understand if she feels rejected but, hey, this is a civilized country. She must learn to keep her desire for me in check.'

'Fine!' he barked and, from the same pocket as before, produced the same notebook. 'You want to press charges? C'mon, then, I'm listening.'

Slowly, pensively, I stroked and restroked my chin. 'Let me think things over, Garda.'

'You won't be pressing any charges and well you bloody know it!'

'Maybe I won't, Garda. Maybe I'll just let it go, for old times' sake. I mean, she was no great shakes in bed, but I could never fault her for lack of effort. And sure that's *got* to count for something.'

He spun on his heel, began away, then stopped and, 'I'll have you, Stokes! If it takes me the rest of my life, I'll have you!'

I watched, unable to contain my amusement as he guided Carla into the back seat, brusquely summoned his partner to the passenger door, and then went roaring out of the estate.

However, as I followed their path of departure, my smile was wiped abruptly. There, parked outside the home of Ger McEvoy was a black Mazda, a car I knew I ought to recognize from somewhere. Before I'd worked out from where, before I'd even got round to wondering how the police had managed to arrive on the scene so promptly in the first place, the answers came bustling out McEvoy's front door. The man of the house it was who led the charge, and at his side one Brian Forrister, father of my dear departed. The last of McEvoy's various involvements with Angie had ended a long, long time since: how could I know he still maintained any contact with the family? And, on this day, how he must've thanked the Lord that he did.

'Well!' Forrister exclaimed. 'Isn't this a picture? One away in the squad, another one still on the premises. And all with your wife barely cold in the ground. Credit where it's due, Stokes, you're a fast mover.'

'Not as fast as you'd say,' McEvoy weaseled. 'He'd started work on these two long before poor Angie ever . . . I mean . . . he was *at it* while she was alive!'

The old man gasped, but the astonishment wasn't real. He'd already been told. 'Good God. And to think just a few short months ago, I shook your hand and thanked you for the way you stood by my daughter to the bitter end. Now I find out *this*. So? What've you got to say for yourself? I'm entitled to some explanation.'

'You, Mr Forrister, are entitled to nothing. No explanation, no apology, fuck all. There's not a thing in this world connecting you and me now, and that's just how I want it. 'Cos anything I say, anything I do, wouldn't make a blind bit of difference. You've never given me a chance. You've been on my back from day one.'

'You bet your sweet life I have! I know bad news when I see it, and I could see from day one that you were nothing else. My girl could've had her pick, she could've married a gentleman. Instead, she wound up with you.'

'Your girl wound up with a lot of blokes – several of them after we were married, what's more. Including that dickhead,' I said, indicating. McEvoy's mouth twitched, but there was never a possibility he was about to speak.

'Hold your tongue, Ger,' the old man cut in. 'Don't dignify that with an answer. Now, you listen to me, you lowbred cur. There's something I want to know. Is this what you intend telling young Robert about his mother? Is this what he's to grow up believing? You say there's nothing left in this world connecting me and you? Stokes, you're wrong. I don't like it any more than you do, but we've got that little boy in common. And I will not have him brought up to hear my daughter's name blackened by you or your sort. He'll be reared properly, and I'll make sure of that the only way I can. I'll take that child off you. D'you hear? I'll fight you through every court in the land—'

I turned to Neve and said evenly, 'Go get him.'

Seeing her go, Forrister proceeded, but not nearly so stridently. 'I'll do it, Stokes. You think I won't, but you'll see. I'll sell my house if I have to, I'll get the money from somewhere. And I won't be shy about mentioning the kind of carry-on I witnessed here this morning. It may well prove the death of me. But I'll go to my God knowing I did the right thing.'

Neve reappeared with Robert in tow.

'Poor little mite!' Forrister whined. 'Well, don't worry, boy. I'll get you away from this place. I'll fight to the last—'

'Let me save you the bother,' I said, and I eased the child on to the path. 'Take him now.'

'Eh?'

'Take him now. Robert, go to your grandad.'

The child took a tentative step towards the old man. It was difficult to say which was more perplexed.

'You wanted him, well, you've got him. May you both live happy ever after. Now fuck off for yourselves.'

'But you're the child's fath—'

'Fuck off, I told you!' and I slammed my door in three of the blankest faces I have in my lifetime seen.

Inside, in the hallway, Neve took both of my hands in hers. 'You're sure about this?' she asked gravely.

Slowly, I let my gaze linger over her, top to toe. Over the matted hair, the muddied face, the scratches, the bruises, the bloodstains. Scarcely recognizable from the girl who, not very long ago, had put to me that stark choice: her or the child, but not both. Now, wise or otherwise, I'd chosen.

'Brendan? What . . . what'll you do now?'

'I don't know. Although washing myself might be an idea.'

She fell giggling into my arms as, together, we shambled upstairs to the hot tub, throwing off our sodden clothes as we went. Oblivious to, indifferent to, the world outside our door.

CHAPTER TWELVE

But that indifference was a short-lived luxury. In the days that followed, I was making uneasy contact with my in-laws to draw up some points of etiquette, to establish the ground rules. I placed the phone call expecting open war: to my great, and grateful, amazement, we reached consensus without difficulty or delay. It was agreed that the child was better off raised by his grandparents, but that I should have unlimited access. And since we hated the sight of each other, those grandparents and I, it'd be best if we came face to face only when it was absolutely unavoidable. And never, *ever,* when the boy was present; this assertion got no argument whatsoever from either side. The Forristers had already devised a way round this; they'd enrolled Robert in Tots 'n' Teenies, a well-regarded crèche located on the banks of the Liffey among the boat clubs at Islandbridge. I had no objection to meeting the weekly bill in full. In return, I could visit Robert there when I pleased, even bring him home to Jamestown Square for a day, a weekend, or as long as the humour took me. All his grandparents asked was that, as a courtesy, I let them know in advance whenever I intended assuming custody. I couldn't quibble with this. And so, on the very next Wednesday, I bundled up all of

Robert's bits and bobs, and dropped them to Island-bridge, to the Tots 'n' Teenies reception, there to be collected by the Forristers when they called for the child later that afternoon. My haste might have been a little unseemly, but I needed the wardrobe space: next day, Neve Shipperly moved in, lock, stock and barrel.

And with that the last piece of the puzzle, having been pared down to size, was seen to fit beautifully. No grey day job, no more truck with life among the lowly. No slatternly spouse, no inconvenient affair, no loose ends remaining in that line. No children, but a bed-warmer not all that long out of school. No great wealth yet, or recognition, but a ship of mine on the horizon, looming large. I only had to sit back and enjoy as the world about me breezed by, even-keeled and easy. The proofs of the novel came, for real this time. The editor, a Welsh girl named Rebecca, had enclosed a short note saying that it was so perfect, she strongly recommended it be tinkered with only where absolutely necessary. I reread, adjusted maybe a comma or two, then returned it to Taurus. When next I'd see that text, it'd be between covers with a price tag attached. Meanwhile, I spent my days in the continuing search for a sequel, though the less said about that search, the better. I no longer had Robert and his histrionics to blame, but I now identified a new and more diverting scapegoat: the upcoming inquest. It was slated for Kilmainham Courthouse on 21 May. I couldn't foresee any great difficulties. But I've always found it's those kind, the unforeseen, that bite the deepest.

That morning beamed warm and hazy. My suit – I still owned just the one – was sober in cut and colour, and quite the thing for such an occasion. But not, however, for such weather: it was likely to get stuffy in that courtroom before the day's business was through. Neve stayed away; I didn't need the moral support. And I sure as hell didn't need a jury of my peers, my supposed equals, seeing what I'd got and they hadn't.

As it transpired, proceedings were perfectly straight-forward and along expected lines. There was testimony from myself, from the policemen who answered the emergency call, from the medical people and from Forensics. The verdicts, too, were entirely predictable. Angela Stokes, née Forrister, had been unlawfully killed. James McDermott had been killed in self-defence. Each was duly recorded by the coroner. And with that, the book was closed.

Indeed, with the outcome so rarely in question, I'd spent much of the day scanning the crowd for faces I recognized. There were the Forristers, naturally enough, noses in the air, pointedly shunning me for part of the time, glowering in my direction for the rest. McEvoy sat with them, basking no doubt in the recent blow he'd struck against me. Blissfully unaware that he could hardly have done me a bigger favour if he'd been trying. Alan Bradshaw was near the door, out of the way, keeping the head down, as was his custom. About the gathering, I spied several other familiar faces, people I knew from the mill, people I knew from the removal and burial, people I knew but didn't know from where. Then, as I chanced to glance over my shoulder to the upper gallery, I caught sight of Garda Denis Cambridge. He would've been hard to miss, so prominent was the seat he'd taken. To see him there did not surprise me: he might have had no direct involvement in the case, no legitimate obligation to be present, but since when did an interfering busybody like Cambridge ever need anything so legitimate as an obligation? Still, I was glad he'd come. It gave me untold delight imagining how his blood must've boiled to hear me exonerated completely, with commiserations for my loss, commendations for my bravery. Then among all these fragrant musings, an ugly weed raised its head: could that possibly have been Carla Whitty up there by his side? When it was decent to do so, I risked another, a better look round. It was her, right enough. Craning forward to whisper in his ear. Cocking her head for the whispered reply. Holding his hand in hers.

So, they'd got it together, I thought, and then thought nothing more of it. The love life of either party was no concern of mine. Not any longer.

Matters concluded, Bradshaw came shuffling through the crowd to say he was adjourning immediately for drinks, and plenty of them. Ten minutes, I told him, and I'd be there too. Before then I had hands to shake, small talk to make, flesh to press. One national newspaper was represented outside: I paused to have my picture taken, to comment that the truth was now firmly established, to express my sincere gratitude for this. Pretty soon the crowd had dispersed, the show was over. It had been a most satisfactory day's work, I told myself, as I strolled up Grattan Road en route to the Black Lion, to my old mucker and a long-overdue pint or five.

'Bit of a result, that,' came the voice from behind. I stopped. I grimaced. Would this bastard ever let up?

'What can I do for you?' I clipped, deliberately refusing to turn. He seemed not to mind, and skipped round me so we now stood face to face on the footpath.

'I said, it's a bit of a result, eh?'

'If you mean the right result, then certainly, I agree.'

'Nah. I just meant it's a bit of a result for yourself. Nothing more, let's be clear on that.'

'And let's be clear on one other thing, pal. If the result is in, then generally speaking the game is over, yeah?'

'Yeah . . . I suppose I can't blame you for hoping so.'

He smirked. So did I.

'I notice you've got very friendly with Carla all of a sudden?'

'What's that to you?'

'Nothing. I just hope you'll both be happy.'

'Well, I already am. And I like to think she might be too. Good Jesus, after some of the vermin she's been involved with lately, the girl is due a change of luck. I asked her, by the way, if she wanted to say hello to you just now. But she wasn't keen, for one reason or another.'

'That's a shame,' I said airily. 'And, y'know, you probably should be getting back to her. I bet she's missing you already.'

I pushed past him and continued determinedly on my way. Just as determinedly, the footsteps followed.

'I read that book of yours. Very impressive.'

I pulled up short and sharp. Again he came skipping round to face me.

'How did you come to see it?'

'Carla has a copy of the manuscript, remember? But I really did enjoy it.'

'You'd no right, that's my property.'

'Carla says you told her she could lend it to whoever she liked.'

'That was then. Now, I want it back. It's mine, and I fucking want it back!'

I went by a second time. Undeterred, he dismounted the path and began tracking me stride for stride.

'Of course,' he said reasonably. 'I'll drop it round. But what's your problem? Can you not stand to hear a little bit of praise for what you've done? Christ above, what kind of author are you?'

I kept walking.

'On the level now. I'm not much of a reader, I never have been. But if I could lay hands on a few more books like yours, that might all change.'

If anything, I quickened my step away.

'But y'know the best bit? Afterwards, Carla took me through it, page by page. And she'd say, like, this character is based on my uncle, and that's my uncle's friend, and this here is a neighbour from back in Mayo. Really brought the whole thing to life for me.'

'Glad to hear it,' I said, without looking to left or right.

'Then every once in a while she'd come to a scene and she'd say, "This actually happened. This incident did take place. Strange thing is, I never told Brendan about it. Somehow, he seemed to just know. It's like he's got this uncanny ability to describe – describe *perfectly* – arguments, punch-ups, sessions and pranks that he couldn't possibly have ever heard of.' Still he followed along at my shoulder, now shaking his head in mock astonishment. 'That's quite a gift you've got there, Mr Stokes. Truly remarkable. I'd almost say miraculous.'

'Miracles happen all the time, Garda. Bigger ones than that, what's more.'

'Really – for instance?'

'For instance, an ugly spud like you finds a woman who's prepared to be seen out in public with him. That tops anything I've ever heard.'

Instantly, I flashed him a wide, sidelong smile, bade him good day and walked on. Alone now, his footfalls dogging mine no longer. Then just as I began remarking how tamely he'd surrendered the last word, he called, 'Stokes!'

I did not look round.

'You stole it, Stokes. You stole the dead man's book.'

'Prove it,' I called back, then turned to face him one last time. In full and brazen defiance, knowing he could not. Knowing he never would. Knowing that only three people might've provided the proof, the *real* proof, he needed. Knowing that all three were dead. Their evidence had gone with them to the grave. And somehow the policeman himself seemed to sense this. It was through his frustration, his humiliation and his fury that he ranted, 'You're a thief! A common thief! That's all you are, a lowlife scumbag and a common thief!'

I let him rant. I waited till he was done, till he could take full account of this, my final word *ever* on the matter.

'Garda,' I said evenly, 'names will never hurt me. And

you don't have the sticks or the stones. Until you do, stay the fuck off out of my way.'

Next morning, I was hung-over. Incredibly hung-over. I knew nothing of the previous night except that I must've fallen foul of my woman: I woke to find myself in Robert's old room, contorted into his little cot, my left foot wedged between the bars at the bottom. I was fully clothed, save for a shoe that I never again did manage to locate. The air stank of sweat and stale beer, the mid-May sun made the whole world blaze bright as a Nazi interrogation lamp.

The postman, I saw, had been and gone. He'd left a large brown envelope with an English postmark. It came from Taurus's London office, the proposed cover for *Remember Me, Fair Eleanore*. Somebody somewhere had gone to a great deal of trouble: the lettering was lower-case and edgy, typed like a bank-robber's demand slip. Underneath lay a riot of scenes from the story, all hand-drawn and in living, violent colour. Such craftsmanship did the heart good. Less so the note accompanying, which reminded me, as if I needed reminding, that I'd put my name to a two-book deal. That time was of the essence, as my contract had been at great pains to stress. And the time agreed upon was one year to the day. Which meant that a sequel, or at least a draft, was due inside the next couple of weeks.

Rereading this note, with its terrible urgency and vague menace, it was difficult not to laugh. Because our agreed-upon second book was not about to happen. It was that simple, and I'd long resigned myself to the fact.

Taurus weren't going to like it but – hey – there was no point in all of us upsetting ourselves.

When I came to check my answering machine, it transpired that the phone had rung, had rung out, and I'd slept through that as well. A message awaited: my mother was coming. My father, too. They'd be travelling to Dublin one week on with Cathal Ó Domhnaill, Earlsgrove's own historian and Gaelic scholar. Months earlier, I'd let that jackass talk me into chairing a seminar he was putting together, some bullshit about the Republican tradition in South Kilkenny. Evidently, that was now almost upon us, and Ó Domhnaill needed to see me prior to the red-letter day. To give me the benefit of his expertise, no doubt; to advise as to how I should discharge this great responsibility. The prospect of even an hour with such an insufferable man did little for my general humour, or for the headache that was only worsening as the day wore on. Still, I told myself, he *would* be bringing my folks. And with their long-standing dislike of bus and train, when might they next get the chance to visit? To see the house, maybe even to meet the girlfriend. Already, I was bracing myself for my mother's disapproval – Neve was a long way from the good, solid lump of a countrywoman she'd been commending to me when last we'd spoken. But the introductions couldn't be postponed indefinitely. And the sooner they were made, the sooner she could begin working on a change in her attitude. As she would need to, because I was changing nothing, budging not an iota.

The days ground by. And as they did, the unease quietly grew. Nothing to do with my parents – their

impending visit hardly even rippled the pond. But that
cursed book situation was another matter entirely. We
were on a certain collision course, Taurus and me. And
as I leapt into bed each night beside the MD's daughter,
it was hard to disregard them. Hard to forget what a
massive company they were. Impossible to believe that
they drew up these elaborate contracts to have them
scoffed at willy-nilly by the likes of myself. It only stood
to reason that if I broke our agreement, they'd make me
rue it. They'd probably make me rue the day I was born.
Break that agreement I would, however, unless
somehow, from somewhere, I could find *something*. But at
every cast the trawl net came up slack, empty as it had
gone down. My working environment I could no longer
fault: all distractions had decisively been dealt with in
their turn, making conditions well-nigh ideal. The
problem, then, was nothing external. Rather, it was
writer's block, plain, simple and disabling. The
occasional curse of all the greats, it had certainly picked
its moment to lay me low, for if ever I needed to deliver,
that moment was now. Though making such an excuse
to the people who mattered would cut little ice.
Publishers have no appreciation of the creative process,
or of the kinks that may sometimes appear in the supply
line. Indeed, it's been my experience that most would fail
to recognize real creative talent if it walked up to them in
the street and introduced itself. And the contracts they
award simply do not make allowances for ailments they
never can, never will understand.

And so back I went to a routine that was sickeningly
familiar. Hollow-headed and hapless, I would take, and

retake my seat before the screen. Thinking, typing, deleting; agonizing, typing, deleting; getting nowhere, whistling 'Dixie', pissing up the proverbial rope. Praying for some inspiration, then gradually lowering my sights till I was praying for some interruption, some reasonable excuse to down tools for the afternoon. In the middle of the fifth such day, the doorbell chimed. It was music.

Outside stood Cambridge in full regalia. Under his peaked cap he wore a bad look, smug and disconcerting. Whatever damage I'd recently done to his self-esteem seemed well healed.

'Your manuscript,' he announced, drawing it from under his arm like a sword from a scabbard.

'Thanks.'

'No, thank *you*. A wonderful read. You on your own?'

'Why d'you ask?'

''Cos I'd like to come in, if I may.'

'I take it you've got that warrant we spoke about?'

'I haven't, I don't want to search the place. But I would—'

'Look! We've been through this before. If you've got questions, I'll be happy to give you my solicitor's number.'

'No, no, it's nothing I need to ask you, more something I need to show you. If you want to see it, that is. If not, you won't need to ask twice – I know my way out of here. It's like you say, I've no warrant, so you're the boss.'

I turned side-on and flattened myself against the jamb. He removed his headgear and brushed past. Undirected, he made his way through to the living room, where he reclaimed the very seat I'd run him from just a few weeks before. And, like before, I sat opposite. 'Okay,' I said formally. 'What've you got?'

He exhaled loudly, snuggled low into the armchair and steepled his fingers under the point of his chin. 'Couple o' nights back, Carla and I were going through old Andy's stuff. She'd never bothered up till now, 'cos she guessed there'd be nothing there of any value. And she was right . . . *almost.*'

Involuntarily, I twitched a little. He saw this and continued, with a grin, 'We came upon this one box full of used typewriter cartridges. I'm sure you know the story; he wasn't comfortable making face to face contact with the outside world, so he preferred to leave notes and the like. Only his handwriting was completely illegible. So Carla had bought him an electronic typewriter. It used disposable ribbon cartridges, which were quite expensive, so she kept him supplied with these too. But when she looked into that box the other night, one thing struck her. For a bloke who, as far as she knew, typed only shopping lists and letters to the landlord, he seemed to have got through an awful lot of these cartridges. Together, we took a closer look. What we found, you won't believe. Or, rather, *we* couldn't believe.'

Butterflies big as crows fluttered round my stomach as he took from his pocket an almost plain white box, not much bigger than a deck of playing cards. 'The machine he used was a Sharp Q-110. And, strictly speaking, it took only same-brand accessories. Sharp ribbons were what Carla always bought him – among his belongings, we found several. But we found even more of these,' and he held up the box for me to see. 'E-X-O-C-E,' he spelled. 'Knock-off gear. Not illegal, but not to be recommended. Really inferior quality, produces a terrible typeface – probably like what I saw in your flat the first day ever I met you.'

He stopped, daring me to protest. When I wouldn't please him, he went on, 'Now, why did he have these? And why so many? Well, it's obvious, isn't it? He was typing something big, something really substantial. He knew he'd need a moxy load of ribbon; way, way more than Carla was in the habit of giving him. So, because money was tight, he went for the cheapest, shoddiest old tat he could lay hands on. Now I'm sure you're wondering, why did he not just mention it to Carla? She'd have been more than happy to stump up for all the good stuff, the Sharp gear, that he needed. But he never said a word, he didn't want her to know. Whatever he was writing, y'see, must've been so sensitive, so incredibly personal, that he couldn't even speak of it to his own flesh and blood.'

These guesses were good. I prayed God they were only guesses.

'What *could* it have been, then? What was he working on that was such a closely guarded secret? Just for the fun, I took one of the Exoce cartridges and I spooled it out.' Gently, gingerly, he lifted the flap on the small white box and removed the solid black plastic oblong. Above the upper corners, two short arms extended, and between these ran a taut, thin stretch of typing ribbon. Cambridge took this with thumb and forefinger and pulled it like a carpenter's measure-tape. 'Spooled it out, just like this. And what did I find? Well, because it's disposable ribbon – y'know, throw away after one use – each character that's typed on it leaves a clear and identifiable impression. To figure out what it's actually written, all you need is a little patience and the ability to read backwards. Any fool could do it.'

With great ceremony, he held the loop of ribbon up to the light and began. ' "The angel's face, the soft pale skin, the green two-piece swimsuit and neither piece big enough to wipe a man's eye, the nipples you could hang wet duffel coats on . . ." That ring any bells, Brendan? It should – the "wet duffel coats" bit is kind of a giveaway. It's shortly after Ned and Ellie meet for the first time. She accidentally takes his latchkey with her when she goes swimming. He has to follow her to the pool and have her paged. And she appears at the reception desk looking like, well, just like old Andy describes. His descriptions are all over those other tapes as well. For us, it was just a matter of putting them in sequence and, whaddya know? We'd got ourselves a book!' He beamed at me. 'Y'see, Brendan, you didn't think of everything. Not quite. Nobody ever does.'

'This . . .' I began to gibber '. . . this is all bollox. It's . . . it's a vendetta, an ongoing vendetta. And a bloody frame-up, that's what it is!'

'You reckon? And how, pray, have you been framed?'

'I dunno . . . I don't fucking know . . . you . . . you had access to the typewriter, didn't you? You . . . *and you had my manuscript as well!* That's it! You typed the whole thing, you bad cunt, just so you could—'

'Don't be ridiculous. Those other cartridges are in the lab, and all have been done for fingerprints. There was only one set on each – Andy's. Not mine, certainly not yours. Only his.'

'Well . . . well, in that case, you've trumped me. I don't know how you did it, I just know you fucking did it. 'Cos I wrote that book, end of story.'

'Actually, the end of the story is the only bit you did write. Oh, you changed the names, and you corrected a spelling here and there.'

'*The end of the story is the only bit you did write.*' What was he saying? Had they failed to locate one – the last one – of Whitty's spent cartridges?

'You're a top-class speller, I grant you, but there's no money in that, is there? Andy Whitty was the novelist. And apart from a page or two at the finish, we can reconstruct that novel line for line.'

I fancy my expression was blank as a death mask. But behind that mask, I was calculating at a rate of knots. As sure as God, the missing cartridge didn't just contain the book's conclusion. It also held Whitty's last will and testament, in which he bequeathed the manuscript, and all revenue it might ever generate, to Shafty McDermott.

'The big, gory suicide scene. And the *epilogue*,' he sneered. 'Epilogue, indeed. We couldn't find that ending anywhere among Andy's tapes and, frankly, I wasn't at all surprised. Something so pretentious could only come from a tosser like you.'

But where the hell was it? This was absolutely critical. If they were to find that ribbon, and find what was on it, then they'd know . . . well, they'd know plenty. And what it didn't tell them, they'd not be too very long figuring

out. But where could it be? Suddenly, a most prepos-
terous thought struck me. It was still in the machine! The
last ribbon, just after being put in, only a fraction used,
practically new – why would the old man remove it? It
was still in the machine, it had to be, it was obvious . . .
so obvious that the cops hadn't thought to check there.
Yet.

'And as for your claims that some of the material
evidence has been tampered with, forget it. You must
know that every typewriter ever made produces its own
distinct typeface, each as unique as a fingerprint. The lab
boys have been over Andy's Sharp Q-110, and stripped
it down to bits the size of shirt buttons. Brendan, it typed
those ribbons. Not only that, it typed them a long time
ago. From the microchip and circuitboard inside, they
could tell that the thing hadn't been switched on in two
full years.'

He was lording it now, believing he'd got me check-
mated, cornered into submission and into silence. In fact,
I was furiously reappraising. It was *not* in the machine,
obviously enough. But if not there, then where? Where,
for Christ's sake?!

'Two years!' he gloated on. 'Since before Andy Whitty
died. So, my friend, the case against you is as clear and
as watertight as it could possibly be.'

Not in the machine. The cops didn't have it. I didn't
have it. Whitty's old flat had since been searched, then
gutted and refurbished, so it wasn't there either. But it
had to have gone somewhere, didn't it? And what, or
where, or who remained? Why, only Shafty! Had Whitty
given it to his late great henchman? As a further keepsake,

another scrap of accreditation, along with the handwritten jotters and the note of bequest? If so, it was long lost to posterity: maybe swept up by the Corporation Sanitation Department, maybe chucked on a barrel fire under a canal bridge one cold winter night. Either way, things didn't look quite so bleak for me all of a sudden.

'What's wrong, Brendan? Got nothing to say for yourself?'

I had plenty to say for myself. And I knew I'd better start saying it quickly, better throw this dog a bone. Then smother it in gravy and, with a little luck, he just might go away wagging his tail behind him. 'Fair enough,' I choked. 'You've got me.'

I looked away, ran a hand through my hair and began to mutter, 'Those ribbons. Those blasted ribbons. I knew he liked to hoard them. I knew they were disposable. So why the fuck did I not dispose of them then, when I had the chance?' I looked back to him again, my brave face on, a loser but a good loser. 'I just didn't imagine they'd ever matter, that anybody would be bothered checking them out. But I can guarantee this, my man – if I'd known it was you I'd be contending with, I'd have been a good deal more thorough.'

He shuffled a little in his seat, then sat upright.

'Garda, I've got to ask you one thing. Somehow, you had all this figured from the minute you came on board. I mean, that letter you sent me—'

'Oh, you opened it, then?'

'Absolutely ingenious, addressing it to old Andy from a major publishing house – of course I was going to open it. And, yeah, it did put the willies up me. Which I'm sure was the intention. After I'd read it, I destroyed it, in case you're wondering. It was all so outlandish, I reckoned I'd be safe enough. 'Cos these conclusions you'd drawn, out of thin air, were so deadly accurate that it, well, it just didn't make any sense. You seemed to know, yet you couldn't know. So . . . how did you know?'

He shrugged. 'I just . . .' he blushed. 'A gut feeling, I suppose.'

'A gut feeling,' I whispered ruefully. 'Indulge me a moment, eh? You'll have your full confession in due course, I promise. But, first, I'd like to test those instincts of yours a little further. Why d'you reckon the old man never finished the book?'

He sucked once or twice between his front teeth. 'That's something I've been turning over in my head,' he said, still on his guard, but clearly flattered by this respect, this recognition. 'I don't believe he died with the work in progress. If he had, we'd surely have found one of the book cartridges, the dodgy ribbons, left in the machine. There was a ribbon in it right enough, but it was a Sharp, a good one that Carla had got for him. Nothing on it but a list for the off-licence and a letter to his doctor, saying he needed a new prescription for chilblains.'

Hallelujah, and let's hear it for his chilblains! I crowed inwardly. That tape – *that* tape – is gone! And because it's gone, I'll ride this storm out yet!

'So go on then,' I said, all ears. 'Your best guess. Why did Andy Whitty not finish his book?'

'Well, I've talked this over with Carla. And she tells me that the original incident twenty years ago – his girlfriend's suicide – traumatized him really badly. It seems that, overnight, he went from a regular, happy-go-lucky kind of guy into . . . into the sad, alcoholic shambles he ended up. So I would say that he began his story, maybe as a way of recapturing his youth.' He was showing off now, and quite enjoying centre stage. 'Y'know, reliving his glory days. Very probably. It was good for him, it occupied his time, it was theraputic, it must've been hugely enjoyable – until! Until he came to the part where, in reality, his whole world caved in. And there, it all got too much for him. He chucked the book aside, and just gave it up as a bad job.'

I shook my head, near speechless with admiration. 'Y'know something, Garda? You really ought to get that gut of yours insured. 'Cos, believe me, it won't see you too far wrong.'

'You reckon that's how it might've happened?'

'I *know* that's how it *did* happen.'

'How? How can you know?'

I smiled, sat straight and began, 'Whitty was aware that I wanted to be a writer. I suppose he could tell by all the manuscripts that kept coming back through my letter box. So one day – much to my surprise, 'cos I'd hardly ever spoken to the fella – he invited me in for tea. Said he had a story to tell about his time spent working on the buildings in England. And as neither of us appeared to have anything better to do, he asked if I'd be agreeable to look in on him every once in a while and give him a hand with it. Now, if I'm honest, I didn't much fancy the idea. But he was old, and lonely, and this seemed to mean a lot to him so I thought, what the fuck, why not—'

'Wait! A hand? What exactly did this "hand" amount to?'

'I'd help him to phrase things. To sequence events for better clarity. His grammar wasn't always what it should've been. And, yeah, I'd fix his spellings, when he asked. If he didn't ask, I didn't interfere, I'd let him bungle on, as you've no doubt seen.'

He nodded, eyes narrow.

'Like I've said, I was only obliging him in the beginning. But as the action began to gather pace, I could see it had the makings of a stormer, a damn sight better than anything I'd ever managed, and that's the God's honest truth. So my interest, and my input, became all the greater. It started out with a peek over the shoulder once a week or so. By the end I was there every day, every time he plugged in that typewriter. More than that, I'd be rattling at his door in the early morning, enquiring if he'd started. And if he hadn't, then why hadn't he?'

'Did you ever discuss writing credits? Or royalties?'

'No. Not even once. We were both so completely caught up in the story. And we were almost there, the finishing line was in sight. But then he announces that he's stopping. That he doesn't want to go on. That it isn't right to make capital out of Ellie's death. That if this is to be her memorial, he'd sooner she wasn't remembered at all. And that was it. His mind was made up. No debate would be entered into.'

'So what did you do?'

'What did I do? Jesus Christ, I begged him. I pleaded. I said, "Give it here to me and I'll finish it. Get out, go for a drink, by the time you get back, I'll be done." But no. 'Twas wrong, 'twasn't meant to be. Well, at this point, I'm not proud to say, I lost the rag. I called him all the useless, good-for-nothing fuckwits, whose life was one fiasco after the next – and now! Now that he has the chance to get something right, a single worthwhile achievement in his whole sorry existence, he bottles it!'

'What did he say to that?'

'He . . . well, he put the run on me. Told me to go, and never again to set foot across his threshold. I told him not to worry, that wild horses wouldn't drag me across. I think I may have said as well that he could take his book and stuff it, that it was an even bigger waste of space than he was. And, Garda, that's how we parted, that's the last time I saw him alive. About a month later, I got this smell coming from his flat. I tried the door and when it wasn't answered, I broke it in. That was when I found . . . I guess you know what I found.'

'And that was when you took his manuscript.'

I set my jaw and said, 'Yeah. You want to know where I took it from? From a black refuse sack overflowing with empty beer cans and cider flagons. Who was ever going to find it there? And even if someone had, what was it? A big wodge of atrocious typing and pure dunce's spelling. The ramblings of a disturbed old shut-in. It would've wound up in the skip either way. Yeah, I took his manuscript – sorry, *our* manuscript. I do have some little claim on it, you must admit. I wrote the ending, I co-wrote the rest, I salvaged it from the rubbish tip, I fixed it, I polished it, then I hawked it from publisher to publisher till I found one who'd agree to take it on. It's

down to my persistence, and mine alone, that it'll be in
the shops for Christmas. Are you going to try and tell me
my name shouldn't be on the spine?'

He faced away, then faced back sulkily and grumbled,
'Andy's should be there as well.'

'And so it will be. The cover's already done, but I'll get
it redone, how's that? I'll talk to Taurus during the week.
In fact, I'll do it now if you like.'

He sat sullen, brooding. He'd arrived believing he'd
got me landed. For all intents and purposes, I'd slipped
his hook. The voice was heavy with dejection, with
defeat as he said, 'Hmmmm. All very plausible. But I
can't help thinking how very convenient it was for you
that he should die when he did.'

'What? Are you accusing me of *his* murder too?'
Instantly, I realized I'd let something slip.

The policeman perked up. 'I've never accused you of
anybody's murder, Mr Stokes. Why? Should I have?'

It was either a timid, damning retreat or a face-down,
bold and brazen. 'You think I killed my wife, don't you?'

'I didn't say that.'

'And I didn't ask if you did. I want to know if you think
it.'

He made no answer.

'Garda Cambridge, I killed James McDermott. Not
only do I admit it, I take pride in it. But I did not harm
my wife. Good God, losing that woman cost me my only
son and—'

'Woah! Just back up one second! I wasn't there,
admittedly, I'd left the scene by then. But I have it on
good authority that you couldn't wait to get rid of the

same son. You turfed him out that morning, like he was some bloody intruder!'

I didn't lose even a single word. 'No, you weren't there. If you had been, you'd know how I was provoked. You'd know that in the heat of the moment, I had to call the grandfather's bluff. I really didn't believe that the old bastard was genuine about wanting the child.'

'You've made enquiries about getting young Robert back then, I assume?'

'Every other day, Garda. I swear to you, every other day. But it's not looking good. You see, I gave him up in front of witnesses. Anyway, it's not just the child, it's Angie herself. Despite everything, I did love her.'

He recoiled slowly, theatrically.

'Yeah, yeah, so what was I doing with Carla, in that ca—'

'Carla, and your other bird.'

'Neve? No, sir, you've got that wrong. I never laid a finger on Neve, not till long afterwards. There was Carla. Only Carla. And, okay, I shouldn't even have been involved with Carla. But she's a very attractive young lady, and I defy any man to say he'd have done different. I mean, you didn't turn your nose up when the opportunity arose.'

Now, again, he made no answer.

'You want the truth, Garda? I bitterly regret how things ended between Carla and me. I should've been straight with her, I know. But I didn't tell her, I didn't tell either woman about the other because I wanted to hold on to them both. It was selfish, and it was stupid, but somehow, these things have a habit of working themselves out, don't they? She's finally got herself a decent bloke, the kind of man she deserves.'

Though he continued to regard me with suspicion, I fancied I could see just the merest hint of thawing. I ploughed on, 'Y'know, it's funny now when I remember waving my fist at old Andy, telling him that this book was his one and only chance to leave his mark, to accomplish anything in his life. But I was mistaken – he's done something, maybe, better, hasn't he? 'Cos in a round-about way, he's brought you two together. And that's no bad legacy.'

That thaw, definite and unmistakable, was now well under way.

'And when you consider it, Garda, you've not done badly out of all this either. You've proved the hunch, you've secured the confession, and you've got the girl. Now maybe that gut of yours is telling you otherwise, but I can see no reason why we should go on being enemies, you and me.'

And with that, I rested my case. For a long time, a long, *long* time, he stared at his shoes, fiddled with an earlobe, said not a word. At last he lifted his gaze. 'Will you tell me something, straight up now, no bullshit, no *plámás*?'

'If I can.'

'What kind of bloke was he, Andy Whitty?'

'Well, as I'm sure Carla's tol—'

'Carla didn't know him. She saw him once a week at most. And then he'd be out and about, on his best behaviour, done up in his finery, God between us and all harm . . . No, I mean what was he really like? Back in his lair. Behind closed doors.'

I spent a moment weighing up what answer he most wanted to hear. Then, 'Right, straight up, here goes. For starters, he was highly intelligent. I'd even say gifted. Under different circumstances, and given a fairer shake, he might've been a famous – a world-famous – literary figure. I've no doubt about it. But, more importantly, Andy Whitty was a gentleman. A gentleman of the first order. You know as much, for God's sake; he spent all that time on his book, then refused to finish it because it came down to a matter of honour. And I could protest all I liked, he was only ever going to listen to his conscience. So what was he really like? Well, I wish I had half of his talent. And, before you say it for me, half of his integrity too.'

But he didn't seem interested in any such cheap shot. 'I can tell Carla then, in all honesty, that she's no reason to feel ashamed.'

'Ashamed? Good Jesus, I'm the only one who ought to feel ashamed. For falling out with him the way I did. For sitting alongside him, day in, day out, and failing to realize that the guy was so hard up. Now, I wasn't exactly flush at the time myself but between us we could, at the very least, have run to some proper typing ribbons. Not to have the poor oul' divil trawling around the hucksters' shops for that cut-price junk.'

'It was worse than that, y'know,' the policeman said. 'He could only afford them on a use-or-return arrangement. And sure enough, shortly before he died, he marched back to the shop in Kilmainham, handed over a couple he hadn't opened, and redeemed his two pounds fifty or whatever. Brendan—' he did call me

Brendan '–*that* is hard up. But who'm I telling? Wasn't it you who came upon his entire worldly wealth after his death. And how much was it you found, seven, eight quid?'

I now recalled that what I'd found was about a tenner more than I'd ever declared. But I fought back a tear and said, 'I'll never forgive myself for this. Never. How could I not have seen that the poor so-and-so was a breadline case, with barely enough to keep body and soul together? Indeed, how could I just turn my back on him after we'd had one little disagreement, and not make a single effort to patch things up? But I didn't do that either. Instead, I left him to die alone – bloody neighbourly of me, all right.' I paused to let this helping of remorse be absorbed. When it had been, I topped it up with, 'And as if that wasn't bad enough, I tried to pass off the book as all my own work.'

Sounding now partly disappointed, partly mystified, he asked, 'What made you do that?'

I now saw the ideal opportunity to spin him some information he'd later be sure to unearth independently. 'What made me do that? The belief I could get away with it, mostly. Garda, I went to some extraordinary lengths covering my tracks. To begin with, I claimed not to know the old man, never even to have given him the time of day. Then I rewrote the book, more than once, in styles that were completely different, unrecognizable from the original. Problem was, none of those rehashes proved to be worth a curse. That story works one way and one way only – exactly as me and Andy first set it down together.'

'And where was the harm in going public on that? Coming out saying, "See this book? It's a collaboration, a joint effort." Why'd you have to lie about it, to try deny Andy's input?'

'Greed,' I told him plain. 'Ambition. And a whole lifetime of sweat and toil thrown back in my face, stamped "Thanks But No Thanks". I wanted to be a writer, Garda. Desperately. But I was close to the poorhouse myself, and fast running out of last chances. Suddenly, a gem was sitting in my lap. With this, I knew I could crack it. But not as co-author, not as part of a team. Especially when that team could never again take the field.'

'Yeah, I understand . . . kinda. But you were sleeping with Carla, for Christ's sake. And you knew that by laying claim to all the credit, you were laying claim to all the money. Money that should've been hers. That *would* have been hers.'

I sat back and smiled. This was a fish in a barrel. 'Should've been, yes. Would've been, no.'

'Huh?'

'Andy Whitty died intestate. Without a will, everything passes to his next-of-kin. That'd be Francis Whitty, his one surviving brother, Carla's dad. A man who disowned Andy twenty years earlier. Who hadn't a good word to say for him in all that time. Who wouldn't have crossed the road to piss on him if he was on fire.'

Cambridge nodded slowly, making a clucking noise as he did. I let him mull it over a while, then added, 'Of course you realize that if – *when* – I give Andy his due credit, that's where his share of the spoils will end up.

With a brother who refused even to acknowledge the bloke's existence. While the only person ever to give a hoot about the old man – that being your girlfriend – comes away with her hands hanging. That's just how things work, I suppose, but, well, it hardly seems right.'

More nodding, more clucking, more mulling over. I waited till the injustice of it all had fully sunk in.

'Garda, I've been thinking . . . this is only an idea but . . . let's just say that, instead of a writing credit, I give Andy a dedication in the book. I mean, a massive dedication. Something like . . . I dunno, "Aided by, inspired by, dedicated to the late Andrew Whitty. A remarkable man, a remarkable life. This is his story." What d'you reckon? It'd give him the recognition he properly deserves. But, more to the point, it'd allow myself and Carla – and you – of course, to sit down and make a fair division of the proceeds. And anyone who's not entitled, it'd keep their grubby hands away from the cookie jar.'

He bit his lip, watching me with a growing interest.

I stood. 'Now, as you know, I've already had an advance on the strength of this book. Unfortunately, it's tied up completely in the house. But, purely as a gesture of good faith, let me write you a cheque here and now. A kind of first instalment, just so you'll know that I'm on the level, and that we can do business. Five grand sound okay?'

His brow furrowed, his mouth opened, an expression I could not with certainty decipher. 'Well, Garda, I can probably manage seven and a half, but beyond that—'

'You're trying to buy me off.'

'Sorry?'

'You're trying to buy me off!' and he leapt to his feet.

'No, nothing like that. I'm only doing what any sensible—'

'Christ Almighty, you are some piece of work! Good day, Mr Stokes.'

'Talk with Carla,' I pleaded to his back as he stormed along the hallway. 'Talk it over wi—', but the door had already walloped shut behind him. I raced out and reopened it in time to witness a savage, gear-grinding three-point turn, then watched him go roaring out of the cul-de-sac. Leaving me utterly confused as to where things stood, or what now the state of play. Leaving me to marvel at how there really is no talking to some people. Which was a big pity. Because if there was one man in the world with whom I needed to maintain amiable dialogue, it was Denis Cambridge.

CHAPTER THIRTEEN

Despite everything, I had to assume that we'd entered into some form of agreement, the policeman and I. And that I had my end to keep. For this reason, I contacted Taurus next day. Under no circumstances would they even countenance a co-authorship. I'd signed the deal, I'd taken the loot, I'd bloody well write the books. A dedication, however, was entirely my own business, and could be as wordy and as fulsome as I saw fit. So, down the phone line, I dictated something like I'd proposed the previous day to Garda Cambridge. Now all that remained was for the stubborn hump to come to the table and talk money with me.

His move, then: I could only sit tight and wait. And I couldn't even do that for very long – the following Wednesday my parents were due. As it happened, Neve was forced to miss this grand and great occasion. A branch of Taurus Books was on the point of opening in Northern Ireland, and she'd been seconded temporarily to Belfast. However, she promised that, come what may, she'd be back in ample time to accompany me down home to Earlsgrove at the weekend. There and then, the necessary introductions could be made. Her regret at not being around to meet and to greet my folks seemed genuine enough; I wondered if she'd still be as regretful when, eventually, she did make my mother's acquaintance. But I kept this wondering to myself, and wished her only a safe return.

It was gone midday when Cathal Ó Domhnaill trundled his old Mondeo into the little estate. In the passenger seat sat my father; behind him, I could see my mother shift from one side window to the other, noting every detail of the environs before even the car had come to rest. I was waiting at the front gate and guided them into the parking space allotted. From there, they emerged bearing gifts. Dad had with him a small sack of potatoes, freshly dug, my mother a home-made wholemeal cake. Ó Domhnaill, not to be outdone, had chosen to delight me with some notes and pointers he'd jotted down regarding his forthcoming pow-wow. I thanked them one and all, and together we embarked upon the guided tour. In each successive room, they oohed and they aahed, marvelling at how modern everything was, how plush, how swanky. Back again in the front hallway, I apologized for the absence of my girlfriend. She'd been dying to meet them, I said, but had been unavoidably called away. I went on to explain that, with Neve among the missing, I didn't dare even try cook for them. However, I had booked a sitting at Joel's restaurant, just a short way out the Naas Road. The fare, I assured them, was excellent, the table ready when they were.

'Hold on!' my father swaggered. 'Hold on one bloody minute. What about the man of the house?'

'Wh . . . who?' I faltered.

'Robert, my first and only grandson! You hardly think we came all this way just to see you?'

'Oh, of course. Actually, Robert is in play school.'

'Play school, if you don't mind,' my mother frowned. 'And what time does he get home from this play school?'

I had no idea. I knew nothing of the runnings of the kindergarten Robert attended. Many months earlier, I'd dropped a bundle of the little boy's belongings at Reception. Not once had I been back. 'Listen,' I suggested, thinking furiously on my feet. 'Why don't we drive out there and collect him? I mean, now.'

My parents smiled at each other, their agreement instant. Almost as quickly, I remembered I had a phone call to make. I'd promised the Forristers that if ever I intended taking Robert from school then, as a matter of courtesy, I'd ring and let them know.

'We should do that,' my dad beamed.

'Sure we should,' I said. 'He'll be thrilled to see ye – it'll rightly make his day.'

With that, I guided them out before me and closed the door. To hell with it, there'd be no courtesy call. I could not afford such niceties, not if it gave them the impression that I needed permission to see their first and only grandson.

All the way to Islandbridge, Ó Domhnaill droned on about his bloody seminar. Some of the time I pretended to listen, mostly I didn't even pretend. Mercifully, the journey was a short one. Inside the quarter-hour we were turning left, away from the southern wall of the Phoenix Park and on to the green banks of the Liffey. There I bade them wait while I nipped in for the boy.

'Robert Stokes,' I said to the teenage receptionist. 'I need to take him a little early.'

'Sorry,' her brow furrowed, 'who are you?'

'I'm his father.'

'His father? R . . . right. It's just that I don't remember seeing you before. It's normally—'

'An older man who collects him? That'd be his granddad.'

'Okay. I take it you haven't spoken to his granddad, then.'

'Where my son is concerned,' I smiled, determined to keep exchanges civil, 'I'll speak to who I like, when I like. Now, can you get me Robert Stokes, or do I have to go find him myself?'

'Am . . . the thing is,' she began, most ill at ease, 'the fact of the matter . . . I'll get Mrs Cummins for you,' and she disappeared through a small door at the rear of her glass enclosure. While she was gone, I privately conceded credit due to the Forristers. When they'd chosen this crèche, they'd chosen well. The attention to the individual was thorough, the security highly impressive.

'Mr Stokes? Imelda Cummins,' said the fifty-something, bespectacled schoolmarm, who shook my hand. 'If you'd care to come with me.' She led the way past Reception into a tiny office full of clutter. We both sat, though there was scarcely the legroom.

'I'm surprised nobody's told you, but Robert doesn't attend this play school any more.'

'Excuse me?' I laughed, full sure of my footing. 'What're you talking about? I wrote a cheque for his fees only last weekend.'

'That may well be. But last weekend *was* his last weekend. Just the other day, in fact, we parted company with Robert.'

'Oh?' I mumbled, a little thrown. 'And . . . what? Did his grandparents remove him from the school?'

'No, actually. I'm afraid we had to ask him to leave.'

'Did you now? And why would you do a thing like that? Was he having problems?'

'Not so much having them as causing them.'

'Causing them?' I don't know why my hackles were rising, but they were. 'Just him, yeah? All his fault?'

'Yes,' she said flatly, with steel. 'Mr Stokes, our first priority in a nursery like this is the safety of all the children in our care.'

'But at his age, for Christ's sake, how much of a safety risk does he pose? Like, what did he do exactly?'

'He stuck a plastic knife into a little girl's face. Missed her eye, but not by much.'

I swallowed and flustered, 'Well . . . maybe he was provoked.'

'It was the fourth such incident.'

'Well, maybe he was provoked four times, then!'

'No. He wasn't retaliating. He wasn't even angry. It's this game of his that he keeps trying to make the others play.' She paused. When she continued, her words thudded like fistfalls. 'He calls it *Daddies and Mammies*.'

At once I felt my chest tighten, my breath come quick and wheezy. Garbling something about getting to the bottom of this, I clattered to my feet and went lurching from the office, from the building. Back in the car, I cobbled the excuse that . . . In truth, I don't remember what excuse I cobbled. But right through the drive to Joel's, through a dinner I barely touched, through the remorselessness of Ó Domhnaill and his South Kilkenny Republicanism, through a distracted farewell after the meal was done, I could think only of this: I had to get Robert back. It didn't matter whose baby he was. It didn't matter what an encumbrance he might be. It didn't matter if Neve objected. It scarcely mattered if she turned tail and walked away. I had to get Robert back. *I had to get Robert back.*

It couldn't wait, I decided. Not another night, not another hour. Near the Black Lion, I hailed a passing cab, and directed it to an address at Berkley Lawns, Chapelizod. The early evening was now upon us, the rush-hour in fullest stodge. It was almost six before we got there. Outside the gate of the small, mid-terraced dwelling, I instructed my driver not to go anywhere. This wouldn't take long.

The door was opened by my mother-in-law. 'Michelle!' I puffed. 'I need Robert for a . . . Is something the matter?'

Something was, and no doubt: upon seeing me, her face had turned the colour of her hair. Even the lipstick she wore seemed to dull to ash.

'My folks are over at my place,' I fibbed, panting on. 'They'd like to—'

'He's not here,' she blurted, all a-tremble.

'I can hear that,' I managed to laugh. 'You think you'd get that much peace if he was around? But where is he?'

'Brian went to collect him from school and they haven't come back.'

'School? I was at the school earlier. They told me Robert doesn't go there any more.'

Her bottom lip quivered.

'C'mon, Michelle,' I said, calmly as I could. 'Where is he?'

'I don't know!' and she began the act of closing the door in my face.

I shot a leg in. 'You're lying,' I said, still calm but only just. 'Tell me where they are.'

She whimpered, and put her shoulder, frail as it was, to the door against me. I muscled forward, sending her and it reeling into the hallway.

'Where the fuck are they?' I roared. By the foot of the stairs, hands to her mouth, she stood weeping hysterically. Cowering from me, eyeing me terror-stricken. 'Where are—'

But eyeing also the small phone table low to my left. There beside the set, the directory lay open at an early page: State services, the listing of Dublin's police stations precisely. On closer inspection, I could see a blue X had been drawn near halfway down, adjacent to the Ks. I looked up. 'When did they go?'

She wailed once, twice, a third time.

I came towards her, clenching my fists, fully intending to use them. 'Jesus Christ, when did they go?'

'This morning,' she sobbed. 'Some time this morning.'

I turned through the open door and sped back to the waiting taxi. 'Kilmainham Garda Station!' I barked. 'Fast. Fast as you can.'

*

The traffic, if anything, had thickened. I sat in the back, urging us on, willing us forward, muttering to myself, cursing those around. The driver sensed I was best left alone, and throughout the entire grind said nothing.

At the bottom of the South Circular, progress had halted completely. Three changes of lights, not an inch gained. Though the cop shop was still the best part of a mile away I threw the door open, threw the cabbie a twenty and began to run. Up the hill I pounded, past the army barracks, through the head-lit stream as it snaked out Con Colbert Road, along by the Royal Hospital and left at The Patriot's Inn. I was only dimly aware how my throat burned, how my sides stitched, how my legs ached; my every thought was for reaching that police station with all possible haste. And being ready for trouble when I got there.

The forecourt is tight, with a sharp fall of ground from the reception area to the front gate. Outside Reception, a squad car was parked, a driver at the ready. As I came spluttering up the incline, just yards now from my journey's end, that main door was pushed open. First came Robert, steered from behind by Brian Forrister. Then came Cambridge. Once outside, the policeman glided ahead and opened the car's back door; the other two sat themselves in. Cambridge didn't follow, but rested an elbow on the roof and seemed to be cosying in for a long goodbye. Until he saw me. With what strength I had left, I came lunging, gasping forward; immediately Cambridge slammed the car door shut and strode into my path. Ten years my junior, six-foot odd and built to proportion, running into the man was like colliding with a post box in the dark. I slumped at his feet winded, exhausted and shaken to the marrow. He pulled me up by the scruff and manhandled me aside. At his back, the squad car trundled down the forecourt, out the gate and away.

'Now, how can I help you?' he smiled, almost laughed.

I wheezed, 'I want my son.'

'Really? I understand this is quite a U-turn, despite all that crap you told me recently. So, what's brought it about?'

'I . . . I don't have to explain myself to you.'

'Maybe not. But you're going to have to explain yourself to somebody.'

'Eh?'

'You surrendered custody in front of witnesses, remember? If you want him back, you need to go to court.'

'Fine!' I spat, my breath returning. 'I'll do that.'

'Yeah. Go to court. It'll be good practice for you.'

Desperately, I trawled for something, *anything*, to wipe that grin off his gargoyle face. 'It's not evidence, y'know.'

'What's not?'

'You've been interviewing that child without me being present.'

'We didn't need to have you present. Not when his guardian was—'

'Now, look, I don't know what he's been saying—'

'You know bloody well what he's been saying!'

'—but whatever it was, it's still not evidence.'

'Oh? And why wouldn't it be?'

''Cos he's too young.'

'Matter of opinion, that. And in the opinion of the child's guardian—'

'It's the child's fucking guardian who's put him up to this, who's coached him in what to say and how to say it!'

'That'll be for a judge and jury to decide.'

I took a step away and I sneered, 'A judge and jury! That meant to scare me, is it? Listen, mate, you're not dealing with some greenhorn who's come down in the last shower.'

'I've just been listening to what that little boy's had to say so, believe me, I know precisely what I'm dealing with. Now, Mr Stokes, you'll have to excuse me.'

And he turned away, heading towards the station door.

I could not allow things to finish on such a retort. To his back I yelled, 'I don't care, God damn you, it's not evidence!'

Slowly he stopped and slowly turned again.

'Who're you trying to convince, Brendan?'

'What?'

'If you really believed that, there'd be no reason to go on repeating it.'

'Yeah? Well . . . well, if you had a single thing on me, I'd be arrested already!'

At this, there came another of those fathomless expressions – I wasn't sure if he was about to concede the point, or to put the cuffs on me there and then. Suddenly, without warning or change of countenance, he spun on his heel and was gone. So, too, for that matter, was I.

This was no place to loiter without cause. This was enemy territory.

For the first time in a long time, I failed to sleep the night. Dublin got its head down, then cranked to life again shortly after with the rising of the sun, and still I'd not even begun to drift. I tossed. I thrashed. At one point, I might even have prayed. But nothing would stop my mind ratting endlessly from one dark corner to another. Would save the bed being drenched in sweat as the knots in my gut twisted and tightened the whole night through. Or, what was worst, would ease the terrible certainty that, whatever I now faced, I faced alone. With nobody to talk to, to turn to, to hear my side. To tell me all was well, and that I mustn't fret. Even to tell me that the shit was fast approaching the fan, and I'd better make plans. A living soul with both feet in my camp, who'd stand by me regardless. Like never before, I needed a friend.

Then who should call round in the mid-morning but Alan Bradshaw. Heaven sent, surely; an angel at my table. But what could I say? What could I do? Start alleging to him some massive top-level fit-up? Claim that the cops and the Forristers were conspiring to put words in my young son's mouth? When he himself had heard those very same words from that very same mouth. Freely volunteered, and long before either the cops or the Forristers ever put an oar in. How could I ask for that man's allegiance? Or for his trust? Or even for his ear to bend, his shoulder a while to cry on?

In any case, he'd not come to do much in the way of listening. The flying visit was solely to finalize arrangements for the following day's excursion south. He'd collect me at about six, that'd have us reach Earlsgrove in bags of time for Ó Domhnaill's thingumajig. Which, by the way, he was looking forward to immensely: it wasn't every day he got to hear me mouthing off to the whole parish like I was a regular, big-shot celebrity. Flaunting a regular big-shot celebrity's dollybird, what was more! She would be coming with us, wouldn't she? Yes, I told him, I very much hoped so. Oh, good Jesus, he said, he hoped so too. 'Cos it'd be worth driving the ninety-eight miles for nothing else than to see how she fared among the wild men of Earlsgrove.

It was happening, then: the plan was set and the countdown begun. Tomorrow I'd be returning to home soil a star, the guy who went to the big city and showed them how, the local lad made good. Among family, friends and neighbours with my head held high. With my name halfway to becoming household. With my arm adorned by the type of trophy bimbo befitting a man of my accomplishment. But with a voice in my ear, gnawing, nagging and constant. If the heights are unearned, it pestered, then the comedown is inevitable. And the steeper the pedestal, the further the fall. Tomorrow night, I'd be reaching the top of the roller coaster. Tomorrow night might just tell a tale.

CHAPTER FOURTEEN

All the way home, Bradshaw was unstoppable. Normally
withdrawn – painfully so – in mixed company, today he
talked like a burst water main. Memories, milestones,
tales true and tall: we'd been hitching this route together,
he and I, ever since we were old enough to stick a thumb
out. And now, like it or not, Neve was getting a whistle-
stop by whistle-stop account of our several scrapes and
escapades. There was Timolin: we'd once waited more
than eight hours in Timolin for a lift, standing on exactly
the same spot all that November evening. Or Kilcullen
where, on the journey back from The Stones at Slane
'82, we found ourselves stranded with dark night fallen
and not the price of a drink between us. In blind
desperation, we followed two comically ugly women into
the local pub, hoping to latch ourselves on and thus end
all our difficulties at a stroke. My bird was up for it,
vigorously so; his intended was just as vigorously
opposed, and managed to dissuade her friend also.
Which left the lads to sleep together, alone, under the
black plastic cover of a silage pit. There was Jerpoint,
Christ Almighty, there was Jerpoint! Bradshaw's first car,
an old Escort, seized up and needed running repairs
right outside the abbey in the small hours of the wettest

February morning the Republic of Ireland has known since records were kept. There were all these and many, many more. And then there was Earlsgrove.

I don't know quite what I'd been expecting, but it was nothing like what awaited: the small function room of The Whiskey Vat was thronged. Still a good quarter-hour to curtain-up, and already standing room only – in fact, we were forced to jostle our way in, such was the mob around the main door. Once through that outer circle, the first person I spied was Ó Domhnaill, chief organizer, main man. And he'd seen me too: I could tell by the great wave of relief that immediately broke over him. With open arms, he came sidestepping between the rowed seats and shook my hand. 'My God,' he beamed, 'I was starting to get a little bit nervous.'

'What're you on about?' I beamed back. 'We're in good time.'

'I know that but . . . now, who's this grand girl at all?'

'This is Neve Shipperly,' I told him. 'And you already know . . .' but Alan had left for the bar, and was elbowing his way towards service.

'Your parents are down here near the front,' Ó Domhnaill whispered. 'I can squeeze a chair in for your girl beside them. Anyway, I think your mother wants a word with you before we get started.'

'She does? What about?'

'Something or other that you're to mention in your speech.'

'Oh, Christ, the speech!' I gasped, only now recalling why I'd been invited in the first place.

Ó Domhnaill looked at me like his collar was buttoned

too tight. 'It's . . . just a few words, Brendan. That's all we want. Y'know, something along the lines of them notes I showed you the other—'

'The notes! Have you got them with you?'

'Well, I . . . I have, but did you not prepare anything of your own?'

'And why would I,' I asked grandly, 'when what you wrote is so absolutely spot-on?'

'Yerragh, that may be, but I thought a man like yourself—'

'Cathal, when it comes to local history, there's not a man *alive* who could improve on you. And I wouldn't even dream of trying.'

He blushed a little, seeming to forget his displeasure. Then he led me towards the podium where he handed over the rough draft he'd made, then briefly introduced me to the other speakers enlisted. Before I could begin an exchange of small talk, I saw my mother semaphoring frantically at the left-hand end of the front row. 'Don't forget to mention Uncle Timmy!' she hissed, when I approached.

'Well, how're ya?' my dad gushed. 'Did you come down with Alan?'

'Yeah, he drove—'

'Well, well, well,' came a voice from behind. 'Can it really be so long ago you don't remember me?'

He didn't seem to have aged at all. Far as I was concerned, he'd always been an old man. 'Of course not,' I smiled. 'It's great to see you, Mr Mahoney.'

'How are you, Brendan?'

'Ah, can't complain.'

'My deepest sympathy on your terrible bereavement. You've been in our prayers daily.'

'That's much appreciated.'

'But don't lose the faith, and God'll make it up to you in other ways. In fact, rest assured, He's got something to do with all this success you've been enjoying. Many, many congratulations and long may it continue.'

'Thank you very much.'

'Y'know, of all the lads I put through my hands, most ended up farming or working on the factory floor, some did the Leaving Cert, an odd fellow stayed on till third level. But one, and only one, ever achieved anything of real note. So, young man, take a bow. Thanks to yourself, I can hold my head up, good as any of them.'

'Any of who? I thought you'd packed it in years ago.'

'Oh, I have. But there's a club for retired teachers in Waterford city. We play some golf, take the occasional trip to the theatre, organize outings – sure, anything to be doing something.'

'Ah.'

'And for years I've had to listen while the others dropped names of TV personalities, stage actors, solicitors and surgeons – listen, and sit quiet in my corner. But not any more! Now, I just say, "You know, of course, that the author Brendan Stokes is a protégé of my own!" Gives them something to chew on, let me tell you.'

He chuckled to see me redden so.

'That's . . . that's nice for you,' I said.

'It is,' and he suddenly furrowed to a frown, 'because back in your time I knew that, for the vast majority of the boys, this was where it ended. Once they'd finished with me, they'd finished with education in every real sense. So if they didn't catch it in Earlsgrove BNS, they never caught it at all. For that reason, I made it my life's mission to ensure that nobody left sixth class without being able to read, write and do arithmetic to a reasonable level. I would not compromise on that, which is why I was, maybe, a little heavy-handed at times.'

'Not at all. You were no more strict than you needed to be.'

'Yeah . . . I used to worry about that, y'know. That I was so preoccupied with forcing the weaker kids up to a certain standard, I didn't meet the requirements of the gifted ones. That being so rigid, I was stifling any creativity they might have. Take your own case, for example. I watched over you for eight long years, and not once did you even flash across my radar! It shames me now to admit it, but I never remember thinking you were anything out of the ordinary. Brendan, I had you down for one of those perennial back-markers. Another face in the crowd, nothing more.'

'I hold no grudges, Mr Mahoney. We all get it wrong from time to time.'

'We do, I suppose . . . What used to worry me most, though, was just *how* wrong I might've got it. Because, as best I can, I try keep track of all my past pupils. By and large, they seem to have done pretty well for themselves, thank Heaven. But nothing special. Not even one of them. I used to wonder if that might've been down to me.'

I thought I could see his eyes begin to brim.

'But then you come along with what I believe is an outstanding novel and . . . well, my conscience is clear. I was right to devote myself to the slow learners, because real talent will rise to the top regardless.' He reached out and clasped both his hands round my forearm. 'You may find it hard to believe, but this means more to me than it could ever mean to you. To you it's just a book, the first of many, I'm sure. But to me, it's the vindication, and validation, of a whole lifetime's work. And I've come here tonight, Brendan Stokes, to thank you for that.'

'Nonsense! It's me who should be thank—'

'Now, I've said what I came to say. My very, very best wishes to you for the future. So, if you'll excuse me, I'll take my seat and wait on your words of wisdom.'

I watched him shuffle away. He had aged, after all. Good God, he'd aged.

'Uncle Timmy!' my mother hissed again, insistent as before.

'Who?'

'Uncle Timmy. Don't forget him!'

'And who's Uncle Timmy?'

'Timmy Denton. From over Ballynooney way. He fought in the War of Independence and was shot by the Tans, Lord have mercy on the man. A cousin of your own.'

'Right,' I said, puzzled that I'd not heard the name before, delighted now to have this personal angle to boast. 'Listen, I'll talk to ye later, I think they're anxious to get this thing started. My girlfriend, Neve, is at the bar, Alan'll introduce ye. Be nice to her now, mind! Timmy Denton,' I said, recapping for my mother's benefit. Then

I turned away towards the waiting podium. Immediately, at my back, I heard the rumble of a chair being vacated, then my father breathlessly calling, 'Brendan!'

I stopped.

'He wasn't her uncle, he was related to her mother's people through marriage. And did he fuck fight in the War of Independence! He was a halfwit who went around with the Tans, pointing out the safehouses where the rebels were hiding. 'Twas the IRA that shot him.'

'You're kidding!'

'Now, if you want to mention him, that's up to you. But, by Jesus, don't you dare let on to the neighbours that he's anything to do with me or my family.'

'But . . . what'm I supposed to say, then?'

'That's your business,' he said, and then he said no more.

Ó Domhnaill was coming to his feet and calling the proceedings to order. 'Reverend Father, ladies and gentlemen,' he began, 'may I start by welcoming you all here tonight to the Vat for this seminar to commemorate, and to celebrate, the part played by the people of South Kilkenny in the struggle for Irish freedom. I can *not* get over the crowd that's turned up, and I'm guessing that 'tisn't just for the history lessons ye're here . . .'

Muffled giggles went rippling around the room.

'And, dear God, 'tis hardly to see myself ye came, sick and tired ye are of me!'

'If you had a little tune to that, Cathal, you could whistle it!' came a cry from somewhere near the bar. The entire gathering broke out in loud guffaws. Ó Domhnaill himself smiled, taking it in good part.

'Aye,' he said eventually. 'I'm right, then, it's not me. And 'tis hardly just Professor D. S. MacAongusa, head of history at Waterpark College . . .' Here he paused for the applause that came, late and polite '. . . or Mr James Loughran, who's travelled from Clashmore in the County Waterford to be here, and James is a Republican in a line that stretches back directly to the great Warrior Gael Thomas Francis Meagher, or "Meagher of the Sword", as he was known.'

Here a stop for more applause, this smarter on cue.

'So that leaves only the one. Now, some of ye might've heard of this fella already . . .' another giggle, nervous and expectant from the floor '. . . all the way from Knocktubber, and for those not so well up on their geography, that's a small townsland about a mile and a half up the road . . .' laughter, loud and raucous, the crowd was loving this '. . . a fella I'm sure we're all very proud of. It's a good few years ago now that we waved him off to Dublin – of course, he was just an ordinary working man then, a humble fitter. Am I right, Brendan?' I nodded. He continued, 'But he's come a long way since, and anyone who can read a newspaper knows that he's on the verge of really, really great things. Unfortunately, you'll know, too, that he had a most horrific tragedy in his life recently. But through it all, he conducted himself with dignity and courage, and brought nothing but honour to this little parish of ours. And I'm certain that in the years to come he'll continue to represent Earlsgrove around this country, around this world, with even greater honour. And that's why *we* are honoured to have him here tonight. Ladies and gentlemen, to chair this forum, would you welcome, please, one of our very own, Brendan Stokes.'

Amid the eruption, I got to my feet. The ovation was sufficiently sustained to allow me iron out Ó Domhnaill's notes on the lectern before me and give them a rapid once-over. By the time the last of the hubbub had died I was ready, ready as I was going to be.

'Reverend Father, ladies and gentlemen . . . old friends.'

One clap. Enough to trigger another damburst, long and thunderous. As it reverberated, I scanned the hall, humbly, graciously, and . . . Jesus Christ, by the door!! Or . . . maybe not. The light there was bad.

'I . . . erm . . . thank you all ever so much for the warmth of that welcome . . .'

Another glance, hard as I dared without appearing too obvious. No sign – not hide nor hair. She was gone, if she'd ever been there.

'Especial thanks to Cathal for those very kind words of his . . .'

One more look, just to be sure. No, nothing. A case of my imagination working overtime, what with the stress I'd lately . . . *There*! It was . . . it *was*! It was her!

'Ah . . . sorry, where . . . am . . . oh, yeah. The way he tells it, you're honoured to have me here. Well, let me tell you . . . tell you . . . tell you what? Tell you that I'm the one who's honoured, that was it, that was . . .'

Large as life, there could not be another. But what, *what*, was she doing here?

'Now, you'll . . . there was some other thing . . . ah . . . maybe it'll come to me . . . but anyway, I'll just say a word or two about the . . . the . . . the topic.'

My attention, wavering between the speech before me and the spectre at the far wall, was now drawn to a small kerfuffle in the centre of the audience. There Babs Brady, wife of the proprietor, was picking her mortified way through the seating, excusing herself as she came.

'Earlsgrove,' I opened, head down, reading unashamedly, 'is not somewhere that figures too prominently in the history books. You may find mention that in sixteen forty-nine, Cromwell's army stopped here overnight on its way south to sack the walled city of Waterford.'

Babs had breached the front row and sidled apologetically to the dais. A brief message was conveyed, then Ó Domhnaill strode to the microphone and leant across me. 'It seems, Brendan, you're wanted at the front door. Urgently, by all accounts. A bloke called Spielberg, something about movie rights!' and he chortled, prompting the rest to join in. I acknowledged the gag, then, 'Terribly sorry about this. I shouldn't be long, but maybe you'd better carry on without me.'

Off I set towards the exit, shaking hands to left and right where I passed, exchanging nods and winks with those off my immediate path. Not once did my front fail me, not even when I reached the door, grabbed Carla Whitty by the upper arm and frogmarched her before me into the lamplit night. 'This better be fucking good.'

'Trust me, it is. It's about those ribbons that my uncle—'

'Christ, not here!' and I forced her further along the pavement, away from the alehouse window.

'Okay, then, where?'

Desperately, I looked the street up and down, both sides. 'Alan's car. It's not locked.'

'Fine. Or mine's not far, if you'd prefer.'

'What? You're driving?'

'Well, it's Denis's.'

'Denis's? In that case, you'll understand if I pass on the offer. C'mon.' I walked her briskly to where Bradshaw had parked by the public phone box. After both car doors were closed behind us I said curtly, 'Right, let's make this quick, eh?'

She stared ahead a while, into the haze of the streetlight and the darkness beyond. 'You know how we found my uncle's novel on those spent typewriter cartridges and—'

'Yes, yes. It's my novel, incidentally, but, yes, I've been through all this with your beloved.'

'You know how he could only afford those substandard cartridges, and that he had them on a use-or-return basis?'

'I'm well aware that your uncle was in dire financial straits. Again, it's something I've discussed with—'

'And you know how the last tape, the one with the book's ending on it, was missing?'

'It was *not* missing. It couldn't be found because it never existed. Because your uncle wasn't able to finish that book. Because it was I who—'

'It's not missing any more.'

'—who took this mish-mash and . . . *what?*'

She laughed. Long, low and drily, she laughed. 'It's turned up, Brendan.'

'H . . . how?'

'I'm very glad you ask. Y'see, it transpires that my uncle bought those tapes from a shop in Kilmainham, owned by a man named Sarhan – a Moroccan, I think. In the course of his enquiries, it was Denis who tracked this Mr Sarhan down, and the pair hit it off quite well. Especially when they discovered that they're actually neighbours. His house is just across the road from where we live in Dolphin's Barn. Small world, eh?'

She paused to leer, to lord it, to watch me wilt.

'Anyway, just last evening, Mr Sarhan knocked on our door. One of his customers had returned a ribbon cartridge to him. He'd bought it as new, but found when he tried it that it was partly used. And Mr Sarhan, God bless him, knew right away that this tape must've come back for refund, and the only person he'd ever agreed to such an arrangement with was one impoverished client named Andy Whitty. So much for gratitude – the old man had pulled a fast one. He'd used only the tiniest part of the tape, that little you'd hardly notice. So he chanced his arm. He wrapped it in the plastic cover, stuck it back into the box, mixed it in among those others he'd not opened and returned it to the shop. Claimed his money back, cheeky as you like. Sly old devil, wasn't he?'

In my throat, something sour and sickly was rising. I swallowed hard, but to little avail.

'Mr Sarhan had been diddled, but that wasn't what bothered him. 'Cos he remembered how the police had been round, asking questions about old Whitty. So he thought maybe he'd better hand them over this tape.

And why traipse all the way to the cop shop, when there's a perfectly good copper living just the other side of the street?'

After another gloat in my direction, she put a hand into her blouse pocket and drew out the cartridge. Black, rectangular, with a length of ribbon stretched between two protruding arms. 'Allow me to read you what it's got,' and she began to pay out the ribbon. Slowly. And with relish.

Too slowly and with *too* much relish. Because, watching these theatrics, it suddenly struck me: this was theatre. Or, more precisely, this was bollox. Whatever, it bore little resemblance to any known form of reality. If they had found that tape, it'd be in evidence control, well under wraps. If they had found that tape, I'd be in custody, well under arrest. And if, for some reason, they'd decided to first confront me with it, they'd hardly send a nurse to do their confronting. This, then, must've been her attempt at a trap. Hatched, no doubt, in that diseased little mind of hers. And now carried out as a solo mission, probably because everyone else thought it too ridiculous. I began to laugh aloud. She looked up with a frown.

'Carla, girl, you may not be the sharpest tool in the box. But please don't assume that I'm just as fucking stupid as you are.'

'Huh?'

'You're going to try tell me that tape's the real thing?'

'Just hear me out a minute and I'll prove it.'

'Sweetheart, you've studied the manuscript. You know well how the book ends. Now you're going to pretend to

306

read it to me from that ribbon, like you were seeing it for the first time. What? D'you reckon that'll spook me into some great big confession? Catch yourself on, for the love of God!' and I shaped to get out of the car.

'Oh, no, no!' she cried. 'To hell with the book, have a listen to this.'

In the very poor light, I could see nothing. She herself was squinting as she began, ' "To whom it concerns, I, Andrew Whitty, do hereby bequeath to my good friend James Shafty McDermott, the original draft . . ." '

The more she read, the more it felt like my head was on the inside of a well-padded crash helmet. Sounds became fuzzed, indistinct, and I saw as if through a darkly smoked visor. My very thoughts were shambling and unsteady, but when at last they stood to order, it all became crystal. She had the words. There was only one place she could possibly have come upon them. She'd got the tape. The genuine article.

'This is most disappointing, Brendan. All the way down, I was looking forward to hearing how you'd go about talking your way out of this one. And what? Nothing? Nothing at all?'

Here she stopped and drew aside, inviting me to try a run at the perimeter fence. When I failed even to shut my gaping mouth, she went on, 'He tracked you down, didn't he? After you'd had your picture in the paper. After you'd had this huge advance on the strength of a book that he owned the rights to. And he confronted you with the will that proved ownership. What did he want? I guess it must've been money, yeah? Hush money, or he was blowing the whistle. And that's the reason you had to get rid of him. The real reason. The only one.'

I would scarcely have been able to change my expression, even if I'd wanted to.

'But, if that be the case, then why should there be a second victim? I mean, how does your wife's murder fit into all this? Well, however, it wouldn't have had very much to do with poor old Shafty. In his entire life, the man had no history of violence. All he did have was a pathological fear of the sight of blood – I'm assuming we both know where that condition stemmed from. But, anyway, why would he want to harm her? It wasn't as if he'd been disturbed burgling the place – he'd come through the front door, with every law in the land on his side, to claim only what was due to him. So, if not Shafty, then who? You were the only other person . . . *Sorry*! There was one other. Little Robert. Incredible, isn't it, that the kid's been telling it straight from the word go? "Daddy stabbed my Mammy," That's what he kept repeating in the Kilmainham police station on Wednesday last. That's what he said to the Gardaí the night of the murder but, at the time, they weren't able to make it out. It was there all along, but nobody thought to look, because nobody could even guess at a motive.' She wagged the ribbon cartridge before my face. 'Reverend Father, ladies and gentlemen . . . old *friend*! I give you, the motive!'

She sat, still leant forward, now unsmiling, unblinking. My best response was a long time coming. When it did come it was purely token, purely to put some tiny dent in that cocksure arrogance. 'Taking a bit of a chance, then, aren't you?'

'Not really. You won't try anything, not just yards from your adoring public. No, Brendan, I think I'm safe enough. What do *you* reckon to it all?'

And this, I knew, was precisely what she'd come in hope to see. Me begging. Me crawling. Me threshing about in her net, scrabbling for a loophole that wasn't there. I couldn't deny her the moment. But I didn't have to give her the gratification. 'Fair enough,' I said, matter-of-factly. 'I'm making no comment. So whatever it is that happens now, let's get it over with.'

Somehow, she seemed unprepared for this development.

'Come on, come on! You're the one holding all the cards, it's your move.'

But it was becoming ever clearer that she didn't have a next move. I pressed on, 'Like, isn't this where lover boy jumps in and reads me my rights?'

'He's . . . he's not here,' she faltered.

'Well, one of his buddies, then.'

'There aren't any.'

'Eh? So . . . you've come all this way, on your own? Why?'

Her eyes darted nervously to every nook and cubbyhole of the car's interior.

'Carla, why are you doing this?'

No reply. And none forthcoming. A most outrageous possibility occurred to me. 'Does Denis know about this tape, Carla?'

The teeth gritted, the head shook.

'Was he not there when the shopkeeper, this Sarhan, dropped it round?'

'He was gone with his mates on a four-day stag to Holyhead.'

There were tears, but only in her voice. Above my head, the clouds parted and a little light shone through. 'Things not going the best?' I ventured, but that only caused the stare to harden, the mouth to clam tighter still. It was pushing my luck, but I pushed ahead. 'Well, if it's any consolation, you're not the first person to hitch their wagon to the wrong horse. Take it from one who's done it before.' I stopped, sighed, considered the gamble, then went on, 'And who's recently done it again.'

With that, I looked wistfully into the darkened distance. From the corner of my eye, I saw her turn to me abruptly, all curious, then turn away again, as if determined not to be drawn in. One eternity later she blurted, 'He's been such an absolute shit lately. Working late, drinking later, coming home for a change of clothes and a bed – and not always doing that either. He'd been on double-shift overtime for the past three weeks. But he promised – *promised* – that when it ended we'd go away together. So it ended – only then he remembered this stag party. He'd clean forgotten to mention it all along – slipped his mind completely. The booze cruise to Holyhead, a four-day stopover in Wales, him and a dozen of his mates. Strictly boys only. Well, if he wants it boys only, that can certainly be arranged.'

This, I calculated, might yet be salveagable. Provided I played it shrewd. 'You realize, don't you, that he'll go berserk when he finds out? I mean, that you've shown this to me before him.'

She nodded.

'Or maybe that's the whole idea, is it? To get back at him?'

'Partly. But more so . . . Oh, Jesus, I must be mad!'

'No, no, please. Go on. Whatever, I'd like to hear.'

It took her several breaths, deep and slow, to summon the courage. 'Denis is . . . he's not the one. Oh, he's a decent enough guy, in his way. And I'm sure he'll make some girl a very good husband. But I'm just as sure that girl isn't me. And never will be.'

I, too, drew a deep breath and soothed, 'If that's how it is, you're better off getting out sooner rather than later. Believe me, you're doing the sensible thing. Like the saying goes, "As God made us, he matched us." Carla, the right man *is* out there.'

'I thought once upon a time that might be yourself,' she said, without looking.

'You did?'

'Yeah. I know what we had wasn't ideal, but it's the happiest I've been in my life. I was with somebody who was somebody – it made me feel like I must be a somebody too. It was never like that before. And it's never been the same since.'

I shifted a little, but never even thought of interrupting.

'Then, of course, you had to go and hurt me, betray me, lie to me and play me for a mug. By rights, I shouldn't be able to stand living in the same town as you. But here I am, sat by your side, having come one hundred miles just to . . .'

'Just to . . . what?'

She laughed. 'I'll say one thing for this God of yours, He's got some twisted sense of humour.'

'What d'you mean?'

'Well, why else would He pair us two off in life's lucky dip? Why would He fix it so that it's you I can't get out of my system? All the decent blokes out there I could've fallen for, but it had to be . . . Jesus, y'know, I was right first time. I *am* mad!'

Tread softly, tread softly, I told myself. No need to say a word, she might just talk me out of this whole bind, unprompted.

'Now, with so much time on my hands lately, I've been giving this plenty of thought. And . . . hey, we get one chance on this earth. And it seems to me that we're allotted one person, and only one, for our own. Bit like Ned and Ellie in my uncle's story, come to think of it. Problem is, though, how far should you go in the real world to bag yourself that one person? Should you be prepared to swallow your pride, and your dignity, and all your self-respect? Should you be prepared to overlook things like dishonesty? Like infidelity? Like . . .' she held the tape aloft '. . . like this?'

'Well,' I stammered, 'if you can never be happy any other way then, yes, I reckon you should.'

'Hmm. Thought you might say that. So, now for the sixty-four-thousand-dollar question. Brendan, if the answer's no, please, please, tell me. But d'you think there's still a chance, any chance, for us? For me and you?'

Good Christ, I thought, she *is* mad. Certifiably insane. And may she never recover! 'Oh, my God, yes! A chance? Carla, I never stopped loving you. But that morning, you didn't let me explain—'

She shushed me with an open palm. 'You'll have your opportunity. But let *me* explain something first. Brendan, if we do get back together, the ground rules are going to change. In a *major* way. Last time out, you were the star, the glamour boy, the one who screwed about where and when you pleased, wiping your feet on this besotted poor fool. Next time round, we'll do things on my terms. 'Cos don't forget, old buddy, I'll always have the goods on you.'

I melted back into the seat giddy with relief, light-headed on the let-off. Yes, I was selling my soul; yes, I was doing a deal with the devil. But I'd wait my moment, then welch on it too. I'd weaseled out of tighter corners.

'You hear me, Brendan? You ever lie to me again, *ever*, and I will grass you up without as much as a second thought.'

'I promise you, Carla. As God is my judge, I swear it. It's going to be so good, me and you back together.'

I leant across to kiss her but she shied away.

'Okay, not so fast. Before we take this any further . . .' she stopped, she turned, she glared '. . . and seeing as how I'm going to be filling the woman's shoes, in a manner of speaking, there's one thing I want cleared up here and now. Why did you kill your wife?'

'B . . . beg your pardon?'

'I'm warning you, Brendan! You'd better be straight with me or, well, this little village doesn't look much, but I bet it's got a police station. And I bet it wouldn't take me long to find it. So I'm going to ask you just once more – why did you kill her?'

Like a falling chimney pot it hit me: she was wired!

Sure as fate, the bitch was wired. In the dim, I looked. Her blouse was sheer and flimsy. Revealing nothing apparent.

'Why did I do it?' *Hand to shoulder. Tentatively.* 'You really want to know?' *Hand to broad of back.* 'Okay, then, here it is.' *Hand to midway along spine.* 'May the Lord strike me dead if I'm lying, but . . .' *Hand to beltline. Nothing. She was clean. Clean!*

'Well?'

'Eh?'

'What's the delay, Brendan? Stalling for time, while you concoct another of your—'

'Just let me finish, will ya?' I drew away. 'You asked for the truth, I'm coming to it. The truth is, I did it for you.'

'You did it f— Aw, Jesus, what *do* you take me for?'

'Carla, on my mother's life. The tramp, McDermott, showed her proof that the book wasn't mine. And she threatened to pocket all the royalties for herself, or else she'd expose me, because she knew I intended leaving her . . . for you.'

'For me? And what about that painted slut back there in the hall?'

'Huh? Neve? Will you have a jot of sense, for God's sake? She's the boss's daughter. D'you not recognize a career move when you see one?'

She shook her head dizzily.

'Look, it's cynical, I know. But business is business. That girl's father is managing director of one of the biggest publishing houses in Europe. If I could convince him I was about to become family, then I was a shoo-in

for an enormous book deal. And I do mean enormous –
a seven-figure sum was even mentioned. Once my name
was on that contract, then it was all legally binding, and
I was set up for life. To marry you. To have the kind of
future we'd always spoken about. I couldn't tell you my
plan, you'd not have understood, you must see that. And
I came this, *this* close, a hair's breadth away from pulling
it off—' here, exasperation got the better of me a
moment '—but then you had to come blundering into
the house that morning, like a raving lunatic, and—'

'What? Are you trying to tell me you were romancing
Lady Muck just to get yourself a deal?'

'And for no other reason.'

'But didn't you already have a two-book deal?'

'Carla, d'you think I'd be satisfied with two?'

'I think it'd be nice if you were to start with one.'

'I *had* one – as far as the world was concerned. I'd
made the breakthrough, I'd done the hard part.
Suddenly, there's this flea-eaten beggar man threatening
to take that away from me. And, by his side, the trollop
who was standing between me and the life I'd dreamed
of with . . . with the woman I love. Carla, how could I
pass up such a chance to get rid of them both and have
done with all my problems in the one act? Especially
when I could so easily rig it to look like self-defence.'

She thought it over. Then she eyed me warily, but not
without a certain admiration. 'I'm no expert, but when
you did rig it, you rigged it like a pro. I mean, getting yer
man's prints on to the knife, how was that done?'

'He had this big bundle of your uncle's handwritten
jotters all trussed up – he used the kitchen knife to cut the

string. After I struck him, I just caught the handle with the sleeve of my jumper and . . . you know the rest.'

Her eyes widened and, slowly, she gasped, 'Christ. But . . . how? Like, how could you manage to think so clearly, and so quickly, in all that pandemonium?'

'You'd be surprised what you can do, Carla, if you want something bad enough. And from the minute you first walked through my door, all I ever wanted was you. Not just for myself, but for little Robert too. You can't have forgotten how he worships you. The other stuck-up cunt made me get rid of him. Can you believe it? Made me abandon my own—'

'Right,' she said distractedly. 'So that'd explain the string Forensics found. The one they lifted my uncle's prints off. But what became of all those jotters of his?'

'I burned them, of course. It took a while, and a good drop of lighter fuel—'

'You mean . . . you didn't call the cops right away?'

'No.'

'And how were you going to account for that if anyone asked?'

'Nobody *would* ask. Because with such a big fire in the room, with all that heat, nobody could ever say for sure what time the deaths occurred. Or who bit the dust first.'

Her smile was broad. I allowed myself an even broader one.

'But, Carla love, none of that's important now. All that matters is, I'll have you and Robert back where you both belong. D'you know, my parents called up to see me the other day, and I had to tell them some cock-and-bull yarn about the little lad being at a birthday party on the other side of town. That's what I've been reduced to, lying to my own mother and father. I've put up with a lot lately but, girl, I've put up with all I'm going to!'

I leant across and snaked a strong arm about her shoulders. In less than a heartbeat, her defences had fallen and she'd snuggled against me, her head on my chest. I pressed my lips into the tumble of her hair and whispered, 'I give you my word here and now, princess, you won't regret this. Not for one minute of one hour of the rest of your life.'

She raised her head mischievously. 'And I'll see out my days in the lap of luxury?'

'Like you've never dared imagine!'

'D'you really think, though, that your writing will keep bread on our table?' she asked, with no change of tone. 'I mean . . . are you any good?'

''Course I bloody am!' I replied, half-joking, whole-in-earnest, and a wee bit indignant with it.

'Well, Brendan, I've heard that to be able to describe, you must first be able to see. And, frankly, your powers of observation definitely need work.'

What a strange thing to say, I remember thinking. But then she suddenly sat upright, away from me, and, 'F'rinstance, as we walked up the street just now, you never noticed the car that was following us.'

I jerked round. As I did, the interior light of the vehicle parked behind came on. I recognized Cambridge at once; a split-second later I'd also placed the other one, the same officer I'd ordered from my flat that day, many months before, when a drunken Ger McEvoy had come rampaging. Both were grinning. Then, like it was something they'd rehearsed, both waved.

'I owed you that, you bastard!' Carla slavered. 'I fucking well owed you. We're not quits yet, pal. But by the time I've testified to what I now know, we'll be pretty damn close. Then we'll—'

She checked. She froze. She realized, at precisely the same instant I did, that she'd left the tape out of her hand and on the middle of the dashboard. She lurched, but she was late – I'd beaten her to the grab and, in a twinkling, was out and on my way. The advantage was mine now; I was on home ground. Across the street I sprinted and up the steep little boreen, the shortcut to the village church and graveyard. At my back, I could hear consternation as car doors were thrown open and hobnailed heels came clattering up the cobbles in my wake. They were younger, and they were gaining, but only I knew the lie of the land. Near the brow of Chapel Hill, I came to Foskin's Footbridge. Underneath runs the Rowlogue, a fast-flowing tributary of the Suir. Once there, I began to furiously unspool the Judas tape, scrunching, smearing, manhandling, doing all I could to obliterate whatever it might hold. Then, with my pursuers almost upon me, I stood back and flung the thing as far as I was able into the downstream, into the darkness. Cambridge slapped a heavy hand on to my shoulder, his partner seized me roughly by the collar; far off to my right came the merest, meekest splash. The tape was in the brook. It'd take just minutes to reach the great river. Next stop the broad Atlantic. Which left nothing to be feared but Carla Whitty's testimony. My word against the word of a woman scorned, and very probably deranged into the bargain. Meanwhile, with eyes adjusting all round, the two policemen peered southward down the stream, shook their heads disconsolately, then both turned fiercely to me. At once, and in unison, they erupted, bending double with the laughter, holding sides, slapping thighs, choking for breath.

In the darkened distance, Carla must've heard their braying. Through the still of the night came her faint call, 'Denis?'

With difficulty, he drew in a lungful and gasped, 'Up here!' Then, to me, his face ablaze with merriment, 'You moron! You fucking knobhead! D'you honestly think we'd risk our most crucial bit of evidence like that? No way, mate! The tape is safely under lock and key in Kilmainham. I mean the real tape. The one that's going to put you behind bars.'

'Well, your woman is going to have a part to play in that too,' the other remarked, to Cambridge but chiefly for my consideration. 'She did get what she came for, yeah?'

'So she told me just now.'

'Everything?'

'The whole story. Direct from the horse's mouth.'

'You should try hang on to her, Denis, 'cos the girl's a marvel. She must've carried it off to a T, right down the line. Let me tell you, that takes talent.'

'Talent my arse!' Cambridge joshed back. 'Y'know, the old man's will was only two lines long, but she spent damn near the whole of last night learning it by heart.'

319

'You can't blame her for being thorough,' said the other. 'I mean, it was pretty important that she knew it word perfect.'

'That was what I thought, too,' Carla said, stepping among us. '"To whom it concerns, I, Andrew Whitty, do hereby bequeath—"'

'Yeah, yeah, yeah,' Cambridge sighed. 'Very clever. But will you remember that confession you heard tonight just as accurately?'

'Oh, have no worries on that score! By the way, Denis, didn't I warn you not to risk putting a wire on me?'

'Why? Did he check?'

'Too damn right he did. Felt me up good and proper.'

'Can't say I blame you, buddy,' said the other. 'One last decent oul' grope, and why not? 'Cos where you're headed next, there won't be very much in the way of intimate contact.'

'At least you'd better fucking hope there won't!' Cambridge cracked, and now all three dissolved in absolute paroxysms. Around me the guffaws swooped and swelled, amplified, it seemed, by my silence, my final admission of defeat. Not since short-trouser days had I cried, not through the hundred caustic rejections, the thousand petty cruelties of a faithless wife, the single soul-deadening realization that the son I called mine was another man's child. But now I felt a tear, hot and acrid, come rolling. And thanked the Lord that the night was dark as it was. Small mercies.

'Brendan,' Cambridge coughed at last, 'this village of yours is a delight, and I'm sure we'd all love to stay a while longer. Unfortunately, there are people in Dublin who're going to be very anxious to have a word with you. So, if it's all the same, we really should be making tracks.'

Down the hill they flanked me, through the gloom and back towards the light. Nobody spoke till, just inside the orb of the first streetlamp but still hidden from public view, I stopped, forcing them all to stall.

'Can I ask one favour?' I said quietly.

'What?'

'Can I go back in there – to the pub, I mean? There's a crowd waiting on me, and I'd better make some kind of excuse.'

The policemen conferred with their eyes.

'What'll you say?' the other demanded.

'I dunno, I'll . . . I'll think of something.'

Again the men exchanged eye contact, but seemed a long way from a decision.

'Look, c'mon, if I just disappear into the night, there'll be search parties sent out to find me. It'll be easier if I just go in there and say, whatever.'

'All right,' Cambridge agreed. 'We can do that.'

They wheeled me round and began left up the street. Once more, I put the brakes on. 'You don't need to come in with me, do you?'

'What? And just turn you loose in a gathering like that? You must be bloody joking!'

'Garda,' I said, 'my parents are in there, and they've done nothing wrong. They're old people, they're not wealthy people and they never had very much to crow about. This night is probably the high point of their entire lives. And now you want to end it for them by marching me off to jail in front of the whole parish? Gimme a break, mate. You've got parents too, don't you?'

'Hey, I sympathize, I genuinely do. But you're a double-murder suspect! We can't let you out of our custody.'

'Out of your custody? Christ Almighty, it's not Caesar's Palace – there's just a front and a back door to the place, and with two of you guys, well, where d'you suppose I'm going to run to?'

'I don't care, I cannot—'

'Denis,' Carla intervened, 'it's okay. If Jason takes the back, you cover the front, and I'll go in with him.'

Cambridge rolled his eyes, shook his head and puffed resignedly. 'I don't like this. Not one little bit. Oh, c'mon then, for fuck's sake. Jason, you go ahead and find that back door. Right, you, let's get this done, and let's get out of here.'

'Thanks,' I said earnestly. 'And thanks, Carla.' But she continued walking without so much as a glance in my direction.

Inside the Vat, she tailed me through to the function room where the crowd, if anything, had grown. Cathal Ó Domhnaill was blustering away about the Battle of Carrigshock, his arms flailing the air as though he was performing a re-enactment. Like before, I began to push through those people congregated around the doorway, this time with Carla holding grimly to a fistful of my shirt. In the middle of the crush, I turned to her and mouthed, 'I have to use the toilet.'

As I did, Ó Domhnaill spied me from the podium,

called a time-out from hostilities and said, 'Ah, the man of the moment returns!' I saluted, raised an index finger to indicate that I needed a minute, then pointed towards the gents. 'Sound as a bell!' he acknowledged. 'The call of nature. Happens to the best of us.'

A laugh went up from the audience as necks everywhere craned to look. And Carla let me go.

The toilet was empty. The mirror riveted to the wall above the wash-hand basin was old, chipped, more brown cloud than reflection. I slipped off my shoe and, with the heel, hammered firmly near the bottom. A sliver the size of a nail file broke off and fell into the sink. Hurriedly, I took it with me to the one and only cubicle: there I bolted the door and sat myself down.

A shudder ran the length of my spine as I touched the glass point to my jugular. One jab, I knew, just one good firm thrust, and all arguments were settled. But somehow, the thought of blood, gushing out where the stubby chisel went in, arcing against the near wall, dribbling from the corners of my mouth, made me quail. It was excessively gruesome, unnecessarily gruesome, when the late Andy Whitty had, in his book, presented a far more humane alternative. Slashing the wrists was slower, but relatively painless and ruthlessly efficient. So he'd written and he was, after all, quite the authority. He had seen it at close quarters.

The gash in the left wrist opened deep and easily. But with the hand adjoining suddenly wet and slippery, gripping the glass blade was difficult, so making the cut in the right wrist involved a good deal of sawing. Still, it couldn't have taken much more than the minute, I'd

okayed with both Ó Domhnaill and with Carla. Now I
sat myself back.

The effect wasn't immediate, but prompt nonetheless.
First I remarked how cold it was becoming, how the air
temperature seemed to plummet. Next came the
lassitude, the increasing exhaustion as, like with the onset
of deep sleep, consciousness wavered. From outside
came a burst of applause, but muffled and distant and
hazy. The lavatory door opened then and some people
walked in. They talked, loud but indistinct. They
laughed, raucous but fuzzy. Then as the last of the light
went out and the volume ebbed to nothing, I just about
caught one of them say, 'Look! There on the ground!
What the fuck . . . ?'

EPILOGUE

For reasons I can't explain, I wasn't too terribly surprised to regain consciousness here, in this tiny private room of St Vincent's Hospital. Nor did the assorted tubing that fed into me or drained out come as much of a shock either. But the chain that attached my left ankle to the iron bed frame did jar just a little.

The room is stark, naked white. Only a small opaque window in the door offers any form of view. Looking through it now, I see that the policeman stationed outside has just stood again. Stretching the legs, I guess: he does this several times each hour. He's here strictly in the interests of security, to prevent me making a break for it. The hospital staff, on the other hand, are monitoring me round the clock, as I'm still on suicide watch. Though I don't think I'll be attempting that again just yet. I don't think so. Not just yet.

It's been almost two weeks now. Here in limbo time's stood still, as I've been considered too unwell to face a proper committal hearing. But outside these walls, the world's gone on apace, and a cracking old pace at that! Taurus have already moved to retrieve their seventy-five thousand advance, so my house is on the market; interest, I understand, has been lively. But while they're keen on having their money back, they're just as keen to see the book published, though in its original form, with all characters named as the author intended. Naturally, that's delayed the launch date. But with the kind of publicity it's generated, the column inches its commandeered, the life of its own it's seemed to assume, *Remember Me, Fair Eleanore* will emerge from the womb a full-grown behemoth. Only yesterday, one newspaper reported that if advance orders were anything to go by, this book was likely to be featuring at or near the top of the bestseller list for a long, long, *long* time to come.

All of which, inevitably, raises the question of the profits, and how they ought to be distributed. The intended beneficiary, of course, was the late-lamented Shafty McDermott. But when he met with his untimely end, not only was he intestate, but he alone was left of his name and race. No next-of-kin could be unearthed. The various Whittys did have undeniable claims on at least part of the fortune looming, but with lengthy and rancorous litigation in prospect, they came to a decision that was both honourable and praiseworthy. All monies accruing from *Eleanore* will now go to a special bursary set up to award an annual prize for the best novel written by a non-professional, first-time author. Those in regular day jobs, along with those in no jobs at all, will be considered. Anyone who's ever earned a shilling at the typeface is out of the hunt. The ironic thing is, if I ever decide to write again, to flog this dead horse one more time, then I'll be more than eligible. Now, wouldn't that be something?

Alan's called – called twice, to give him his due.

Otherwise, I've not had a visitor. Oh, there's this duty solicitor – court appointed – who drops round from time to time, but I don't count him. My girlfriend hasn't been here. In point of fact, my girlfriend hasn't been seen. Nor has one – not even one – of the scores who thronged The Vat to shake my hand, clap my back or touch the hem of my garment. Not a man among them has come to ask if I'm dead or alive. Not Cathal Ó Domhnaill, he who sang my praises louder than any. Not even old Master Mahoney. It didn't take him long to disown the jewel in his crown, the glowing validation of his entire working life. Eaten bread really is soon forgotten. My parents, of course, haven't forgotten. But they still don't own a car, and they continue to detest public transport. Otherwise, I'm certain . . . I'm just certain, that's all.

I've spent, therefore, these past two weeks in virtual solitary confinement. But if that solicitor of mine is to be believed, then not for very much longer. According to his best guess, there may well be developments as early as tomorrow. It seems I've at last been passed fit to face the court, where charges will be read and a trial date set. Pre-trial, I'll be taken to one remand centre or other; post-trial, I fully expect to be taken to the cell where I'll spend the greater part of the rest of my life. And tomorrow, I understand, is when this whole chain of enchantment kicks off. Tomorrow they unlock me, unplug me, and get me out of here. Away from this garish, whited sepulchre. Back, for better or worse, to the land of the living. Back to the grind.